ALSO BY Shelby Hearon

Armadillo in the Grass

The Second Dune

Hannah's House

Now and Another Time

A Prince of a Fellow

Painted Dresses

Afternoon of a Faun

Group Therapy

A Small Town

Five Hundred Scorpions

Owning Jolene

Hug Dancing

Shelby Hearon
Life Estates

Shelby Hearon was born in Marion, Kentucky, lived for many years in Texas and New York, and now makes her home in Burlington, Vermont. She is the author of thirteen novels, including *Hug Dancing* and *Owning Jolene*, which won an American Academy and Institute of Arts and Letters Literature Award and will soon be released as a film. She has received National Endowment for the Arts and John Simon Guggenheim fellowships for fiction, an Ingram Merrill grant, and has twice won the Texas Institute of Letters fiction award. She has taught in numerous writing programs, including those of the University of Houston, the University of California at Irvine, the University of Illinois at Chicago, and the University of Miami, and currently she teaches at the University of Massachusetts at Amherst.

Life Estates

a novel by

Shelby Hearon

VINTAGE CONTEMPORARIES

Vintage Books

A Division of Random House, Inc.

New York

VINTAGE CONTEMPORARIES EDITION

Copyright © 1994 by Shelby Hearon

All rights reserved under International and Pan-American
Copyright Conventions. Published in the United States by Vintage Books,
a division of Random House, Inc., New York, and simultaneously
in Canada by Random House of Canada Limited, Toronto.
Originally published in hardcover by
Alfred A. Knopf, Inc., New York, in 1994.

Portions of this novel were originally published in
Countryside, Shenandoah, and *Southern Review.*

The Library of Congress has cataloged
the Knopf edition as follows:

Hearon, Shelby, [date]
Life Estates/by Shelby Hearon.
p. cm.

1. Friendship—United States—Fiction.
2. Women—United States—Fiction. I.Title.
PS3558.E256F75 1994
813 .54—dc20 93-13977 CIP

ISBN-10: 0-679-75796-1

ISBN-13: 978-0-679-75796-2

Book design by Robert Olsson

Manufactured in the United States of America

146684614

for my sisters
with love

Life Estates

ONE

~~~~~~~~~~

THE PHONE WAS RINGING when I came in with Gentle
Ben. It was fine dog-walking weather, still chilly in the early
mornings here in the foothills of the Blue Ridge. Pulling
off my zip-front jacket, I was thinking that I did not want
to talk to anyone, wishing instead that I was in my car
headed for the pine forests, the Wild and Scenic River overlook, the sight of Georgia. They'd all been calling me, early,
late, even at the shop, since Nolan died: my family, the
lawyer, bankers. As if my time were now a blank sheet of
paper on which they needed to write their messages.

"Sarah," Harriet said. "I was afraid I'd missed you and
was going to have to go through that girl at your shop."

I was glad to hear from her. Pouring myself a cup of
coffee, I pulled a wicker chair over to the kitchen windows,
where I could look out on my peach trees, and sank against
the seat while Ben, my broad-faced black Sandyland labra-
dor, settled at my feet. My trees were much in need of
feeding, already leafy, full and green, the Georgia Belle,
the Monroe, the Tyler, the O'Henry, as dear to me as kin.

"We were out trotting," I said. I did not rise to the defense
of my partner, knowing that we were all "girls" to Harriet.

"Do you have a minute?" she asked.

"No rush."

"I wanted to warn you. Don't wear any jewelry."

"Do I ever?" I had to smile at that. I was in my baggy faded chambray dog-walking pants, a worn workshirt, a sweater which had once been called, in the catalogue, cobalt blue, and was now a much-washed Sarah blue. I lifted my French braid, thinking I must pin it up for the Texas trip. I was too old for so much hair. The plait was a compromise; I couldn't bring myself to cut it.

Harriet and I had kept to these twice yearly reunions, me going to see her in April, East Texas's finest month, her coming to see me in October for western Carolina's glorious fall, since our children were toddlers. We had let nothing stand in our way, and this loss-filled season, we'd agreed, would be no exception.

"I mean it," Harriet said in her determined voice. "Public places these days are full of idiots, criminal idiots. We've had a rash of stickups, nothing like Houston naturally, but still—creeps following women home from the malls because they spotted a Rolex watch on their wrist or diamond studs in their ears, women in jogging clothes who didn't even realize they had a piece of jewelry on. Following them right out of the parking lots and attacking them in their own driveways. One woman, I heard about this at Birthday Club, had a stud ripped right out of her ear. Another almost had her finger cut off because she didn't get her engagement ring off fast enough. Following people home from the airports, can you believe it? Watching them get their new cars out of short-term parking."

"I promise to look worthless." I could hear the fear in her voice, but could not recall how long it had been there. Was it just since Knox died, since she was living alone?

"You're teasing, I know," she said, "but I'm scared to death to go out anymore. We had a woman right here in the county, somebody's neighbor, who was carrying in her groceries and her .22 caliber single-action went off and shot her in the eye. Slipped out of her pocket. You try to defend yourself and look what happens. I'm sleeping with Knox's Browning lever-action 308 deer rifle next to my pillow until I get a gun of my own."

I had a little trouble with that, imagining Harriet, small, blond, in her emerald green bedroom, in her green satin robe and mules, hefting a shotgun on her shoulder. An Annie Oakley heading for bed. It must be that a husband, even sleeping across the hall, had seemed a protector. I asked her, "Is it being there by yourself?"

"No. Yes. Not really. I don't know, Sarah. I don't. The world does seem less user-friendly since Knox died. I guess I feel like I've lost my job. Wife. I'm unemployed. That's enough to make me jump at my shadow. What about you? You're the one—"

"I'm taking it slow," I said. "A day at a time." In truth, I didn't know how I was doing. Nolan and I, who had begun in heat, had ended up with a coolness between us for which I was still sorry. It was disheartening to lose someone before you had the chance to make things right, to go back and take a different path. The fault, I thought, was not his—I gave him that—nor even, I wanted to believe, mine, but rather that of the encasement we had coexisted in: marriage.

"You had time to get used to his going," Harriet said.

"Yes." It was true. I'd done most of my mourning while he was dying. The bad prognosis—cancer of the pancreas—had come the middle of November; then, while we were still trying to get used to the idea, talking to Nolan's doctor, Harriet's husband, Knox, had wrapped himself around a hickory tree on a curve he'd taken drunk or sober for thirty years. We had all been stunned, numbed by the suddenness.

Harriet's tone brightened. She didn't like to stay too long on gloomy topics. "Isn't it amazing, when you think about it, incredible really, how the two of us have always done everything at the same time? I mean, gone off to boarding school at Miss Pritchard's, dated those cadets named Stewart with an 'e' and Stuart with a 'u,' been in each other's weddings, married bankers, had our boys and then our girls the same years, got separate bedrooms at the same time. You even got your tubes tied when I had my hysterectomy. Now, imagine, both of us widows. It gives me the goose bumps, things working out that way."

"I think about that, too," I said, looking out at the trees. Thinking perhaps that a close friend, after all, was someone who had gone down the same road with you, who'd made the same stops along the way. Grateful that Harriet had walked my lifeline with me for forty years.

"Well, not *every* single thing," she amended, vexed. "We aren't both grandmothers. That's the exception, but don't get me started on our girls. Me, the boy-crazy one, having a daughter thirty years old who is not only not married, she's not even living with anyone. And you, who could never even remember whether you had a date or not, having a brood hen with four babies already."

"Maybe they were switched at birth, our girls." This was an old joke between us, one I often made when Harriet got on the subject of our daughters.

"It does make you wonder—"

"They're not us, that's all."

There was nothing to say which helped. If Harriet had been nearby, I'd have given her a squeeze, a Carolina hug. It was fine as long as we talked about her son, who wasn't married either, but she didn't worry about him. It was her Pammy, so different from her, who was the Achilles heel of Harriet's lovely legs. How she had expected and expected for her daughter. Through the years of summer camps, high school honors, sorority pledging, law school, every step painful. Because if things went fine, then it was such a relief, such a reprieve, but then the next stage was already upon her, and this time Pammy might not do it right. Now the job with one of Houston's mega-firms was forgotten, it was time for marriage and children. I sometimes thought that Harriet's very breasts were less flesh to her than her daughter's smallest choices.

"It seems strange," she said, her voice faltering, "nobody at either of our houses but us. I can practically hear that hound of yours breathing. Remember how we used to talk on the phone with the kids screaming in the background, people knocking on the door, husbands hollering where was their breakfast, or their supper? We used to talk about how grand it would be to have phone booths in our kitchens. Remember?"

I admitted, "It helps to have Ben."

"Maybe I'll get me a cat. Knox never liked cats. Some long-haired Abyssinian or Persian who'll sit up here on my pillow sham and lick her whiskers."

"You don't mean that." I couldn't imagine Harriet tending an animal.

"I don't. Fur balls and shots and shedding all over my clothes. But it's a nice image. With a little jewelled collar."

"Then you'd have to hire a guard."

"Oh, Sarah, can you believe we're about to have a visit with no children, no husbands? I know this probably isn't all right to say, so soon after Nolan—but I'm so excited you're coming. I'm so thrilled that it will be the two of us again, just like old times."

LATE, I LET myself into Rooms of One's Own. Katie, my partner, was sitting cross-legged on the floor, doing her controlled breathing. When the door opened, she rose slowly, not using her hands.

"I was on the phone to Harriet," I said.

"I'd think you had enough on your mind these days without carrying that woman around."

"We go way back," I said. I didn't feel the need to rise to the defense of my old friend, knowing that any traditional homemaker was "that woman" to Katie.

"How about way forward?"

"She's scared," I explained.

Katie and I had on the rust jumpers we wore to work, with white T-shirts since it was a spring day. We'd decided when we started the shop that dressing up every day, having to think about that, what to wear six days a week, was going to be a drag. "Let's do uniforms," I'd suggested. And we'd each bought three heavy cotton jumpers with dropped waists and pleats almost to the ankles. We'd also got mammoth brown cardigans for when it was really cold and we were out traipsing around the county looking for ideas for new wallpapers.

We sat behind the counter on stools and Katie filled our Rooms mugs from the thermos of coffee. "I should have bought donuts," I said.

My partner, a slender woman with café-au-lait skin and her hair currently worn high in a rooster comb on her head, looked younger than her years, our years. She had no children and no husband—maybe that was her secret. She was glad to live alone, having raised all her younger brothers and sisters. What she did with men was her business, although in the fifteen years we'd run the shop, I'd met two who were serious contenders. One, a local contractor, had been in the picture until last year. The trouble was, Katie was too smart and too good-looking for any available man in the area, and I felt some responsibility that the shop had held her here in South Carolina. The good side of that was she had security, and a house on the road out of Mineral Springs, our hometown. (My house was on the road into Mineral Springs. The county still had these firm but invisible boundaries.)

"What Harriet misses most I'm most glad to be rid of," I told her, looking around the shop.

"I expect that means a husband."

"Being married. The title." I stirred around my already mixed feelings about widowhood, trying to separate my real grief over Nolan's going so young, not yet even sixty, with my equally real relief at finding myself, after thirty-three years, unattached. "I don't think I knew I felt so bound. I'd got the right to operate the shop as a femme sole, got him to put the notice in the paper saying he wasn't responsible for my debts. Got his accountant to give up and let me file a separate return. Got my name, the Cooper name again, on everything I signed."

"You got your own credit cards."

"I did."

I turned the pages of the sample books stacked on the counter, full of familiar interiors: the Clarence House, the Wickam-Valentine House, the Grange, the White House of the Confederacy. "I didn't understand before that once you marry, you are never again not married. You can legally change your name, you can take back your maiden, as they say, name, but you are never single again."

"Some of us figured that out watching our moms."

"I'm a *husbandless wife*. A *widow*. I'm married to a man underground. I feel I'm destined to be the Widow Rankin until I'm buried with Ben beneath some peach tree."

"Join the club. All of us get defined by how much husband we've got. I'm an old maid, you're a widow, that's two names for being without one. Divorced is a third."

I emptied the thermos into our cups.

"Hey, we quit working for your man anyway," Katie said.

"We did that." I smiled, remembering those days. How long ago that seemed.

I'd hired a cleaning service through the employment agency twenty years ago, when Nolan, nearing forty, a new vice-president, had begun to entertain bankers and clients in our home, once my grandmother's. I'd been in my dog-walking pants (Rogers it was then, Will Rogers, my first black lab) when the doorbell rang. And there was this black woman dressed in a taupe suit and heels, handbag and carryall under her arm, standing at the door.

"Yes?" I'd asked, confused.

"I'm the Pegues Cleaning Service."

I straightened up and stared. "You look like you should be hiring me."

"Today you've hired me."

I let her in, but gestured to her clothes. "How can you—"

"I came from a real estate closing," she said. "I'll just be a minute." And before my eyes she slipped into walking shoes and a smock, tied a scarf around her cropped hair. "There," she said.

"Is anyone else with you?" I'd expected, I suppose, half a dozen men with brushes and brooms, pails and mops. A crew to scrub the place top to bottom.

"I'm it." Katie had looked around the downstairs, talking as she looked. "I work for a realty company most of the time, cleaning up houses before they show them, or after they show them if there's an open house. But some weeks are slack, and I got this idea of getting myself some work for the lean times, as a party service."

"Was that hard to do?"

"Was what hard to do?"

"Set up a business." I was at that time railing almost daily at the credit strictures on a married woman. Angry that anything at all—getting my tubes tied (which was on my mind), buying stock (which was on Nolan's), even ordering bath towels and sheets—required either a husband's signature or, at the least, use of a husband's name.

"Not if you're single," she answered.

"Is that right?" And I felt envy along with my admiration that she'd taken her finances in her own hands so firmly, this pretty young woman. "Well, I can't even get myself a credit card in my name."

She nodded. "At the closing it was the woman's money made the down payment, and it was the woman's money was going to pay the house note, but the home was in his name."

Listening to her, I felt I'd never been single, not in a business way.

"You want me to start upstairs or down?" she asked.

"Up. I'll show you. I'm Sarah."

"Katie."

We shook hands on that bit of bonding, that trading of first names. But it was five years later, when we were used to cleaning the house together, in tandem, talking as we worked, that we got the idea for the shop. It was a Monday morning when we were getting the house ready for some monstrously important function, some cocktail-reception-dinner for all the bank directors and their spouses on a Friday night. We'd given over the whole week to it, which wasn't anything out of the ordinary. Cooking ahead, scrubbing and polishing and sprucing up. Getting flowers. Seeing what dishes needed to be borrowed or rented, if furniture needed to be moved in or out to allow for traffic flow. What to do if it turned cold—it was late March, the week before Easter, and sometimes on the edge of the mountains you could get a cold snap, a sudden drop in temperature that made garden parties into unpleasant shivering affairs where everyone felt locked out of the warmth of the house. We'd decided to hold the whole thing indoors.

I remembered the moment exactly. Katie was putting paste wax on the huge gateleg table, and I was cleaning the glass doors of the heavy breakfront. We had a checklist for every day of the week; tasks that would stay done were that day's, Monday's, chores. I looked up, rubbed my forehead, tired already, and asked Katie, "Why're we both working for this man?"

Katie had put down her can of wax and gestured with the soft cloth. "I don't know, but what I do know is that your wages are better than mine."

"That's because I do double duty in bed."

"He didn't ask me did I want that job. For what you probably get, I might have accepted."

We'd looked at each other, two women both turning forty, serving the functions of wife and hired help respectively, and then put down our cleaning supplies and headed for the kitchen. The cook, a German woman I hired for big parties, wasn't due to show up until Wednesday. We had the big old room to ourselves. I fixed a pot of coffee, percolator in those days, and we moved wicker chairs over to the windows. I was still smoking then, and had a cigarette. Katie got a notepad from her handbag.

"What could we do instead?" I asked her.

"What've you got in mind?"

"What do women do to make money—"

"You want a smart-aleck answer or census figures?"

"—that isn't going from the frying pan to the fire?"

"They type; they deliver mail; they clerk; they answer phones; they sell beauty supplies; they fill prescriptions; they lick envelopes."

"They clerk. Anybody can clerk. You don't need training for that."

"You going to work at the five-and-dime? I'll come see you, buy some mercerized thread from you."

"What if we clerked in our own place?"

"What place is this?"

"Katie, think. You know how to start a business. You *are*

a business. What could we sell that would make money? That wouldn't take all our lives to get an inventory? That we'd already know how to sell?"

"You tell me."

"I want us to sell something that people like to buy and are always going to continue to like to buy. But where we offer something a little better, a little different. What do all women do? They fix up their houses. Come on."

I walked around the whole downstairs and then the upstairs with Katie following. I was trying to see with fresh eyes the old home that had been Mother's back before she spent most of her time in Antarctica, Brazil, Nigeria, tracking arachnids. That had been my grandmother's before that. It took two trips before I saw what my eyes hadn't seen before. The fabrics, the patterns: on the beds, at the windows, on the walls.

I'd repapered the rooms myself when Nolan and I moved in as bride and groom. There'd been some awful paper, turn of some century, big prints of trees, meadows, horses, ponds, which Mother must simply have ignored. That was upstairs. Down, there'd been birds of paradise, bouquets and palmettos. Nobody could live with the wrong wallpaper. Every woman wanted to put her own taste on view, and— here was the important part—every woman was permitted to pick out wallpaper. Husbands did not pick out wallpaper. They picked out the cars, voted on the furniture, even had a say about appliances, but the walls and windows they left to her, the wife. That seemed a revelation to me.

"We're going to open a wallpaper store," I told Katie.

"Before or after the bank director's party?"

"During. We're going to take this whole week to figure it out while we work."

And we had. We'd set up ground rules—in a rush to right old injustices, to offer credit where credit was due. No bank cards, no husbands' names on checks, no decorators, no copying some friend's house. We would divide up the customers between us, each following a room from start to finish, and pool the costs and profits. All of western South Carolina, the upstate area, was full of old homes, historic places where John Calhoun had slept, lived, or his father-in-law or his sister, nieces, whoever, had resided. Lovely old places all roped off, in the historical registry, tended by guides. All of them with wallpaper.

We decided that papers based on these old patterns and faded colors would be our specialty. We would photograph the papers, enlarge and study them, rough out our own variations, the colors, the pattern repeat, and have a commercial artist translate it for us, a manufacturer, preferably a woman, established, who would do our rolls. Custom designs.

"Every woman can create a room of her own," I'd said, and then of course the name of the shop was born.

It had taken work, some wrong starts, some dismal first reproductions, before we found our present team. But we'd had the right idea at the right time.

The week we'd spent planning it, I'd done homework reading at night, learning that there was quite a precedent for what we were venturing as businesswomen, as partners. South Carolina had been unique in the early nineteenth century in allowing women to declare themselves femme sole traders, to separate their commerce from their husbands' control and responsibility. In those days, women mostly went into bonnets, corsets, artificial flowers, but they set up shop nonetheless. And not just white women; free black women ran coffeehouses, oyster bars, kept boarding-houses.

The sign over the counter, SARAH COOPER AND KATIE PEGUES, PROPRIETORS, still filled me with pride.

Sometimes we spent half a morning sitting here, warming up, flipping through thick pages, looking at wallpapers. Then one or the other of us went on calls, checked out rooms, took pictures, made estimates, while the other minded the shop. We never left it unattended if we could help it. Women were apt to drop in, even from out of town. They didn't call ahead. It wasn't like a hairdresser's or doctor's appointment that had to be scheduled. Deciding to fix up a room was always somewhat spur-of-the-moment, urged by some event, spurred by some discontent.

We had customers now not only from Greenville, Spartanburg, Columbia, but from as far away as Asheville, Charlotte, even Atlanta. Still, the bulk of women who came to us were from small Carolina towns like ours—Williamston, Greer, Seneca, Pendleton—women who decided to drive down to Rooms of One's Own to see if something could be done with that dark dining room, that old bedroom which still had the tape from the kids' posters on the wall, that half-bath carved from under the stairs.

Then they could count on lunching at the Mineral Springs Depot, a homestyle cafe that sat atop a hill and was housed in what had been the actual depot, in another location, back when our town was a famous spa, the destination of eight trains a day.

WHEN THE PHONE RANG, Katie answered, as she always did when we were both in the shop. A kindness for which I was grateful, especially lately.

"Yes, ma'am, Ms. Cooper," Katie said. "She's right here." Then Katie smiled before she spoke again. "I expect you told me to call you that, but every time I start to say 'Edith,' then the whole entire thing wants to come out,

'Edith Huntt Cooper,' and I get stuck on the mouthful."
She nodded. "I expect I can." She handed me the phone.
"Your mom."

"Hello." Mother had been out of the country when Nolan
died, but had made two trips down in the months before.
Widowed some twenty years younger than I was, she'd been
attuned to my wobbling feelings.

"Checking in, dear, before you go to Texas. How are
you?"

"Taking it a day at a time." I hesitated, thinking she
deserved more than that. "Distressed and relieved—"

"That's not uncommon."

"The widow's weeds are choking me. . . ."

Mother paused. "You don't mean that literally, do you?
I didn't wear black when your father— But you are speaking metaphorically."

"I am. At this hour of the morning."

"Your sister said the memorial service went well."

"It did. Bess was kind to come help with the little boys."
My sister, a horsewoman, had missed Carolina's William
of Orange Triple Crown, a big event, to be with me, and
tend my grandfatherless grandsons.

"Just remember, you haven't taken suttee," Mother said
firmly. "Remind yourself you've lost a recreation not a voca-
tion."

"It's that I've lost the husband but not the title."

"How well I remember."

"I think I'll take Gentle Ben and drive around the state
parks this afternoon, get out of town."

"Do that, by all means."

"Any other suggestions?"

"Put your wedding ring in a drawer."

"I put it in Nolan's cuff link box."

"Eat your meals in a new location. Set your alarm for a

different hour. However you felt about him or feel about him now, there's going to be a hole where he used to be."

I was touched, as I often was by my mother, who had seemingly not a hostile bone in her body and not a single bad idea. "Thanks," I said. "That's helpful."

The amenities over, Mother began to talk about her work. "I've a chance to go back to Patagonia, based in Tierra del Fuego. I'd be in the field, tropical forests. Exciting work. I've decided that seventysomething is the perfect age to travel. One has the resources and the reserves, yet one still has the stamina and curiosity. I think this is my favorite decade; I'll be sad to leave it."

"You've done a fine job with all of them so far."

"Thank you, dear. Should I drop down to see you on the way?" Mother was in Washington now, able to be on the spot when opportunities arose.

"No, I'm fine. Sorting it out."

"Good, then. Tell Katie that I intend to call her Ms. Pegues until she gets my name right."

"She says, Hang in there, Edith, baby."

"She said no such thing."

"Thank you for calling."

I'd long ago forgiven my mother for sending me off to Miss Pritchard's; for not knowing that her elder daughter would loathe boarding school from first day to last. I knew Mother's intent had been that I get as good an education as was possible, to her way of thinking at the time; just as she'd sought out for Bess a place where there were horse trainers and shows. I also knew without a doubt that if she, Edith, had ended up there herself, she'd have crawled out the window and down the ivied walls and never come back from the genteel prison all of whose resources went to protecting its inmates' good names, good reputations and good behavior. I had no doubt that in part my recalcitrant attitude

was a result of my anger at being locked up for four years
in one of the country's best marriage preparatory schools.

"You had two other calls before you got here," Katie
remembered.

"Everyone is calling—"

"Will Perry said whenever you're in the mood to take a
dog to the country, let him know."

I smiled. Nolan's seventy-year-old physician was an old
friend. "Did he tell you that his pup and mine—not pups
anymore—were from the same litter?"

"I expect he meant himself."

"Probably he did. Old dog, old tricks. He doesn't want
me to hold him responsible for Nolan's dying."

"And Theo Kenton said tell you to call first thing when
you got in."

I hated even hearing Nolan's lawyer's name. "You don't
have to go through that reading of the will, do you, if there
are no surprises?"

"You're asking me? I was the beneficiary of my mother's
will. I got my brothers and sisters."

"I don't understand what probate is or why we have to
talk about all that again."

"He said call when you got in—"

"All right, okay. Thanks for not dropping that on me right
away. What he wants to tell me is that I'm still married,
that I'm still Mrs. Nolan Rankin and that there's nothing I
can do about it." I put my hand on the phone, but I couldn't
bring myself to lift it.

Katie stood, stretched. "If you're going to take your drive
this afternoon, I think I'll clear out now and have a look at
that zigzag paper upstairs at the Calhoun house at Clemson.
I got an idea something like that might work for Morrison."

"What's she doing?"

"Turning her bedroom into an upstairs sitting room. She

says she can't have anybody over for a cup of tea or a visit because her son's friends fill up the downstairs. She's going to move her bed into what was a spare room."

"I thought Morrison's son was as old as mine."

"So? He's living at home. Back home. Still home. Home. Hey, it's a grand house. Why move?"

"I thought you hated that zigzag paper."

"I've been reassessing it. It's gold and silver—gold and gray to be correct. She wants pink and cocoa, rose and cocoa. And first I was thinking along the lines of something patterned after a French brocatelle, but that's too formal. This would be different, sophisticated but cozy. The trouble is, I can't recall what formed the pattern. It might be tiny rows of flowers? I need to see."

Katie and I divided up our customers according to our sixth sense about who could work best with whom, as well as who could get enthusiastic about a particular room. But Morrison was not only an unlikely candidate for Katie, for some years she'd refused to be a client of Rooms at all. She'd come in—eight years ago? nine?—swept in, brushed right past Katie as if she were the help, stomped up to me at the counter. Explained that she wanted to match a wallpaper that a friend of hers in Savannah had. For me to order enough for a twenty-by-twelve-foot room with twelve-foot ceilings with moldings—she'd have a paperhanger pick it up. For me to send the bill to her husband's office; he was a developer.

I'd explained that, first, we didn't duplicate friends' papers, that we were a custom outfit, and, second, that we did not bill husbands. I explained how our system worked: we had a large ledger in which every woman had a page, and in which we wrote what she had contracted for and which she signed. Then, if she paid on time, she could do up another room when she was in the mood. If she didn't, then her account was closed. I explained that we didn't take credit cards, and, furthermore, that we didn't want to see any proof of solvency or need any identification. The client's signature was her word.

We'd worked that out because neither of us wanted to penalize the woman—of which there were legions fifteen years ago—who had no credit of her own, who didn't have her own bank accounts or charge cards in her name. We figured that if a woman had sixty days to pay, she could get the money somewhere. And that she would welcome the chance to work out her own financial arrangements, no questions asked. Word had spread faster than chicken pox.

But Morrison (we never used titles—Mrs., Ms., Miss, Dr.—a woman was just a last name to us until she became friendly enough to be a first name) had stormed out, taking care to slam the door. Not staying to hear that, third, we used our own paperhangers, a pair of women we'd trained ourselves.

Neither Katie nor I thought we'd ever see Morrison again. But then about a year and a half ago, her husband, Poindexter Morrison, Sr., had dropped dead. And she'd appeared in the shop, contrite, her finances in shambles, her son, Junior, absolutely no help, terrified. She had remembered the terms, the offer of Rooms of One's Own.

She hadn't made a peep, her bulk tottering on high heels, when Katie said, "I'll be glad to help you."

Instead, she'd said, getting the name off the sign above the counter, "You might want to see the room first, Ms. Pegues."

"Take your time," I told Katie now. "Detour by Ashtabula if you're in the mood. I don't need an audience to get mad talking to the lawyer."

"You want me to pick up a sandwich?"

"No, I'll get something on my drive."

I went to the bathroom in the back, thinking how glad I was I'd quit smoking fifteen years ago, and wondering if you ever reached a point where you didn't want one anymore. I washed my face, put water on the back of my neck, put some color on my lips. Freshening up.

I resisted the impulse to stall further. "Theo?" I said into the phone. "Sarah."

I pictured him, the great messy hulk of an attorney, lounging at his desk, belly hanging out, hair crisscrossed over his bald spot, spanking new bright red suspenders and red bow tie to make him think he was one of the new breed. Wingtip shoes he'd forgot to trade for Nikes. He had something sly on his mind, I could tell from his money-sweetened tone.

"Sarah, how are you? Getting ready for your trip to Texas? Or have you already been? Don't tell me. I don't want to hear a single Texas tale today. But you're doing just fine, aren't you? That's what I hear."

"What is it, Theo?"

"I've got Nolan's will before me."

"And—?"

"I don't believe you ever saw a copy of this most recent will. I'm fairly certain of that."

"We drew up joint wills, years ago, each leaving everything directly to the children."

"That's right, you did. Back when you opened up your little gift shop. That was the idea, you'd have your own thing and so forth. Am I right?"

"Wallpaper."

"Right. We did the paperwork then, everything in order. But Nolan never took that too seriously, I'm guessing. I'm guessing he never thought that was the end of it, just a whim. The long and short, here, Sarah, is that he wanted you to be provided for. He wrote a new will, the very next day, as I recall. He didn't see any need to upset you with it; still and all, he didn't want to pop off and leave you in a fix. Prescient, as it turned out."

"What are you telling me?" I tried to keep my voice calm. His kind could never say a thing straight out.

"Everything to you, life interest. Lock and stock. Meaning everything. To the kids after you're gone, what's left. The residual." He paused and must have been taking a swallow of something, as if he were speaking at a podium. "Now, he wanted me to restrain you from flying off the handle when you got the news. He expressly wanted me to keep you from making any hasty decisions."

"Such as telling you what you could do with that will."

"I believe that was the gist of his concern."

I moved a sample book, looked at our pleasant space. "I don't have to take the money."

"Life interest," Theo explained with patience, "means you skim the top, give the bulk to the kids. That's fair to both generations, all parties. You can't liquidate the assets. We didn't think you'd have an objection to that, a life interest."

"I don't have to take it." I tried pacing while holding the phone, but the cord didn't reach. I sank back on the stool. Picked up the empty thermos and considered hurling it. "You don't have to accept an inheritance. You know those tidewater people refused the land their granddaddy left them because they figured it would cost millions to drain it and clean it and get it so they could sell it."

"You read too much, honey." I could imagine him mopping his fat brow with a monogrammed hanky. "A life estate, it's yours. You die, you pass it on."

The only estate Nolan had held for life had been laid to rest in the cemetery. "Draw up what you have to to convey it directly to our children," I said, "George and Fannin."

"This was his will, Sarah." Theo's voice had grown testy. "I'm looking at it, witnessed and signed. You know what that means, his *will*? It means his *wishes*. It's the same as saying he wanted his ashes spread over the steps of the state capitol or scattered on Sassafras Mountain. Think it over; sleep on it."

I stood, as if ending the conversation. "You sleep on how fast you can execute the transfer."

"Will you come into the office? Let me talk it over with you? Explain the details?"

"I'm overheating, Theo. I'm going to let you go." I did not sail a sample book across the room, only hefted it to get an idea how far it would go. I tugged my braid: maybe this was why I didn't cut my hair.

Hanging up the phone, I considered Nolan. Wondering why he had had to make it so difficult, had had to go behind my back in this way. Why he'd had to have the last say. There was no way this wasn't going to get out, have tongues flapping. Theo Kenton would be telling this to his partners over big gin drinks filled with those little onions that looked like mothballs. Gibsons. He drank Gibsons.

My children would think me militant and utterly out of line not respecting their father's wishes, disregarding a life estate. At least in Edith Huntt Cooper I had a mother who wouldn't give a fig about what I did or didn't do with a husband's money. Who would not give it a passing thought. How dreadful it would be instead to have one of those parents who said, How can you possibly do this, dear, you're breaking my heart, you have to think how it will look, and more. I'd been blessed, having such a mother. A woman who had not one time ever suggested that she wished her daughters had done other than go into wallpaper and horses. Who, rather, had conveyed relief that we'd found something we liked and so did not begrudge her her own work. A mother who would not have turned a hair if we'd sold corsets or bonnets, run boardinghouses or taverns.

I'd said it to Nolan at least a dozen times before he fell ill: I don't like the way the world is set up. Men on the embalmer's table paying off their wives' mortgages, setting a little series of loophole trusts in motion. Men, stretched out, breathing their last, envisioning the financial complexities they were about to put into play. It used to be, I'd argued, Heaven and Hell that a man thought about on his deathbed; now it was life estates and residuals.

When he was dying, we hadn't talked of wills at all. We'd talked instead about putting a new horseshoe pit down by the peach trees. About the annual party for bank stockholders, and if he should make a little speech over dessert. About Fannin's boys, and was her husband, Johnny, going to be able to care for them. About George, and were his investments shaky.

How was it possible that there had been so little communication between us that he could have changed a will and never mentioned it for a dozen years? Or more? How had we come to that, leading lives so separate that in the end even our thoughts were separate, our words no longer conveying where our minds were. Oh, Nolan Rankin, how could you? Why would you?

I left the shop less in anger than in grief over what was lost.

HEADING OUT OF TOWN in my generic gray Toyota, I thought, as I often did, of towns such as ours, possessing a past far grander than its future.

Mineral Springs before the Civil War had been the site of the most famous spa in the country, so in demand that

eight trains a day deposited travellers come to take its me-
dicinal iron-rich waters. The legend was that the planter
who owned the land had been "riding through his prosperity" one day when he got drowsy, dismounted and, napping,
dreamed he found a fountain with healing properties. When
he awoke, he parted the vines in a damp spot nearby, and
discovered a crystal clear spring, laden with iron like the
fabled chalybeate springs of Asia Minor. Now there were
more people in the hilly green cemetery where I had recently buried Nolan than lived in the entire town. The old
train tracks had been torn out, the depot moved and turned
into a cafe, nothing remained of the hotel but a few pieces
of the foundation, and the spring itself was now only a
trickle of water that bubbled up in a low fountain sheltered
by a frame springhouse.

Only the sunsets seemed to me to belong to those early
days—in our part of the state, each night, summer and
winter, as if the atmosphere reflected the iron-filled bedrock
below, the departing sun covered the horizon with carmine
color like lava flowing forth across the sky.

I had three drives I liked to take. One led to the Wild and
Scenic River overlook on the Georgia border, and the sight
of the blue ridge of mountains in the distance; one followed
Long Creek Road—past the Chattooga white-water-rafting
rapids, the signs for boiled peanuts, hot cider, scuppernong
grapes, salmon eggs, winesaps and roseapple honey—to the
cottages, picnic tables and wild animal smells of Oconee State
Park; one wound toward North Carolina, curving up along
Lake Keowee, around a chain of smaller, interlocking lakes.

Unless I had Gentle Ben along, used to a set routine, I
didn't have to choose until the road forked north and west
and then again west and northwest. Unless he was with me,
I could let the car decide. Whichever road I took, I climbed
red clay hills dense with the scent of pine. Whichever way

Life Estates

I went, I found a beautiful part of the world, nestled on the rolling remains of the oldest uprising on the continent. My love for its sights and scents never lessened.

One of the pleasures of "riding through my prosperity" was being out of touch with the rest of my life, beyond the reach of those who called, and called upon me. When I was in the car, all I had to do was drive—as long as I didn't get myself in a wreck, or lost, which was possible on Long Creek Road since each of every two forks on the dirt two-lane also said Long Creek, so that you could go in looping circles, eating up your gas, past the same boiled peanuts sign three times before you put your mind to it and took care to peel off at the right time and hit the state road again. But that was my choice when I was driving; no one else was there to mind. No one else had to be taken into account.

It was a freedom I'd seized upon years ago, and no matter what was going on at home or in the shop, what or who was falling apart or crowding in, no matter who was in need or want at the time, I always gave myself at least one weekly drive. Sometimes, bad times in the past, I'd racked up as many as three hundred and fifty miles in one day, but, even so, it was one of the greatest rewards for the time spent.

Usually on a workday I'd swing by the house to change and pick up Ben. He liked the ride; he knew the stops, the soup and sandwich diner, the state park with its smells to track in the spring, its leaves to burrow under in the fall, the overlook, Rae's truck-stop cafe. Today, at the last minute, I'd decided not to. This was a private trip; I was driving to bury Nolan. I'd take Ben instead on a long after-supper walk, watch the strawberry sunset while he stalked shadows in the brush. I knew if I went by the house, he'd want to come along and I would be reminded of all that needed doing.

It was time to feed the fruit trees, but I would do that Sunday. Sundays I was accustomed to working outside in the orchard and garden alone. Nolan had liked to spend the day dropping by to see cronies, maybe pitching a few horseshoes, watching sports on TV, shooting a couple of garage-door baskets. Then he'd take me to supper at the Mineral Springs Depot, where he'd see the same men again, eating out with their wives, and they'd talk across to other tables, catch up with each other again, and in this way make it through the weekends to Monday.

Taking a break, I pulled off the road at the little diner that offered lunch for $1.75 and outside bathrooms. I liked to stop for a cup of coffee to drink in the car; or to stop with Ben so we could take a leak and stretch our six legs. There were a lot of old homes on the hilly streets behind the car, and at one time or another Katie and I had paid admission to the ones with historical markers, or knocked on the doors of the ones occupied, wanting to see inside them all. Curious what they had on their walls; how they'd fixed up their rooms.

Back in the car, the grade of the road growing steeper, I decided to go first to Oconee State Park, and that made me wish I had brought Ben, that he was on the seat beside me, eagerly anticipating a romp.

One of the treats of my drives was listening to the call-in radio shows, hearing the troubles of other lives told in strangers' voices. Plus I got a lot of local color, of the feel for where people were in our neck of the woods. South Carolina was a complex place. It might be the only state in the country which was both for guns and for abortion rights, against gun control and against abortion control. Although it had a sort of logic if you thought about it: you mind your business and we'll mind ours. The state confused outsiders and politicians, because the press and the rest of the media were hung up on some fixed idea of what was "liberal" and what was "conservative." Operating on the mistaken idea that voting was along those lines. I often thought that the two political parties here should be called "Give Us a Hand" and "Butt Out." Listening to the call-ins, I knew that people sounded as racist, sexist and provincial as they were thought to be; yet I also knew that, in practice, blacks and whites, men and women, now worked together to keep the outsider out with the same vigilance they'd once used to keep each other out. It was progress of a startling kind, if you lived here and if you knew where to look.

Driving with the window open, my arm on the sill, I caught the big hour-long main event of the afternoon: gun control. The staple topic when local events were slow, and there was nothing on national news but natural disasters and general elections.

The first caller did the kick-off speech on the constitutional right to bear arms. The second updated the numbers: more people were killed in vehicles every year than were killed by firearms, so why didn't they come out with legislation for car control? The deejay was going along, having a good time, knowing that the majority of listeners were sick up to here with all the criminals running around loose. He suggested that, well, now, Canada had a tiny percentage of shootings and they had strict gun control. What did the next caller think of that? He thought that was because they didn't have no blacks in Canada. Moving briskly along, the deejay asked the next voice, a woman, if she didn't think that, to use an example, the terrible mass shootings in the cafeteria in Texas last fall weren't due in part to lax gun control. She said she did not; that if the people in that cafe had had their own guns, you could bet your ass they'd have finished that killer off before he got a one of them.

I turned off the radio. It was standard fare.

I passed familiar names on dirt side roads, Apple Barn, Berry Farm, Bear Hollow, and turned right at the fork between Sumter National Forest and Oconee State Park. At the picnic area, I parked and got out to stretch my legs. I'd never taken a cabin here, but I thought that one of these weekends soon I would. They had kitchens—I could see the chimneys—or at least they had wood-burning fire-places. How grand an apple- or cherry-wood fire would smell here in the pines high in the hills. Ben and I could walk and eat and pile up under blankets at night and have easy dreams.

I sat at a weathered table, wishing I was in my old pants instead of my rust jumper, and opened the lid of the diner coffee. No one else was around on a weekday spring afternoon. The outdoors was all mine. I could see wild flowering bushes through the trees, and smell some faint heavy scent almost like magnolias. I'd held myself together so tightly while Nolan was dying, wanting to be there with him all the time, and, equally, often wanting to be far away. I'd not wished him to go so early, so quickly, a man not yet sixty, cut down (as they always said as if talking of a felled tree) in his prime. With time left he should by rights have had. I'd not wanted things settled between us by default.

I THOUGHT BACK to how tickled Harriet had been to learn that both of us had got separate bedrooms the same year. She, in her rose-colored way, had put a romantic face on their move, hers and Knox's. There'd been too much shar-ing of bath and bed, she said; it had got too ordinary. Then they'd given each other a bit of privacy, and soon they were having late night visits to her green satin room or Knox's male quarters. What could I tell her except that it was an-other coincidence—Nolan and I had moved into different bedrooms, too.

What I had not said, had not wished to tell, was that in

our case it had been hurtful, bitter, frustrating, and had changed nothing at all for the better. This was—what?— eight years ago. I must have been forty-seven, Nolan fifty- one.

What precipitated our decision to sleep apart was an acci- dent, one of those chance incidents.

I'd come home late; Katie and I had been going over the books, preparing for tax time. I'd run out of steam, and had decided to call it a night sooner than I expected. Nolan didn't hear me come in; he was up on our bed, looking through a girlie magazine. He had his pants on, a drink on the lamp table—a hefty drink, clearly not his first—but was just looking. I was caught by surprise. I knew the skin magazines were all over the newsstands and the airports; I'd just never thought about it, had grown up without a brother in the house. I sat down on the side of the bed, relieved almost, thinking that here was a chance to say some of the things to him that I'd been too hesitant to say before. Sex was difficult to discuss; misunderstandings were too easy.

I took off my shoes and hose and the rust jumper from the shop. It was about this time of year. (Perhaps that's why his dying in March had had a painful echo to it.) I'd told him that I understood his looking, that all sex was a sort of regression to some degree. That the way it worked for me was different. That perhaps, now, we could do what he liked and what I liked, too. I undid my hair, which in those days was pulled back on each side with barrettes, and took off my white blouse.

In my bra and panties, I told him, "What I like, what I fantasize about, is getting out of the shower, still damp, my skin prickly hot, and being wrapped in a towel and carried to bed. Like a girl, you know?" I'd asked him, "Maybe you could do your magazines and then come wrap me in a towel and we could"—I'd stopped, watching his face, then gone doggedly on with it—"go slower than usual, do some things we haven't done before?" I'd made it a question.

Nolan had closed the pages and shoved the magazine under his side of the bed. "Don't make a big deal of it, Sarah," he said. "I was just window-shopping. I wasn't planning to buy. Come on, let's have a drink and eat. I was waiting for you."

I'd tried again to address where I was, later that week, while it was still fresh (after the skin pictures had gone from under the bed). "Take your time with me," I'd said. "I like to go slow; I like to have time to let my mind get in the mood, get excited. I'd like to do it fresh from the shower. Will you wait? Then I'd like you to put your mouth on me, get me ready."

"Jesus H., Sarah, what's got into you?" Nolan asked, embarrassed. "Can't we just have regular sex without going into all that stuff? Can't a man just have plain sex with his wife when he wants to without all this fuss?"

I'd flown into a rage. "Why does plain sex mean you get to come at the speed you want, and I don't get to come at all? Why doesn't plain sex mean both of us having some? Why is plain sex just you thinking about your dick?"

Nolan had got out of our bed, pulled on his pajama bottoms and gone into Fannin's room. (Where were the children? Off at school? George at Sewanee, Fannin at Duke? They must have been. What did they think when they graduated and their parents took over their rooms, swapping things around, making the old master bedroom into a sitting room/guest room?)

That had been a dreadful time between us. I'd been full of anger for days, weeks. But when I went for my Texas visit with Harriet in April and admired her newly decorated emerald bedroom, I'd kept my own counsel about our decision to sleep apart. Out of habit and temperament keeping my private life private.

Nolan and I had had grudging sex at first when I returned, usually following some bank party when he was tanked up and so could pretend that none of that other business had ever happened. When he could coax his wife—that being his version of the problem—to put out. "Come on, hon," he'd say, "give me a little." As if I were the one reluctant, as if I were the one not interested in sex, not more eager than he for satisfaction. Later on, he would come into my room if he wanted to do it, and go through the motions of touching my nipples and slipping his hand between my legs—a couple of pinches, a couple of rubs, as if he'd learned all the sexual moves of the depraved and enlightened—and then he'd lumber up on top of me and saw away until he came.

I'd seen it as a choice: I could be bitter or I could be agreeable. I could tend my own body in the shower and be glad for whatever additional warmth in bed his body offered, or I could rage and stew, throw my towel across the room, take all the bedding off my narrow single bed and drag it downstairs to the sofa. I'd tried both. In the end, going along had won out; if you were going to cohabit you had to coexist.

By that time, anyway, I'd already got Nolan to agree to separate tax returns, separate checking accounts, separate names; to agree not to list me as his life insurance beneficiary ("That's sick," I'd said, "for a man to think he should support a wife from the grave"); to leave me no inheritance ("I will not, I am not, going to benefit from your death"), or so I thought. I had already made clear that I had no love of and a lot of dislike for the institution of marriage. I wasn't going to relinquish what little intercourse we had.

What made the break so stupid and so sad, and brought

my anger back whenever I thought of it, was that sex was how Nolan and I had got together in the first place. I'd been seventeen, he'd been twenty-one, finishing up at Chapel Hill. His family had come to visit mine in Mineral Springs over Easter; our sisters were school friends with a mutual interest in horses.

I'd been alone in the house with him. Where had the rest of them gone? The lakes? The state parks? I had said I wanted to stay behind and wash my hair, so I must have planned it out. As soon as the front door slammed, before the rest of them could even have got in the car—they might have returned for something, have called out to me—I'd gone into the back room where Nolan was staying and closed the door. He'd been on the bed in blue-jean shorts and no shirt, studying. He was that sort of big North Carolina boy with black hair, blue eyes, broad shoulders and clean looks I couldn't resist. And old enough to know the score.

"Do it to me," I said, peeling off my baggy blue shorts and chambray shirt.

"You're crazy," he said, bolting upright. "They'd kill me. All of them. My folks, your mom."

But he had. Right then and there, on the lumpy guest bed. It hadn't taken two minutes before I realized I had more experience than he did, but I didn't say so. And, later, when he found out, he seemed shocked but excited by it. Him getting a girl who'd been around, he didn't mind that. Except that maybe, on some level, he did. Maybe that was the reason he never loosened up with me later, after we married, the reason he was afraid to find out what it was I really liked, because maybe I'd learned to like it before him. Or perhaps that wasn't it; perhaps he just thought it was always going to be the way it had been the first time. Me stripping and him climbing on and going wild with how willing I was and how exciting that was, with how fast he came.

You would think, with a start like that, long before anybody said anything about love or marriage or making a family, when we were taking it whenever we could, and, later, when our families knew we were "dating" and we spent weekends together, rushing to get into bed when he came to see me at Duke, when I went to see him at Chapel Hill, where he was finishing his M.B.A., you'd think nothing could mess that up. I had thought we were made for each other.

How could it not have worked out? How could I have grown so angry at him? How could Nolan have become so rejecting and rebuffing toward me? If I had been outside it looking in, could I have said, Stop, wait, this moment you are taking a wrong turn, taking a dangerous step, here's where you're going to make trouble? I had never suggested we see a counselor, fearing that one would only tell me to be a better wife, and knowing that there was no chance Nolan would have hauled his ego into some therapist's office and said, My wife and I are having trouble in bed. He'd have died first. He had.

I was never with another man after Nolan. The only institution I was less fond of than marriage was adultery. Adultery being a diversion created by marriage to maintain itself, a distraction to keep a woman or man from ever questioning the basic contract.

I'd tried in vain to convey this to Nolan: my faithfulness. My dislike of, distaste for, adultery as something which adulterated and therefore made marriage palatable. I had tried to no avail to reassure him he would never have cause to worry on that score. But he did not believe me. He was jealous of impossible, implausible, boring and gross men of all sorts who were chummy with me at bank affairs. Jealous even of the gay architect (what Katie and I called "a real man's man") with whom I sometimes had lunch to talk about the houses we'd both worked on. He was jealous even of Harriet, *Harriet*, my oldest friend, to whom, he was convinced, I confided everything. Despite my assurances, and despite the fact that he could have observed that I was not the sort who confided everything to anybody or anything much to anybody.

Jealous men, I had come in time to believe, had once been jealous boys. It became a part of their personality. It seemed to me that Nolan must have been jealous of something as a child. Some kid who had the best shooter, or Marvel comic, or trick of holding a basketball in one hand. Something. (Perhaps that was the personality that went into banking. Bankers were always guarding their assets and coveting yours, weren't they? Wasn't that the job description?)

Oh, Nolan, I said aloud, burying my head in my arms on the rough wooden table, I'm sorry. I truly am sorry.

MY FIRST EXPERIENCE of sex had been so generous, so freeing, I had assumed that was the way males and females were made.

I'd been sixteen; it was the start of my junior year at Miss Pritchard's. I'd fallen head over heels in heat with my history teacher. His name was Ned, Ned Brown. He was ten years older, all of twenty-six. Just a boy, but a grown man to me then. I'd hung around him after class, gone by to talk to him—which was not at all encouraged—whenever I had a free moment. Finally, one day I'd made him a proposition.

I'd closed the door to his office—Mr. Brown he was to me then—and suggested we become lovers. I knew that he would never tell anyone, I said; he'd be dismissed if he did.

And he knew that I would never tell because I'd be expelled at once and my mother would feed me to the spiders. It would be our secret. I had never been with anybody; he could teach me everything.

He'd replied, panicked, "You're trying to get me fired, Cooper. You're tired of school and wish to go home." He'd stood and pressed his palms on an open book.

"You know you want to do it with me," I said boldly.

"I may know that. I also know I wasn't born without a brain. Girls tell everything. They're conduits. That blond who's your next of kin will know by nightfall."

I was offended and said so. "I don't tell anybody everything; I don't tell anybody anything."

Ned had walked around the other side of his desk and stood close to me, still looking ready to bolt. "Where do you propose we carry on this way, and when? This is not only crowded as a zoo, it's also public as one."

"I've thought it all out," I told him. I was in a skirt and sweater set, pretending to be heading for study hall. "We'll meet in the practice room, the back one on the third floor. You can go up there from the faculty office wing here and I can go up there by the back classroom stairs. We'll do it in the afternoon the days that everybody goes to the military institute to have their pretend dates in the parlors. Or when everybody goes to the movie matinee in groups of four to meet boys in the theatre. They'll all be busy. The girls trying to get off where the chaperones can't see; the chaperones trying to watch what the girls are doing. There are always two or three of us who don't go on these trips. Oddballs. Loners. Nobody pays much attention. They know we aren't pyromaniacs, just misfits. We play the piano, or we read books that aren't assigned, or we write long letters home telling our mothers about the wonderful time we're having."

"You've got it all worked out."

"I have." I took a step toward him so we were almost touching. "We have to open the door now; you'll get in trouble. Do men always want to kiss with their tongues?"

"Here," Ned said, "I'll demonstrate."

He taught me so much about my body, made me so comfortable with its wishes. Told me: "You have to do some of the work, too," and showed me how to do my share. Told me: "Take your time; sex is in the brain and the brain doesn't like to be rushed." "But we have to hurry," I'd said the first time, when we were huddled together on a pile of overcoats on the floor of the second piano practice room.

"We don't," he said. "If they come in here at any stage in the proceedings, then we'll be drawn and quartered, tarred and feathered, shipped out. If they don't—then we have world enough and time. Or, at least, we have the afternoon."

I'd said, "Teach me everything. I don't know anything."

"We'll start by naming," he said. "I'm Ned, not Mr. Brown, you're Sarah, not Cooper." He'd put his hand on me, on my panties. "What do you call this?"

"My 'down there.' " I'd tried to make it a joke, but that was the truth. I was jumpy on our piled-up coats, electrified at having his hand on me.

"But what if your 'down there' ends up 'up here'?" He'd let it be a joke.

I tried to remember what other girls called between their legs. Mostly they didn't, or they didn't tell anyway. I thought of Harriet, who was always telling me about how some boyfriend, some Stewart or Stuart, wanted to get his hands on her treasure, wanted to feel her treasure, sure wished he could get in her treasure. "My treasure," I said to Ned, thinking that sounded terribly worldly.

He'd acted as if he wanted to laugh, but he hadn't. He

was one of those dark, soulful-looking men in white shirts that girls eat their hearts out for, just this side of tubercular, but kind, his pale lips able to make the gentlest possible smile at my inexperience. "You hoard treasure; you want to give this away."

I'd reached up, then, and yanked his head down by his black hair, bringing his ear to my lips. "Pussy," I'd whispered.

"Very good. Now we can begin the education of Henry Adams," and he'd put my hand on him, already hard.

We'd only got together a dozen times. It hadn't been as easy to beg out of every outing as I had anticipated, and I didn't want to raise suspicions. Then, at the end of the year, Ned told me he wasn't coming back.

"Time I got that Ph.D.," he said. "That way, the next time I'm seduced by a student, I can at least be sure she's in graduate school."

He'd dropped me a couple of cards my senior year, telling me to take care of myself, wishing me happy graduation, signing them *Henry A.* I told Harriet at the time they were from some cadet, that I couldn't even remember what he looked like. Harriet, who believed me, thought that thrilling.

Later, I told Nolan there had been someone first, but not who. I had to tell; he knew I was using birth control. I didn't share with him my early terror when Ned had tried rubbers, nor my boldness in going to Mother's old doctor and obtaining a diaphragm through a mixture of coaxing and coercion. Counting on his desire to keep me from getting pregnant to combine with his wish not to upset Edith H. Cooper. At first Nolan seemed flattered that someone with experience had sought him out. And that he had a girlfriend who wasn't a virgin. But after we married, his attitude changed. Every word I said, everything I confided I liked, everything I already knew how to do, he used to bank the fire which had flared so swiftly between us.

Living with someone that jealous, I'd learned to keep my mind blank, to keep even my thoughts clean. I'd learned to think of my mother, of my father as I remembered him, of my grandmother, of Bess, my sister, young, rocking herself back and forth after our daddy died, papering her walls with pictures of horses. I'd learned not even to dream of that year with Ned Brown, lest some of the remembered coupling creep into my stirring, my voice, my response.

I poured out the cold coffee and rose, still smelling a heavy waxy smell under the resinous pines. There was no use in dealing with regrets. Today was enough for today. Not that that was true; you never really lived only in the present. I wouldn't be out there among the peach trees weeding and feeding but for the memory of last year's harvest of fruit. You were always thinking about what you'd done before and what you were going to do again. Unless, with Alzheimer's, you'd come to the end of your past; unless, dying like Nolan, you'd come to the end of your future.

DESCENDING THROUGH THE red clay hills with their blanket of pine, I felt back in my skin again—if not at peace with myself, at least not at war.

Part of the pleasure I found in these excursions into the Blue Ridge was the echo of a summer long ago. I was four. It was before Bess was born, when just the three of us, my mother and daddy and I—Mother laden with the baby but still agile in walking boots—spent three months in a log cabin in north Georgia. While my daddy, MacDonald Cooper, gathered data on the WPA in the four-state area— Georgia, Tennessee, the Carolinas—my mother and I spent our days eating peanut butter sandwiches by the creek, which ran by our cabin and tasted of iron, and gathering fresh needles of short-leafed pine for a sachet to put under my pillow at night. She young, slim, tanned from the wind and sun, I in my shorts and canvas shoes, covered in insect repellant, a smell I can still sense beneath the odor of pine.

I remember the thrill of hearing my daddy come back in the early evening, hearing him call out to me, "Where's my Sarah?" and turning my head to see him, amazed to find I could tell direction by sound.

I remember touching a tree, trying to make sense of all its parts. The rough trunk big around as a cider barrel, the sharp-petalled cones, the needled branches, some hanging as low as my head. *Tree*, once a shape in a coloring book, now a reality containing many parts. I remember at night, when the resin-filled logs were fed into the stove and burst into flame like torches, thinking that the very tree itself contained fire.

I kept that summer deep inside me, even after baby Bess was born and we settled in Mineral Springs, after my daddy's heart was torn apart, and after I watched Edith Cooper go back to the pine forests and begin her work there with silken webs glistening with dew, spun on a pile of pine needles. Intricate patterns that I, a schoolgirl by that time, was forbidden to disturb.

I had that summer still, and could recapture its wonder and contentment each time I drove high into the aroma of these woods. Even when I tended my gardens and fed my fruit trees, it stayed with me. Even when I covered the walls of forlorn and abandoned rooms with countless paper forests of lilies, peonies, roses, climbing vines, it was there as well.

TWO

⟋————⟍

I HAD TAKEN Mother's advice, and now woke at a different time and breakfasted in a different place. I'd begun to move through the mornings with some ease, no longer going in and out the back door without a sound so as not to disturb someone resting upstairs. No longer stirring and baking in the kitchen in fear that the smell of the food would be painful to someone who couldn't eat.

This morning in the first light, before heading for the Greenville airport and Texas, I carried my plate of scrambled eggs, toast, peach preserves and my coffee out the front door and sat in a rocker on the porch. This was new, eating here in the mornings. Just in sight to my right were the peach trees, just in sight to my left was the county road and, across it, my neighbor's apple orchards. Before me, the winding gravel drive circled a large oak. Dogs Past ran beneath its branches, darting after scents under the shrubs. (Will Rogers, Thomas Hardy, Gentle Ben's forerunners.) When I had time to linger for a spell, I could watch the mail carrier make her rounds and workers in their ties and scarves head for the highway and city desks.

Fannin, my daughter, had called just before midnight with the news that she was expecting a fifth child. I hadn't slept much after that. I'd packed in a rush, throwing in a linen dress for supper at the Stagecoach Inn, my dog-walking shoes for the back roads of East Texas, and, my mind only half on the matter, had laid out a long, gored blue skirt for today, an embroidered white blouse that Mother had given me after an earlier trip to South America, a wide-brimmed straw hat with streamers, and sandals with heels. Harriet liked me to look presentable.

I was still trying to deal with the news. I didn't know—and perhaps Fannin didn't either—how much of her decision had to do with losing her father. If I calculated right, she was six weeks along, and he, six weeks gone. She hadn't wanted to wake me, she said, and she hoped she hadn't. But she'd just realized I was going off for my "Texas slumber party" and she wanted to tell me before I left. "Don't be mad, Mother," she said, which filled me with guilt.

"I'm not mad," I told her, though I was, of course, as she knew, not heartened by the news. I worried for her health and her stamina, understanding better than she what was involved in raising a child to adulthood. What was she doing, my dark, slender daughter, having baby after baby? What was she thinking of?

I knew what she was thinking, because she'd said it to me and to her Aunt Bess, her confidante. She thought that Bess and I had had lonely childhoods, with our father dead and our mother gone, that she and George had had lonely childhoods, with just the two of them at home. I knew that she wanted to provide for her young a clan of siblings, a pack, the safety of numbers, the warmth of a crowd.

It made me think there was some truth in Harriet's and my joke that our daughters were switched at birth. Harriet, who spent every weekday morning with her group of eleven other friends called Birthday Club, could have been dropped at the North Pole and had a dozen chums by nightfall. She possessed the need to be surrounded by her familiars. Both of them apparently taking comfort in human bodies, whether small or tall, making a fortress around them.

I'd left Nolan's room as It had been when he was alive, for my children, for Fannin's little boys. It might be that she wanted to return there pregnant, to work out her daddy's death in that way. *Rankin* she was going to name it, for Nolan, whatever the gender. "If I can put up with Fannin," she'd said, "my daughter can put up with Rankin."

In the early days when we were together, Harriet and I had talked for hours about our parents. It had provided helpful insight, to see them through outside eyes.

I remember Harriet asking, early on, "How does somebody get into something like spiders anyway? I can't picture a little girl saying in the third grade, I think I'll get famous for studying spiders when I grow up."

And my replying to her, "I think it did happen more or less that way." Then telling her about my mother's favorite grandfather, who used to sit her on his lap and talk about his mother, who'd been a naturalist, a word that young Edith must have seized upon. About how this great-grandmother Fannin had studied primarily carnivorous plants, spending her springs with the Venus flytraps in North Carolina, her summers in Florida watching the southern butterworts eat pollen and insects, her falls abroad observing pitcher plants intoxicating bugs. And how this naturalist had originally been interested in burrowing spiders in the Pine Barrens of New Jersey, but had got sidetracked—flesh-eating plants being more dramatic and easier to get support for. And my concluding, what seemed clear to me, that my mother had felt compelled to complete what her great-grandmother had left undone. Which in part explained the sense I still had that my mother had a calling while I only had a job.

Similarly, Harriet talked to me back then about her father, Nat Sloane, an engineer who loved to hunt, who always had the refrigerator stocked with something curing or basting. She told me how it embarrassed her that there was nothing ever ready to eat, but always pans of game birds with apple wedges tucked in slits to take out the bitter taste, frog legs soaking in cold salty water and vinegar, venison that had to marinate for days. Even, once, bear meat that her dad was trying to make edible. That had helped make clear to me why later she'd chosen to marry someone who hunted for sport, and why her favorite dinner was the Stagecoach Inn's fancy specialty: wild boar terrine, blackened quail, venison au poivre, rabbit cacciatore.

These days, a generation later, Harriet and I mostly talked about a later generation, our children. It made me wonder, watching a pair of produce trucks go by my porch, if our four in their thirties now talked to their closest companions about us, if they recounted Sarah and Harriet stories and shared memories of Nolan and Knox. It made me wonder if their friends replied, So that's how you turned out the way you did, coming from them.

HARRIET FOUND ME at the baggage carousel. She was in white linen shorts, a bright blue silk shirt, her wonderful legs tan as a berry. "You look straight from Tara," she said, holding me at arm's length, smiling to take the edge off her words. "Gone with the winds of change. A hat, yet." Her own highlighted hair was sleek, curved under in what we used to call a pageboy, held back with a blue velvet bow the color of her shirt.

Hugging my old friend, I felt as I always did when I arrived, like a boarding school roommate come to call for the first time. Perhaps we both liked that echo; it took us back in time.

Heading us in her new-smelling Buick away from Houston, the country's fourth largest city (which I thought of as a sort of Los Angeles on the Bayou), Harriet said, "Don't think this ghoulish, Sarah, coming so soon after Nolan's funeral and all, but we're going straight to the family cemetery. We've time to get there for the covered-dish lunch. This is spring grave-cleaning, and Mom is counting on seeing you. I promised her. I use the word *see* loosely, since she can't see and can't hear and for the life of me I don't know why she likes to spend all day at her age surrounded by tombstones and Dad's relatives."

"That's fine," I said. In fact, it seemed a good idea, going to the Sloane plot where Knox Calhoun was buried. I had not been able to come to Knox's funeral because Nolan was in the hospital, and then, when Nolan died, Harriet had said she wouldn't come, there would be a mob, she'd wait for this visit instead. So although we'd made the trip for each other's weddings and for the christenings of our four infants, we had missed out on standing together at the cemetery services. This would help with that. And when she came to see me in October, I could take her to the hillside at home with its fences and kudzu and show her Nolan's stone. "I'm sorry I wasn't here."

"I wasn't there either," she said.

"It was as high church, Nolan's service, as St. Andrew's in its little gray frame building without a single stained glass window can get. Our nice young new beanpole of a vicar was beside himself with such a crowd. I told you half the bankers in South Carolina were there, all with a white rose pinned to their lapels. And that tiny row of grandsons—"

"You had time to plan it properly."

I agreed. "Yours was so sudden."

"At least neither of them had some awful lingering business."

"Yes."

"Imagine, both of us, at our age, widows."

"I'm having trouble with it," I confessed.

"I am, too. And, what's creepy, I find myself still carrying on conversations with Knox. Worse, still speaking of *we*. We had such fun. We ate ourselves silly at your buffet. Thank you for having us. We should know better than to eat late at night. I had no idea I talked in the plural. I've even stood in the middle of the floor and said aloud, Now, where were we?"

"*We* do that, too," I told her, making a joke.

"Maybe it's a queen complex, the royal We. I'm going to have a cigarette, if you want to roll down your window."

"I don't mind."

"You do, too. You wish you were still lighting up. I know. Remember how we used to sit out on your porch watching those ruby sunsets, having ourselves an after-supper smoke because Nolan couldn't stand it in the house?"

"You ought to quit."

"Tell me something new. But I am, I actually am. I'm down to half a pack a day. I figure no handsome younger man—whom I have just met one of—is going to want a smoker, not these days."

"You have some news," I said. This was the way Harriet liked to do, spring a surprise. Have a bit of something new to show or tell me when I came. Sometimes it had been only a piece of jewelry, a new car, a promotion of Knox's, but there was always something saved back, in the nature of a gift. I recognized this as such and asked, "Younger? But that's grand. A new man?" Knox had died in the fall; this was spring.

"Fifteen years younger." Harriet blushed.

"Well, and here I've been trying to work up my nerve to invite Nolan's seventy-year-old doctor and his dog to go for a drive."

"Seventy? Sarah." Harriet made a face. "Sorry. I guess you were a one-man woman so long that anyone else must seem—that you must have to go slow."

"I am going slow. . . ."

Harriet pulled off the highway onto a state road and threw her cigarette out the window. "You don't mind my talking about it, do you? Somebody I've met? I never know where you are about all that. You were always trying to get out of dates at Pritchard's, sneaking off to practice scales on the piano or some other excuse. I don't think you even looked at anyone before Nolan. I always wondered, to tell the truth, how he hammered his way through your barricades. Not that he wasn't the most handsome thing ever."

"But not a ladies' man like Knox. Not that charm." I didn't want to get into my feelings for Nolan, still mixed and raw in my own mind. Certainly I didn't want to talk about where I'd been with men. Her view had a truth to it, in its way, and I let it stand.

We bypassed her hometown of La Salle and headed straight toward the loblolly pines which edged the acres of ancient hardwoods, dark and towering, known as the Big Thicket. A swampy world of egrets and alligators, water snakes and carnivorous plants, where we used to take the four children on day trips when they were small and our reunions included the whole family. I had always found the dense area alluring, the massed sweet gums, sugarberries, hawthornes, cypress, the pale light which reached the wings of wood ducks and the nets of golden spiders as if from an earlier geologic time. I saw it through my mother's eyes. But I found it strange, too. These pines were not the pines of home.

"Heading this way makes me think of your mother," I said. "How is she?"

"Like I said, losing it. I still can't understand how Mom

could have come back here to that falling-down place of her mother's. She's turned herself into a country person, Sarah. It's as if she's never known any other life. She might as well never have lived all those years with Dad."

"He won't be here, will he?" Nat Sloane was one of my favorite people. In recent years he'd been laid up with back trouble at their old home on the other side of the Thicket on the border of Louisiana. I hadn't seen him in years.

"Certainly not, if Mom is."

"But it's his family's plot—"

"Oh," Harriet said, "after nearly sixty years, who remembers? Mom's been a Sloane since Hector was a pup. Besides, they're still legally married so nobody thinks anything. Most of them are so dimly related by now, they don't know who's who."

"I remember everything she fixed for us had a gravy or a sauce on it. Something thick and peppery or thick and sweet." How I had loved Doll and Nat Sloane when we were at Pritchard's. They'd been storybook parents to me: Doll, a dumpling of a woman, always in the kitchen; Nat, a good-natured hunter, bringing home his kill. Both of them ever-present in their daughter's life.

"She still cooks like that."

"Maybe our parents were switched at our births?"

Harriet pulled off the highway onto a two-lane dirt road, and I decided this was as good a time as any to tell her my news. Knowing how she felt about her lack of grandchildren, I knew it would not be welcome. "Fannin is pregnant again," I said.

She slowed the car, then made a brittle laugh. "What on earth will they call it?"

"She says Rankin, whatever the gender, after Nolan." Fannin had giggled, saying that everyone was making jokes about the name for this one. Her boys were Matthew, Mack,

Lucas and Jonathan. They, she and Johnny, hadn't started out intending this echo of the Gospels. Matthew had been named for Johnny's dad, and then the second was called MacDonald for mine and Bess's, shortened to Mack. When the third was a boy, too, they'd dreamed up this scheme. The worst thing, they'd agreed, after reading up on the literature about same-sex siblings, was people getting them mixed up. The boys having to hear, Now, which one are you, little fellow? Now, son, what's your name? Whereas anybody could silently count down: Matthew, Mack, Lucas, Jon, and get it right. Now, Fannin had said, they were saying if it was a boy it would be Acts and if it was a girl it would be Revelations. The rub was that good, serious eight-year-old Matthew had already got into trouble, telling his teacher they were getting a new baby named Revelations. Which had got him a note home suggesting to his parents that such levity was not appropriate for second graders. I'd wanted to tell my daughter that it wasn't appropriate for grandmothers either, but she was smarting already at my fret about her newest pregnancy. Besides, by now the boys had grown into their names, had made them their own.

"I might have known," Harriet said, "we'd get off on daughters the minute we got in the car." She fished around for a smoke. "I didn't tell you my real surprise. Beyond depressing."

I put my hat on my lap and looked out the window. I had gone berserk when Fannin called, thinking of another on the way. Thinking that when this one came in November, Matthew would barely be nine. Surely Johnny, an OB, should have more sense. But I knew Harriet would hardly be feeling sympathy. "Pammy?" I asked.

"I wasn't going to tell you on the phone. Anyway, it can wait; it can wait years, as it happens." She maneuvered the Buick around a series of ruts. "She dropped it on me last week, cool as a cuke, out of the blue on the Bayou. I was down in Houston, having lunch, braving all that traffic and picking up the tab as well, for forty-five minutes of my daughter's time. She showed up late in these heavy black killer shoes that looked as if they were taken off a telephone lineman, black legs, olive drab suit that was way past wrinkled, and a briefcase which must have cost as much as this car. . . ."

I smiled. I knew Pammy's taste in clothes was light-yards from her mother's.

"Then, over coffee—espresso, excuse me—she takes off her jacket and lifts her arm out so I can see where she's had the contraceptive sticks, the tidy fan-shaped implant put in. I thought I was going to pass out right there in the lap of luxury. A Norplant. Making the decision not to get pregnant for five years and not even telling me. Not even mentioning that it was on her mind. She's thirty years old, Sarah. How can she decide that now?"

"What do you think?"

"That all she cares about in this world is making partner at that zillion-dollar law firm, that's what I think. That she hates her mother, that's what I think."

"Fannin says she's going for six. She says children from a big family are more resilient, more easygoing."

"You're always saying they're not us, our daughters," Harriet said, her voice rising, becoming a cough. "But they are. Sarah, they *are*."

"Yes," I agreed.

Harriet lit a fresh cigarette. "At least we can talk about it with each other. What a relief. I used to go crazy bottling it up with Knox. You know how it is: no man wants to hear anything negative about his daughter, since he thinks she's just this side of perfection, or any aspersion on his son, since that's a reflection on his manhood. To husbands you can only say, 'Great kids,' 'Honestly, those kids,' 'I miss the kids,' 'Did you hear from the kids?' That's it—all the allowable sentences about children you can utter to a man."

I laughed. Harriet never stayed down long.

"Here we are."

Harriet pulled in at the Sloane family plot behind a red pickup with a bumper sticker which read STEERS AND QUEERS: NO PLACE BUT A&M. There were a dozen new-model American cars and a couple more pickups, clearly recreational, the wheels too clean, the back ends too waxed, to be really truckers' trucks.

The ground had been cleared long ago for plots, with only a few willows and pecans left for shade and a field of wildflowers available for future expansion. Trees hundreds of years old and a hundred feet high rose past the open pasture.

I followed Harriet toward clumps of men in jump suits and zip-front hunting jackets, and women in pedal pushers, long-sleeved blouses and head scarves. She smiled at all of them, cousins of cousins, most of whom she did not know. The Sloanes had married other names and those names had married other names until by now all the people who knew the kinship lines were underground.

"In the beginning," Harriet said, "Knox thought my family, the Extended Sloanes, as he called them, were a bunch of nuts for coming out here twice every year to weed and rake a bunch of ancestors' bones. But then he really got into it after a while. He'd be out here spring and fall glad-handing distant kin when he didn't have the foggiest notion who they were. And they were always tickled to see Knox. The other men all liked him, they joked around with him.

You know the way country men will make a male club out of anything."

"He was a charmer," I agreed, wondering if she was missing him, wishing him still here offering his handshakes, or if she was fortifying herself against seeing his grave.

Harriet's mother, Doll, was sitting under a pecan tree in the middle of the cemetery. She had on a lavender sun hat, a lavender Sunday dress, and a sweater someone had buttoned across her shoulders. Her hands were holding a cane, and her tiny little feet (how did old people have such small feet no matter their weight?) were in thick white walking shoes.

"Mom," Harriet said, leaning over and shouting at her mother's hearing aid. "Here's Sarah. SA-RAH."

"I know who it is." Doll's soft face crinkled. She reached up a hand to my cheek. "No need to holler. That's a fine hat, honey, your straw. I can't get my girl to wear one. You both look pretty as pictures."

"So do you. SO DO YOU." Harriet turned away, trying to curb her impatience. She looked at me.

I bent down and wrapped my arms around Doll. It didn't matter whether she could hear; she'd never been much for words anyway. I felt years of gratitude well up in me for all the mothering this squat little old woman had provided back in boarding school days.

"You girls are going to stay over with me, aren't you? Stay the night? I'm counting on it. Both your men are buried now; nobody needs you at home." Her voice was slightly metallic, the way with people who can no longer hear themselves. Canned. "Not a soul comes to stay with me anymore. I've got eight beds all made up. You can have your pick."

I met Harriet's eyes over her mother's head. It was her choice to make. My visits to East Texas had coincided with the spring grave-cleaning now and again, but our appearances here had been brief. We'd had dinner plans with Knox; we'd had reservations at the Stagecoach Inn

"Do you want to?" Harriet asked me in a normal tone.

"I'd like that," I told her truthfully, trying to read her face to see if this was all right. "I'm worn out from all the funeral aftermath, all the phone calls which don't seem to stop. I always liked staying at her house, your house, when you were all living together on the other side of the Thicket." I was also thinking that I had not got much sleep the night before.

"Let's do it, then," she said. "I haven't stayed out there overnight but half a dozen times since she moved back here." She bent down and hollered at her mother. "YES, FINE."

Doll beamed and then pointed to Knox's grave, indicating that we should pay our respects.

The polished black double headstone was etched on one side with Knox Calhoun's name and dates. The other side was shiny and blank, awaiting those of his wife. Next to his curved tomb-shaped mound lay a flat grassy rectangle, also waiting. I turned to Harriet, to see how she was taking this.

"I didn't put my name on it," she said. "I think that's ghoulish, creepy. When you see the spouse's name and birth date, then a blank space left for the death date. Besides"—she glanced at me and smiled—"who knows? I might not even end up here. I might be Mrs. Some Young Man's Wife by then."

I studied her, so trim and youthful, so lively and lovely in her shorts with her long tanned legs. Talking of the new man, she seemed the schoolgirl she'd been long ago. As if time had changed nothing.

"I put up a single stone to Nolan," I told her. "A copy of an old one that Fannin had taken a fancy to—it has one of those kneeling lambs on top, you'll see. She had some memory of herself and George when they were little, playing around the plots. She wanted her boys to grow up with that."

Harriet's eyes filled. She said, "How often is she going to drive the Gospel Quartet—excuse me, Quintet—over from Atlanta anyway?"

I wanted to bite my tongue. How thoughtless, to talk about my daughter wanting the boys to have an old-fashioned stone of their grandfather's. When Harriet's feelings were still bruised from Pammy's news.

There must have been fifty people clustered about the grounds. All coming together on this Saturday because some woman married some man named Sloane way back when the world was raw and unsettled. Family tracing was a complicated foolish business, which must have at its heart a denial of death. We and our loved ones may not be around forever, but this place and this kinship will. Our old parents rest under a stone which says THEY WERE THE SUNSHINE OF OUR HOME. Our beloved wife under one which claims TO LIVE IN HEARTS WE LEAVE BEHIND IS NOT TO DIE.

Just then someone in a red jump suit rang the dinner bell, and Harriet's Uncle Bob, her dad's younger brother, came trotting over to escort us to the tables under the tent. He must have been in his late seventies, only a couple of years younger than Doll, but he seemed another generation in his windbreaker and jeans. How was it some people got old, I wondered, so much sooner than others?

"Hiya, Doll, who you got here?" he asked. "Besides my favorite niece."

"You've met Sarah," Harriet told him. "My old friend from South Carolina."

"Sure have. Sorry about your husband, young lady. Sorry for both you ladies. Fellows that age, a crying shame." He gave us all big smiles and smacking wet cheek kisses.

"Happened in my wife's daddy's family. A man outlived all four of his boys. They died from one thing after another, TB, the war, colon. It doesn't seem right."

"Thank you," I said. "It's good to see you."

"Chow down," he told us, holding out his arm to Doll.

There were gallon jugs of iced tea, and soda pop for the youngsters, and two plank tables laden with food. I tried the chicken and dumplings, which Doll had brought, roast pork, fried hominy, coleslaw, yeast rolls, hush puppies and sweet potato biscuits. At Harriet's urging I went back for a smaller dessert plate with a sample of a gooey layered lemon cake called "Better Than Sex," and a meringue, pecan, raisin and whipped cream confection called "So Good Pie." She helped herself to two pieces of the devil's food cake and a bite of the walnut fudge.

"My chocolate fix for the day," she said.

When all of us had tasted all we could, I asked Harriet, "Should we drive your mother home?" I felt suddenly frayed, peopled out.

"Uncle Bob will take her. She likes to stay until the very end. She'll have to have seconds and thirds." She looked across at her mother, a table away. "Then he'll help her make a slow tour of every stone, telling her who's buried where—she doesn't need a hearing aid anymore to know what he's told her so many times—just as if she were the matriarch of this whole clan. It slays me. Then she'll sit back on that bench and watch them lay out pea gravel and rake neat lines in the ground where the grass won't grow. He'll have to stop and debate with a couple of cousins whether to cut down a weeping willow that's putting out unruly roots. It's an all-day party for her. And, except for church, I think it's the only time she goes out of that house all year."

"I need a nap," I confessed.

"We'll go to my house. I want you to see how I've made over Knox's room anyway."

I noticed with amusement in the parking area that someone had taped a hand-lettered sign over the red pickup's offending bumper sticker. This one read POTHEADS AND HOT HEADS: ONLY AT U.T.

WE DROVE THROUGH La Salle, a tiny bit of Texas history which now consisted of one historically marked county courthouse, one Stagecoach Inn on what had been the old cattle-drive trail, one monument designating the spot where the famed explorer, for whom the town was named, had died. Most of the homes lined the main street, which ran south to north; the rest, like Harriet's, were scattered about in the woods outside of town.

I saw that Harriet was keeping a nervous eye on the rearview mirror, and wondered if this was in reaction to the afternoon at the cemetery. It would be enough to make you think someone was after you, seeing all those tombstones, especially one with a polished place just waiting for your name.

"I didn't wear my jewels," I told her, meaning it as a joke.

"They follow new cars," she said, serious. "Don't think I didn't watch out when we were leaving the Houston airport. I'm totally spooked. I admit it." She lit a cigarette. "I didn't tell you what happened yesterday. I could have been a statistic—"

"Tell," I said.

"I was hurrying to meet up with Birthday Club for our morning walk, wearing a blue T-shirt and my white short shorts, working those muscles. My mind was wandering. I was thinking how we tend to look back, all of us, how we replay old tunes, screen old film clips of our earlier lives. I mean, if you think too hard about the fact that more of your life is behind you than in front of you—and it's a little hard to pretend that fifty-five is middle age—it can be a downer. I was trying to pep myself up."

"I've been looking back a bit myself—" I said.

"Just then an unmarked tan van drove by me. The kind you just know belongs to thieves who are out to get an early start lifting a whole suite of furniture or an entire office including wastebasket and light bulbs. You wouldn't believe the gall they have: stealing everything for a weekend at a hunting camp down to the steaks and beer, or every item to furnish a love nest including silverware and wine coolers. I'm not kidding. The driver was a black kid, the passenger a white boy with bad skin. They must have been all of seventeen. When they passed me, the redneck hollered out the window, 'Hey, skinny legs.' That made me so mad, so disgusted at their type, I yelled back at him, 'These are Betty Grable legs, kiddo.' "

I laughed because I could just imagine the scene, Harriet with her hands on her hips, shouting at the vandals. "Did they turn around?"

"Thank God they did not."

"You were lucky."

"Wait till you hear how lucky. It was in the county paper the next day. In the 'Crime Stop' column. Two perpetrators driving a tan van apprehended in the middle of a robbery at a private residence not two miles from my house. They took everything that would plug in or turn on. The sheriff's office reported that they'd confiscated two Tec-9 assault-type semiautomatics. I just about fainted. I've read up on my guns, you know. That's a 9-millimeter with a ventilated five-inch barrel and a thirty-two-round magazine. The kind terrorists use in the movies. Can you believe I stood there in the middle of the road talking back to criminals carrying weapons like that?"

"I can," I said.

Harriet seemed pleased at my response. Throwing her cigarette out the window, she said, "If I'd been carrying a weapon myself I might have shot out their tires." She made a pistol out of her thumb and index finger, pointing it at the window. "The white boy was so young you could see the Clearasil."

"Would you really have shot at them?"

"You don't know what you'd do until you get there," she said, pulling the car around the back of her house, parking out of sight of the street.

Going in the house, I saw that there were now two locks on a door that, to my knowledge, had never even had one before. Surely this was a result of having Knox gone. Surely her whole sense of danger was at suddenly living alone.

The kitchen, as always on my visits, was filled with flowers. Terra-cotta pots with fragrant paperwhite narcissus sat everywhere, on the terrazzo floor, the counters, the wrought-iron table, on the windowsills beneath the green-and-white-checked curtains. Yet the house seemed altered. I couldn't put my finger on why. It had an abandoned air, as if the owners were away. Yet, outwardly, nothing was different. Knox could have been playing golf. Still, there was an absence here. Used to picking up the messages of rooms, I turned in a slow circle, stopping to face Harriet. "What a scare you've had," I said.

She stashed her handbag and hung up her keys. "Let's take a little something to drink upstairs with us. What would you like? Those better-than-sex covered-dish dinners are always drier than a creek bed in August."

"I think I'd like an iced tea," I said.

"I'll have a little gin and orange juice, then. Get my vitamin C."

"The flowers smell wonderful."

"You won't recognize Knox's room. I've fixed it up like a country inn. You'll see. I couldn't stand it until I got it redone. It was like living across the hall from a mausoleum."

"I always liked that room, from back when it was Dwayne's. Sunny, with that window seat."

Upstairs, shoes off, we sat on Harriet's green satin spread, three pillows behind our heads, drinks in hand. I noted the deer rifle propped in the corner behind the lamp table. It was the first time I'd ever seen a gun in her bedroom and it made me uneasy. Harriet was indeed frightened.

"Do you really want to take a nap?" she asked, in a voice that meant she'd like to visit.

"No, I was just having trouble with so many people. It's been a crowded few weeks."

"You seem to be doing great. Straw hat and all. I mean, you seem just the same."

"Did you think I wouldn't be?" I was surprised. We hadn't been together since the men had died, but for the most part our friendship had existed before, around and past our husbands.

She rattled the ice in her glass. "I worry myself sick that *I'm* different, that I'm turning into a Widow. Capital W. I'm terrified that I'll turn into one of Them. There are two other women in Birthday Club who've lost their husbands, each about two years ago. And they started to lose their shapes overnight. I'm not kidding, Sarah. They started to lose their hips and waistlines and get those flat fannies and thick middles you see on old women." She leaned close and dropped her voice. "They began to look just like their mothers. They dress like their mothers and sound like their mothers. And both of them—this gives me the creeps just talking about it—wear *turtlenecks* all the time. Whenever I'm around them, I can feel myself reaching up to my throat, tugging at the neck of my shirt. I keep peering in my closet, terrified that turtlenecks are going to start reproducing in there."

I smiled. "I should have given you a fright by stepping off the plane wearing one."

"Which you don't own."

"Is that right?"

"Theirs are beige. That awful 1950s carpet beige. And aqua, they have them in 1950s kitchen-counter aqua."

I slid down flat, thinking I could have slept until morning. A new grandbaby. What on earth was my daughter doing?

Harriet reached for an ashtray and her cigarettes. "I hate it, actually, being Birthday Club's widow number three. The group has got morbid enough already. All of us talking about our health. We've already had three bouts with cancer and lost one. Plus we've got one member going through what they call 'dose-intensive stem-cell rescue.' And all of us know somebody—a friend of a friend—who's had a stroke and is using a walker when last week she was jogging, or who's got high blood pressure right out of the blue, or developed migraines when she never had a headache in her life, or needed an emergency hysterectomy when she'd just the week before made a speech about all the unnecessary surgery. Or someone who's come down with the depression that eats your insides like a rat."

"But you're all right?" I asked, studying her, so tan and glowing.

"I am. I am definitely Birthday Club's poster girl."

"With the Betty Grable legs." I laughed.

"Don't remind me. That was so *dumb*."

"I think it's our age," I said. "The fifties. It seems to be some obstacle course. Once you make it through it's clear sailing. Look at our mothers: they made it and they're heading for eighty. Look at our men: they didn't make it."

Harriet said, "I went for a mammogram to this woman in Houston we all go to, who's so short she has to stand on a stool to examine you. She said my bosoms were as transparent as glass. She showed me. She put about two dozen X rays up against the light for me to see, and it was amazing, the difference. Some looked like cotton candy, some like lumpy mashed potatoes, some like banana pudding, some like scour pads, and it had no connection to size. No wonder they can't always tell. I had no idea. Did you ever see that?"

I shook my head. I knew I should have such preventative procedures done, including mammograms—the heavy breasts went with the heavy hair in some genetic way. But I hadn't even been for a checkup in several years. That was the luxury of getting your children grown; you could forget about your health. They could get along without you. You didn't owe your children longevity.

"Did you know I heard him hit the tree?" Harriet's voice cracked. She stubbed out her cigarette. "I did. Years after I'd quit lying awake listening for the sound of a car in the drive, the way you worry about your kids for half your adult life, waiting for them to get home in one piece, scared to death you'll hear the doorbell and there'll be some highway patrolman on your porch. You finally get them grown, and then you like cars again. I'd just got myself the sapphire blue Buick Park Avenue. Then—"

"I remember," I said, "all that worrying over ours when they were teenagers."

Harriet took off her bow, smoothed her blond hair, clipped it back on her head. "We'd had those rocky times you have, you know. When the children were babies and I couldn't think of anything but them, and when he was moving to a new bank and that took all his time, I mean, every waking moment. Later, I had those yeast infections, before I got on the estrogen, and he had his prostate problems, the way men do. Those were natural things and I thought we'd got past them. I thought everything had been turned around after that wonderful trip to Aspen we took for our twenty-fifth. You remember. Knox took day hikes with me, and we went to all the pricey restaurants, and he held down his drinking. And we had that divine suite, with two bedrooms and two baths and a view of the mountains. And when we decided to take separate bedrooms when we got home, that seemed a great idea. No more picking up each other's wet towels or opening the cabinet to each other's medicine. No more seeing each other a mess in the morning, me without my makeup and him with a hangover. And no more having to sleep next to each other when things were messy or not in working order. You know?"

"I never saw you happier than after that trip," I said.

"That's what made me so mad. Him plowing himself into a hickory tree on a curve he drove twice a day. I know they did an alcohol count and it was high, but even a heavy drinker like Knox could navigate his way home blind. He'd done it too many times to count, driving home from bank parties that went on too long or from out-of-town trips to see Houston clients. It was senseless and awful, his dying that way."

"It was a hard time to lose him." I was stretched out on what I thought of still as Knox's side of the bed. His end table had always been piled high with Civil War books, his escape reading, stacked beside his half-glasses and a coaster and gold Cross pen. He looked, had looked, much like a Civil War general himself: dapper, small, trim, with wavy brown hair parted in the middle and a neat mustache. Who had he cast himself as? I used to wonder. Robert E. Lee?

"I didn't mean to get morbid," Harriet said, her cheerful self back in control. "It's the idea of being alone. I don't know how to start over. What do women do who aren't in those movies with the improbable plots on some golden pond or travelling alone by the fountains of Rome? Maybe Club Med? Can't you just picture a tropical beach crawling with a herd of flat-fannied women in turtlenecks, searching for men?"

"But you said you'd met a young man."

Harriet tucked her feet under her and turned to me. "Ah. I did. I have. His name is David. David McCord. I swoon— whatever happened to that word?—every time I think of him. I couldn't figure out at the beginning what made him so attractive. Then I had to laugh. I'd been around men my age and up for so long I'd got to thinking they only came bald, fat, diabetic, emphysemic, depressed, or courting cir-rhosis of the liver after forty years of hard drinking. It dawned on me the reason this man was so beautiful was because he's so *young*."

"How did you meet him?"

"It was the strangest thing. I owe this one to Dad, of all people. He, David, is an oral historian, at the university. He'd been to see Dad, to tape his story about that damn radio. You remember that? Of course you do. Can you believe it, someone driving through the Thicket to get that down on tape?"

"I liked your daddy's story," I said.

"Lucky for me, David did, too."

I'd liked a lot hearing how Nat Sloane had put together the first wireless telegraph receiver, as they were called then, in East Texas. Winding twenty-four insulated copper wires around an oatmeal box to get the right wavelength, using a galena crystal. I'd liked hearing him recite the chro-nology, warm up to the finale. The first beep transmitted across the country signalling the hour. The first radio receiver, after World War I, built in the back of a Ford garage, using dry cells and an auto storage battery, which could pick up music all the way from Chicago, Illinois, and Davenport, Iowa. The thrill of completing his first Armstrong super-heterodyne radio in time for the first-ever broadcast of the Rose Bowl game from Pasadena, California. "I worked on that thing, racing time like Lindbergh or Marconi," he would say. And, on cue, I would ask, "What was the score?" "Notre Dame twenty-seven, Stanford ten." I still remembered.

He had reminded me of Edith, not his retelling of his story, but his passion for electronics, for something out there, beyond himself. Nat's fingers winding that wire around a cardboard box to pick up sound was as amazing to me as Edith crouched under a stand of pines, waiting quiet as the spider's web, watchful as the spider herself. I'd wished that for myself and later for my children—but that long-term, lifetime commitment to the daily details that lead to something new seemed out of style.

"Anyway," Harriet was saying, "Dad told him to look me up. 'You young people ought to get together,' he told David. I was so embarrassed I could have died. But David thought it was charming. 'Your father fancies himself a match-maker,' he said. So I told him about the kills in the refrigerator back in Dad's hunting days, and then I took him to the Stagecoach Inn for their game dinner, pretending it was the same." Harriet flushed slightly. "You don't mind my talking about this, do you? So soon after—"

"I'm glad for you," I said truthfully. "Did he stay over?"

"I wish." Harriet stretched her legs. "I guess I thought we'd hop right in bed. Don't be shocked. But he's just getting over a painful divorce, he says, and he wants to go slow. He's into the New Chastity. I wanted to tell him: Not me. I grew up on the Old Chastity and once was enough. I guess it hurt my feelings. . . ." Harriet shut her eyes, then opened them. "I mean, I sort of made a pass."

"But surely he must realize, whatever his age, how lucky he is, to have you interested—"

"I guess. I mean, I think so. He calls a lot. And he says we'll take a trip when his semester is over and we have time to get 'better acquainted.' I hope that means what I hope that means."

"I'm not surprised you found someone already."

"It may seem soon to you. I mean, you— But to me it was a long four months without a man." Harriet clapped her hands and got to her feet. "Come on. I'll show you what I did to Knox's room, although I shouldn't call it that anymore, should I?"

I FOLLOWED HARRIET around what had once been her son Dwayne's room, listening to her and looking at the results. She'd mounted Knox's antique muzzle-loaders on the wall, a dozen of them, and, on each side, put framed photos of her family and his. His Civil War books were cased behind glass where his TV had once stood. The country-looking bedspread and pillow shams in ivory had an old-fashioned look against the gray papered walls. Knox's neat twin beds (Dwayne's before that) had been replaced by a four-poster high off the floor. It was history, that was the message. This room was history.

"I fixed it up so David wouldn't think my husband's ghost was across the hall," Harriet said. "I found all sorts of stuff when I cleaned everything out." She gestured toward the chest of drawers and the closet. "Belated musket shots fired after he died, you could say. For instance, in his wallet, I found the list of my sizes I'd given him when we married, yellow as parchment and permanently creased. My dress size, gloves—imagine, shoes, panties, hat—really. I almost tore it up. You could tell he'd never used it."

I felt suddenly uneasy, guessing what was coming. Knox, the ladies' man, had been careless, foolish.

"Sit over here by me on the window seat," Harriet said, patting a place.

"What else did you find?" I asked reluctantly.

"Oh, Sarah, how do you always know?" She started to light a cigarette but then stopped. "No, I mustn't smoke up this room. Young men . . ." She took a breath. "I found a blouse, stuck up on his closet shelf. This was, remember, November when he died, It was gift-wrapped in red from Neiman's. I told myself it was an early Christmas present." She swung her foot up and down, her toes barely touching the polished floorboards. "It was a silk blouse, white with a big bow tie, and printed all over it were tiny red and black bow ties. Tacky. It wasn't in my colors and it wasn't my style and, it turned out, it wasn't even in my size. It was a *ten*."

I had to smile, I who wore a size ten on my good days.

"It was so wrong, I was speechless. How was it possible, I thought, to live with someone for thirty-two years and still be a total stranger? I held it up against me; it was big as a house. And I could just imagine Knox handing it to me Christmas morning, and me saying all the things you're supposed to say. I wanted to cry.

"Then I remembered exactly where I'd seen one like it before. We were at a bank party in Houston, one of those things with mountains of shrimp and ice sculptures and mobs of people I was supposed to remember. And this old girl came up, clearly having been in banking since paper money was first put into circulation, the sort with humped shoulders and logs for legs. She had on this very blouse.

Knox asked her, sweet as taffy in that way he had, 'Honey, where'd you get that knocked-out blouse, if you don't mind my asking?' And of course she was dying to tell she got it at Neiman's and how much it cost. All the while I was standing there thinking the money would have been better spent on calcium tablets. Knox said, 'I think I'll get one of those for my secretary; she's always saying I don't give her anything.' And I kept my mouth shut, but I knew that Mrs. Beeson wouldn't wear that if her job depended on it. But I told myself that was just an unperceptive male thing to do.

"Then, when I saw the blouse in the box, all that tissue paper, I thought, How could he have imagined I wanted that? How could he? But I guess I knew it wasn't intended for me—" Harriet pressed her fingers to her temples. She'd been coughing as she talked, as if remembering had shut off her air, as if breathing and telling the story were too much.

I didn't know what to say. I felt defenseless in Knox's place. I could imagine myself leaving behind a wrapped package—slippers, a book, a framed photo of Ben—and Nolan, a widower, going into a jealous slump, imagining a recipient in his mind, when the gift might have been meant for him, or our son, George, or Johnny, our son-in-law. It wasn't really that I doubted Harriet had found a gift intended for another woman—Knox did attract females the way a bee attracts honey—but that I didn't want him judged, condemned, when he wasn't here to answer back. "Perhaps he bought it for Pammy," I ventured.

"You're trying to be nice," Harriet said, wiping her eyes. "You know better."

"Speaking of Christmas presents"—I decided to change the subject to give her time to regroup—"do you know that Nolan is still getting the one you sent him? Posthumous potatoes?"

"Great heavens! The Potato of the Month. How ghastly, ghastly, to have a gunnysack arrive addressed to someone dead. Do you want me to cancel them?"

"Not at all." I visualized the hefty burlap bags with their neat New Penny Farms cards attached, giving the name of the potato, the cooking suggestions, the starch content. The Norland Reds arriving just as Nolan began treatment; the Yellow Finns, the day after the funeral.

"I remember I thought my card to him was cute: 'To a real meat and potatoes man.' "

"So he was."

"I always do that, don't I?" Harriet said. "Remember Fruit of the Month? And Chocolate of the Month? Remember Fifty Designer Day Lilies?" She hugged her knees.

"I liked the boxed set of Eight Great Classic Colors discontinued by Crayola. Goodbye to maize, violet blue, raw umber."

"That was a birthday present." She began to pace the floor, went to the door, then sat back down.

"The potatoes will serve to mark the year," I said. "When they stop coming, we'll get out of our widows' weeds."

She made a shaky smile. "Us, in widows' weeds. What were they anyway, weeds?"

I looked around the room that had been Dwayne's and then Knox's, and now was being readied for a young man who might or might not sleep under this roof if not in this space. It was like archeology, like excavating down through layers of the earth. Rooms and their histories, occupants and their antecedents. "Harriet—he isn't here to ask about it. Don't make yourself miserable guessing." I touched her arm.

"What would you do if you found out that Nolan had been having an affair?" Her voice was scarcely a whisper.

"With a size four like you?" I tried to make it a joke.

"I'm serious, Sarah."

"I don't know. There are so many ways husbands and wives miss connections, don't you think?" There were so many ways we were all unfaithful to one another. So many ways that Nolan had been to me, and I to him. Would a sexual lapse have mattered? "I think I would feel the most grief for her," I said, "the other woman. Someone unable to properly mourn."

"I'LL NEVER UNDERSTAND if I live to be a hundred," Harriet said, slowing the car to a crawl on the bumpy two-lane, "how Mom could have come back here to spend her last days at Grandmother's house."

We passed muscadine vine, wild strawberry, Indian strawberry, blackberry in bloom. A loon called in the twilight, and a whippoorwill. High in the trees, owls waited for night. What a lovely time of year this was in East Texas, a lush season not yet the steaming hot summer, crawling with bugs, air so thick that breathing was work. "Perhaps she likes being out here," I said.

"It's a flat-out country place. And that means never-ending chores. I can't tell you. Every time I come out she's got a project. She's canning pears and plums or she's shelling pecans or hickory nuts. She's got the hired man mending a leak in the roof or repairing a gate. Or she's called the county about her water well or septic tank. I can hardly stand being out here for more than an hour."

When Harriet's mother moved back some years ago to tend her own dying mother, she left her husband behind in their house on the edge of Louisiana, where Harriet had grown up and I had visited. With the move, it was as if Harriet had lost not only having her parents together, but her childhood home as well. I thought that part of her resentment about the old country place was no doubt this—anger at all she'd lost. "We don't have to spend the night," I offered.

"No, no, I want to. A slumber party at Mom's house—it'll feel like we're back at Pritchard's. But such endless failures of the physical world give me hives. I guess I'm afraid I'll be next. I can see me moving in when Mom is gone, and starting to call you to talk about how the linoleum is cracking or the flue isn't drawing or the window sashes are rotting out."

Sensing, beyond the pines to the east, the Big Thicket with its massive hardwoods, dim light and oppressive undergrowth, I couldn't imagine Harriet living out here alone.

We parked in the dark on the eroded shoulders of the road, and Doll met us at the door. "You girls sit," she ordered. "I've already got the mats and silver out. I waited to fix things until you showed up."

I could see that she had unwrapped the Towle sterling from the soft maroon bags where she stored it until company came. The last time I'd been here with Harriet, Doll had fried us up a late breakfast, although we just stopped in for an hour, dredging strips of bacon in heavily peppered flour, frying it up in wild-hog sausage fat. Batter-fried bacon, a delicious deep-country treat. "You'd have to be a woman to eat this meal," Harriet had said. "Any man sitting down to this much animal fat would have a coronary occlusion on the spot."

It was hard to realize that then, a scant year ago, both men were alive.

Tonight Doll had fixed chicken and dumplings, left over from the cemetery dinner, hot devilled eggs baked in a thick cream sauce, and, for dessert, fresh gingerbread, much too sweet, swimming in a dark chocolate glaze. She brought us each a cup filled to the brim with sweetened milky percolator coffee. The fact that Harriet preferred decaf and I drank my coffee black didn't matter. Being good daughters, we took what we were offered.

"It's wonderful, Mother, WONDERFUL," Harriet shouted.

"I can fix you girls something else if you're still hungry," Doll said. Her voice rose and fell in the way of someone who can't hear. Out of her Sunday clothes and her sun hat, away from the clusters of kin, she looked wrinkled, powdery, soft and old. Everything about her tonight was white—her hair, her cheeks, even the cotton duster she wore.

She took our plates, insisting that she didn't need any help in her own house. That if she'd wanted a maid she'd have hired one. We watched her through the kitchen door as she tidied up, retracing her steps, going through the slow motions of cleaning. Over her shoulder, she talked to us about the old days.

"Papa used to take a single-shot down to the creek bottom and bring back two or three squirrels. He had a string of outbuildings in the back that were all workshops. He could fix a new blade for the scythe or new points for the plow. He made his own shears and built his own brakes. Most of the time he spent out with a bush-hog trying to clear the land. Back then it was a daily chore; the underbrush pushed up and you cut it back.

"Youngsters played with what they had. My cousin— we'd take two corncobs, put a string between, play at being a yoke of oxen. We'd cut sticks, ride horses. My papa would get him an elm branch—he called it el-um—chew it down into a brush, use it to dip snuff. He died when his horse hit a fence. He hit his head on a rock."

We could hear the sound of pans and her talking to herself. Then she said, "Well, now, that's water under the dam."

Harriet and I smiled. This had been the favorite fight between Doll and Nat in the house where I'd visited, a fight

repeated over and over, sometimes half joking, sometimes
truly angry. Doll would say, "That's water under the dam,"
when Nat went on and on about his super-het, his first-ever
Rose Bowl game. He'd flare up, holler out that water did
not go under a dam, it went over a dam, that, in fact, water
usually didn't go anywhere. That was the purpose of the
dam, to dam the water. To which Doll would answer, drawing herself up to her full five feet one, "That's what I said,
it's water under the dam."

When Doll finished her clean-up chores, we sat on the
sofa and went through the ritual of looking at the old photo
album and opening the flowered drawstring bag and taking
out Harriet's letters from school.

We turned the thick black pages, looking at the pictures
held in place by tiny gold stickers. There we were at fifteen,
sunbathing in the summer in our two-piece Rose Marie
Reid bathing suits; there we were at Pritchard's, dressed for
a formal, both of us in strapless gowns with wide skirts,
both with corsages taped to our shoulders; there we were
bridesmaids in each other's weddings, only six months
apart; here as young mothers in heels and long skirts holding fat baby boys, then in short skirts with bouffant hair
holding wiggling baby girls. Last, posing with our husbands
as beaming couples. Where had those people gone?

I lifted the tissue-thin green Hallmark pages of Harriet's
letters home. How I'd wished to copy them, those messages
that had gushed forth from her pen almost daily, seeming
so carefree and affectionate. Now they seemed to me forced;
cheerful missives never quite reaching their mark.

Dear Mom, I met a new boy named Stewart. He is from
Virginia. He sails in the summer and sleds in the winter.
I'm sure he will ask me to the Cadets' Ball. . . .

Dear Mom, Today in Latin we learned eight ways to say,
The soldier carries his sword. . . .

Dear Mom, Four of us got to go to the movies today
without a chaperone. . . .

Dear Mom, Today I was invited upstairs to eat chocolate
cake with the seniors. I think I must lead a charmed
life. . . .

Outside on the porch, we watched mayflies flock to the
aromatic insect-repellant candles. A light breeze stirred, the
stars came out and, across the road, the pines stood solid
as a canyon wall. High in the air an owl hooted.

Harriet lit a cigarette.

Doll stuck her head out the screen door. "You girls want
separate or together? I've got six bedrooms, eight beds made
up. You can have your pick."

"Mom, we'll take the front room. FRONT ROOM," Harriet hollered.

"It's yours. I've got plenty of quilts in the hall closet. You
know where they are. It'll get cold toward morning. It's
likely we'll get a rain in the night. Did you bring gowns?
There are plenty in the chester there, inside the bottom
drawer."

Harriet rolled her eyes. Since moving back here, her
mother had picked up the old country terms. Chest of drawers, she told me, had become first chester drawers and now
was just chester.

"You let me tend my business in the bathroom first," Doll
said, closing the screen, "then you can take your time. I
drew a full tank of water if you want a bath. There's Cash-
mere Bouquet soap. I put your towels out already, they're
the pink ones on the side of the tub."

"We'll be FINE," Harriet told her, gesturing to her
mother's back, then catching herself and sighing at the
futility. Throwing her cigarette out into the dark among the
fireflies, she slipped her shoes back on. "Look at her," she
said, "stuck out here in the sticks, in nowhere-nowhere East

Texas, beyond country, doing fine. Neighbors bring her over stuffed Russian hog sausage, hired men mend fences and shore up outbuildings for her, and the Sloanes, who by rights belong to Dad, fetch her to reunions and church. You have to hand it to her."

I looked out toward the Thicket to the east. When our children were small, Harriet and I had taken them on day trips into the ancient area, showed them swamp lilies, widow's-tears, carnivorous pitcher plants. We'd photographed golden spiders for Edith. Among the cypress we'd sighted wood ducks and egrets, and heard the thump-thump splash of alligators in the waters of the bayou. I said, "Maybe the best thing our mothers have done for us is to live to an old age."

I took a quick tour of the old country house while Harriet and her mother made their good-nights. I hadn't been out often, and I found it a very pleasing place, with its surfeit of bedrooms, painted in faded flat paint-box colors: ochre, lavender, gray, blue, sage, rose. Rooms which once must have been designated as parlor, sewing room, nursery. I papered them in my mind's eye as they must have looked a hundred years ago. I could see that despite her diminished vision and disappearing hearing, Doll Sloane was far from lonesome here. The past was too present.

The front bedroom had one giant feather bed, and we each sank down as if in separate sleeping bags. I tried to prop up on one elbow, but that only made me sink deeper into the goose-down mattress. Instead, I put my hands behind my head. We were both in sprigged cotton nightgowns which smelled of dried sachet, faintly musty. It was a true slumber party.

Harriet scooted way down and put a feather pillow on

her chest, tucking herself in the way she'd done at boarding school. "The first night Knox and I slept over after Mom moved in," she recounted, "she asked us, 'You sleep together or apart? Some folks snore. I can put you in two rooms or one.' Knox was as embarrassed as a teenager, as if we weren't long married. Then the door didn't quite close—we were in the blue room—you know the way these old frames sag, and he was sure she could hear the bed bang against the wall in the middle of the night. He just about died." Harriet gasped. "Oh, listen to me, the things we say and don't even hear—"

"This is like being back at Pritchard's," I said. "Listen to us, we're whispering as if it were after lights out."

"I know. We could shout and she wouldn't hear." Harriet shifted to her side. "My back's going to pay for this mattress," she said. "I should have tested every bed like Goldilocks."

"I like this room with windows on two sides."

In a normal voice, Harriet asked, "Do you think in another ten years we'll be worrying about our boys the way we do our girls now? Boys are always slower—maybe even at breaking their mothers' hearts."

I thought of our sons, George and Dwayne. "I'm sure we'll see some cracks in the surface from losing their fathers at such an early age."

"I don't miss that, the father-son thing."

"I can't say I do either."

"Our *marketroids*. How on earth? Sons of bankers are supposed to turn out to be potters or forest rangers, aren't they? My Dwayne a trader, and I don't even know what he trades, except that it's foreign things that don't exist yet. Your George betting on miracle materials and getting backers besides. Maybe we were a recessive influence, like recessive genes."

"We never thought about all those Stuarts and Stewarts

at school as having fathers, did we?" I was thinking that when you're young you imagine only yourself to be part of a family. I had talked to Ned Brown a lot about my mother, her spiders, my daddy being already gone, but had never thought for a minute of asking him about his parents. Had not even, I think, considered that he had parents. He was *grown*. Imagine, and six years younger than my son now.

Harriet peeped out over her pillow and sighed. "All those big-boned Virginia boys with stand-up hair and sagging socks—I miss them. Where are they now?"

"The future was open then, wasn't it?" I said. "Open as a fan."

"Remember," Harriet asked, giggling, "how we were the absolute only girls in school without nicknames. That must be why they put us in the same room. *Harriet* and *Sarah* when everyone else was Teeny, Tiny, Bitsy, Midge, Punkin, Puddin, Sugar, Ginger."

"What happened to all those names?" I asked. And to all those girls now heading for sixty.

Harriet hugged her pillow. "You know what I miss? I miss the corsages. Remember how we all had to compare what the Stus sent? To see if we were going to be wearing skimpy split carnations or delectable camellias. You never seemed to care, they were the same to you, even when you got those awful Vanda orchids that looked as if someone had picked bug-eating plants from the Thicket. But I minded. I liked to open that chilled box with its little sentimental card, lift off the layers of waxy paper, and see those real red rosebuds or that melting white orchid. How I loved it—my girlhood of corsages."

"I wasn't so fond of all that," I said.

"I know. Anytime you could get out of anything you were up there in that practice room pretending you were going to be a concert pianist. I don't think you ever even played the piano before or since. You were just trying to hide."

"I confess it." I smiled at her, remembering that I did like our staying up half the night talking after the dances, with Harriet confiding everything about some new boy, what he did or didn't want to do, how far she let him go, how much he wanted to touch her treasure.

Harriet said, "This is going to sound dumb—is dumb— but what I didn't realize was how much of what I did all day, every day, was for Knox. It seems like I spent all day getting ready for him to come home in the evening. I find myself still trying to do it. I mean, I'll be downstairs on the sun porch making plans for supper in my mind, and I'll think, What can we eat? We had that chicken curry, but now the weather is warming up. I'd like to have chicken salad, but that would be chicken two nights in a row. I actually find myself saying things like that, in my head. When I could eat chicken seven nights a week—or never— if I felt like it. I could even pig out on double chocolate fudge for breakfast if I wanted to."

I tried to get into Harriet's skin. How on earth would I feel if I were still waxing that gateleg table for a husband who wasn't there, for bankers who weren't going to come to dinner anymore? Bereft. "I think you took to marriage better than I did," I said finally. "I don't miss that. It wasn't anything that Nolan did, I don't mean that; it was the insti-tution that rubbed me the wrong way."

Harriet tossed her pillow at me. "Oh, you," she said, "with your shop and your Cooper name. I guess I'm just the opposite—even when it was something Knox *did*, I couldn't imagine not being married. I still can't; I feel like a fish out of water. Truly I do." She got out of bed, holding up her gown, tiptoeing as if we really were back at school. She opened the window and sat on the deep wooden sill, sneaking a cigarette.

I pulled up a green-painted chair and joined her. The walls of the spacious high-ceilinged room were a color as faded as old linen, amethyst Harriet had called it. A faint scent of lilac came from the chest of drawers. "Will you be all right," I asked her, "financially?" I was trying to sort out all that she might be missing.

Harriet hesitated. "To tell the truth, I don't know for sure. I thought things were fine. Knox left me a life estate, you know?"

"Life is a life estate," I said mildly. I didn't want to get into Theo Kenton and his red suspenders, or Nolan's change of mind about what could be conveyed from the grave.

Harriet tapped her ash in the wide windowsill and stuck the pack in her nightgown sleeve. She picked at a painted fingernail. "Last week I gussied myself up and went to see our accountant, taking all those boxes of stubs and chits I always do at income tax time. I even—promise you won't laugh—wore that damn blouse that Knox had wrapped. I mean, black, red and white are not my colors, but I thought they might be to an accountant's liking. The blouse was baggy but my skirt was snug. I figured that balanced out. And I didn't think it would hurt, showing off my legs.

"The first blow was when he informed me that he, Freddy, was not *my* accountant; that he'd been my *husband's* accountant. And here I had not even thought to call and ask him if he'd do my return or what he charged. An arm and a leg, it turned out. That was awkward. Then, after he'd smoothed that over and told me he'd be glad to handle my problem, as he called it, he went over my checkbook. Explaining to me that in the past—this immense toad of a man in a striped vest holding him in like a girdle—my expenses had just about equalled the funds deposited in my account. 'Well, naturally,' I said, not seeing what he was getting at, 'that's how Knox and I settled on the amount he gave me to run the house.'

" 'Yes,' Freddy the Frog pointed out, 'but now the expenses are continuing but the deposits are not.' And what did I propose to do about it? He explained in a patient tone that the investments and interest might last me up to ten years, depending on inflation, but that if I sold the golden egg, the bank stock—and who could tell where Texas banks were headed—then I was in worse shape. I could either, he said, cut my expenses in half, or—and he actually snickered, ha, ha—get a job." Her laugh turned into a hacking cough.

"Get someone to listen to that," I said, thinking she sounded like a child with the croup.

"I'm going to quit, cross my heart." She stubbed her cigarette.

I hadn't thought to wonder what Harriet would do for money; it had never occurred to me there would be a problem. Knox was a banker's banker, an enthusiastic financier, a charming money manager. I didn't waver in my objections to husbands supporting wives from the grave, yet what would someone like Harriet do? For that matter, what could my daughter do, with another on the way?

Crawling back into bed, Harriet said, "I imagined myself going to some career counselor who specialized in Returning Women, as they call us. Some little-chinned guy in a black toupee who'd lean across his desk and say, Mrs. Calhoun, I've looked over your life experiences, your aptitudes and interests, and my strongest suggestion for you is: *remarriage.*" She crouped, only the top of her head visible. "And for that advice I'll have to pay a hunk of money which fat Freddy has just explained to me I no longer have."

"It sounds to me as if you've got ten years to be a swinging single before you have to settle down." I said it lightly.

Harriet confessed in a hoarse voice, "I'm scared to pieces, is the truth. I mean, my grandmother was a widow for forty-six years, *forty-six*, and my mom might as well be one, running off fifteen years ago, camping out here in the back-woods of the universe since then." She spoke in a whisper. "I mean it. I'd die before I'd end up like them."

THREE

I WAS PARKED AT the gate to the doctors' parking lot at
quarter till one, waiting on Will Perry. I had Gentle Ben in
the car, and had stopped at BiLo on the way to pick up a
double pack of Gainesburgers for the two pups if it became
a long afternoon. The treat, and pie tins to use as water
pans, were locked in the trunk.

I'd called him yesterday at his office, catching him right
before he left for rounds. His nurse, who knew me only as
the wife of one of his deceased patients, did her duty as the
cop at the door, skillfully screening the survivors.

"The doctor is with a patient," she said. "I'm sure he'll
get back to you."

"Tell him it's Sarah Rankin."

"Ma'am, I can't interrupt him now."

"Let him decide that. Just tell him I'm on the line."

"I'm sorry, I can't do that."

"I'm going to hold," I told her.

In half a minute, Will picked up. "What's going on,
Coop? Be fast. I've got a naked man here and you're de-
laying his receiving good news."

"Want to take the pups to the state park tomorrow afternoon?" I knew Wednesday he had half a day off.

He drew in his breath. "Sounds good. Pick me up at the
doctors' parking lot at the hospital, by the gate. One o'clock.

Make that ten till. If I don't leave then, I'll never get out of there."

"What about Missoula?"

"We'll swing by the house for her. You take care of whatever else we need." He made a hoarse sound, a bark almost. "Food or whatever."

"I know a swell place."

"I could use one." He hung up.

I stroked Ben, who was lying on the passenger seat beside me. Such a smooth sleek coat. He knew we were going to the country; he could unfailingly sense it. I'd had dogs ever since I married. Mother had always had dogs. Scotties, Edith had, and then, later, Cairn terriers. Nice, neat, smart, sporty little dogs who kept pace beside their human. Agreeable dogs. All males. Mother refused to get a female dog; she said she didn't have time to worry about getting her spayed or with dispensing puppies. I'd thought that an awful attitude when I was a girl. Now I wondered if it was behind the generally accepted preference for male children. It was certainly true that reproduction, the danger of it, the possibility of it, a woman's fear of or need for herself or her daughters to bear babies, was always on her mind. Look at Harriet—fretting herself into a state because Pammy was not having children; look at me— getting gray-haired and frazzled because Fannin was having so many, so heedlessly.

Bess had called this morning to say that she'd invited Fannin and the boys to come for Mother's Day. Would I mind? "We've got two foaling," she said. "Plus the Polo Cup matches. They can take over the upstairs and sleep as late as they like."

"You're so good to them," I told her. My daughter liked going to her Aunt Bess's and being coddled. And her sons loved to be around the animals. On neighboring horse farms there were sometimes foxhound puppies or even fox cubs to see. My good Ben was not enough for four pairs of arms.

"You're sure you don't mind? Them coming on Mother's Day?"

"I'm glad. And besides, Fannin is the mother we ought to be thinking of." My daughter did not have her strength back yet after Jonathan; her blood count was low. And her spirits had been sagging since her OB, a Japanese woman, had discouraged the idea of six. "Content yourself with a basketball team," she'd told Fannin and Johnny.

"Where's ours these days?" Bess asked.

"Heading for Patagonia," I reminded her.

Bess's voice had a familiar tinge of hurt. "You keep up with her, don't you? You're proud of her, aren't you? You're not mad she ran off when we were growing up, that she always had to be off somewhere, making three names for herself."

"I am," I said. Then, "Thanks for having them." I didn't want to get into our worn old argument about our mother. I had a lot more guilt than I let on to Bess. I still reproached myself that I had called Edith back from the Pine Barrens of New Jersey, where she was at last doing fieldwork, to say that Grandma couldn't handle things and that Bess was having nightmares. My curly-haired little sister crying out in the dark, her daddy dead and her mother gone, her affection not yet turned to horses.

Bess of course did a lot of mothering herself, and I wanted to send her a gift in thanks. She was godmother to Fannin's four, and I'd thought, if this one was a girl, they might name her Bess. Had I known that my sister would end up fifty-one, divorced and without children, I might have named my daughter for her rather than for the first naturalist in the family tree. But then frail dark wiry Fannin, as Bess or Bessie, would have been a different child.

Life Estates

Off the phone, I found some dessert plates in the Crate and Barrel catalogue, thick white pottery with raised black and white cows in the center. And some cow bowls to match. They would do for cookies and hand-churned ice cream or berry sherbets. Bess always had a houseful of company, down for some event—polo matches, flatland racing, steeplechasing, riding to the foxhounds. Her place, called the "cottage," had fourteen rooms, and two outbuildings which had once been milking sheds and were now guest quarters. That old part of the state around William of Orange still had the look of its glory days as a vacation compound for the rich. Something that had faded from our upstate area. By now, in May, all of Bess's plump sofas and armchairs would be wearing their striped summer duck slipcovers. Drink proof and godson proof.

I patted Ben. Will would be late. He'd been late making the rounds when Nolan was in the hospital; when we'd had him to a supper party he was late. But he would show. I was sure of that. I knew when he left the message with Katie for me to give him a call when I was in the mood to take an old dog for a ride, that he was asking. Well, not asking, he would never do that, having been Nolan's doctor, but just checking to see if the rules had changed.

In a more perfect world, Will and I could have been better friends than we'd been allowed to be for the last thirty-odd years. Marriage didn't just mean unlimited time with one man; it meant no time for other men.

I had not planned to use him even informally as a doctor, now that we were free to be friends, but Harriet had called the night before with troubling news. And I knew that I would want to talk to Will about it. As an informed source, if nothing more.

I was brushing my hair dry, sitting up on the bed, when the phone rang, the catalogues for Bess still lying about. I suspected it might be Harriet, at that hour, and propped two pillows behind my head before answering.

"Guess what?" she said.

She had called often since my Texas visit, usually with good news. Her friend David had made a trip back to see her; he was planning another in order to interview her mother. "I'm not sure I can stand to be there when she tells her el-um stories," Harriet had said, sounding pleased.

"You tell me," I said. "What?"

"I bought a gun. A .22 caliber Colt single-action nickel-plated pistol. I have to wait a week to pick it up."

She'd really done it, not just talked about it. I had some trouble with the idea. I did not like firearms or what it meant for Harriet to have need of one, a personal weapon. Something more than Knox's deer rifle on hand in case of intruders, although I had trouble with that as well. "Was it hard to get?" I asked, needing to make a response. I was wondering what it would mean if my eldest grandson, stalwart brave Matthew, had taken to carrying a brick with him in his yellow lunch box (or Disney backpack). If all his buddies packed bricks along with their peanut butter and jellys. Would I think them angry at the Safety Patrol or afraid of bullies?

"It turned out to be nothing at all. It was like getting paper towels or something at Never Pay. There I was, getting my first gun at this county store, and it was like getting my first pair of heels or my first formal or learning to use my first Tampax. A rite of passage."

"Well," I said. "Do I say congratulations or be careful?" I was wondering if there was more to the story, if she had, as usual, saved the real news for last.

"He kept showing me these .38s, this pasty skinhead at the gun shop, and telling me, 'That's mostly what we sell to the ladies taking the Handgun Safety Course.' It was

insulting, the way he said it, and besides, I didn't want a
.38. I don't plan to be crouching in the middle of the road
holding it out in front of me in two hands, shooting out the
tires of the next creep who calls me *skinny legs*, tempting as
that is. I just wanted something I can shoot right through
my purse at his groin if I'm in the mall, or pull out from
under my pillow if he's in my room looking for the jewels
I can never wear out in public anymore."

"I didn't know it was that easy." Although I should have,
after listening to all the call-in gun nuts. I should have
known that almost anyone who wants to can carry a weapon.

"I told him, 'I think this will do for a starter gun,'"
Harriet went on, sounding as excited as she had in the days
of the cadet balls. "I had to laugh. 'Starter gun!' It sounds
like getting a starter bike with training wheels or a starter
bra before you've even budded out. What is the world coming to? I can't believe I told him that."

"I have some news, too," I said. "I'm taking a drive tomorrow with Nolan's seventy-year-old doctor." I was giving
her an opening to mention young David if she wanted to,
or laugh at me for my staid choice.

"Speaking of doctors," she said, her tone bright, almost
brittle, "I went to one myself."

"Are you all right?" I couldn't tell from her tone. Harriet
had a way of presenting worrisome matters as affairs of no
consequence, of presenting trouble as a lark. Her way, I
used to think, of whistling in the dark.

"I guess. I wish I'd had my .22 with me when I went. I
went because I couldn't get rid of this cough, and when he
said he heard a wheeze, I could believe that. But then he
said something about my fingernails, and got all serious,
the way these young types do. He wants me to go in for a—
I wrote it down—bronchoscopy. Just a precaution, he said,
to look around. He asked me if I hurt. I guess he was

thinking pleurisy, which Mom has had, and he made me spit. His eyes got wide when I did, but I bet he'll find he's got Estée Lauder's new summer shade on his slide when he looks under the microscope." She laughed and it did turn into a cough, just briefly. "I guess the good news is, he didn't tell me that since Knox was dead he wasn't going to be my doctor anymore."

"Should I worry? When do you go in? Is it overnight?" I was trying to sort out all she'd said, making notes to show to Will on the notepad by the phone. I'd been braiding my hair into a loose plait while I talked, and stopped to get a pen.

"No and tomorrow and no. How's that?"

"I may worry anyway," I said, "just because that's my nature."

"I'll let you know. Have fun with your old man. *Seventy*, really."

"Harriet—"

"Bye. Don't fret. I just wanted you to know." And she was gone.

Leaving me troubled on more than one account.

I HAD NEVER BEEN Will's patient, not even in the beginning. He'd taken over—the young doctor then, hard to believe—from Mother's family doctor. When Nolan and I married and settled here in the county, we'd gone to get checkups, in order to get our names on some doctor's records. At that age, so young, the only medical matter on our minds was that I intended to get pregnant one of these days. But it was a routine practice for newlyweds then; you got a doctor, you got a lawyer.

Will had seen Nolan first, given him a workup and sent

him off to the lab. Then I'd gone in. He'd sat me down in his office and declared, "I'm not going to be your internist, Mrs. Rankin. I believe it works best if a couple has separate physicians."

I'd been surprised and disbelieving. I looked at him. What was he then, in his late thirties? He had assumed a gruff air, in order to look older, and stared at me through horn-rimmed spectacles (window glass, I learned later).

"Don't call me that," I said, not used to being called "Mrs. Rankin" and not liking it for any number of reasons. "My name has been Cooper all my life. I'm not used to the new one. You can call me Sarah if you like."

"Okay, Coop," he said. "I'm going to send you to my new partner."

"I don't believe what you just said." I had my handbag in my lap, was wearing heels and hose, as you did in those days. My long dark hair was held back with combs. I was trying to get used to my recent change of status into *wife*.

"That I've got a partner?"

"That you don't take couples. You're not telling me the truth. Besides, you could have seen me first and not taken Nolan, but you didn't."

Will stood up, a broad-chested man with a big rib cage, and a short, trim haircut on his big head which looked as if the haircut were a size too small. The kind of man who looked as if he should be a coach, but never was. He fiddled with his stethoscope, just like the doctors in the movies. I didn't know it then, but he was trying to get used to his recent change of status into full-fledged *physician*.

I stood, too. "You're trying to intimidate me," I said. "I get an honest reason."

"I don't want to put my hands on your naked body."

I smiled, grinned in fact. I sat back down and gestured to him to do the same. "Okay," I told him. "But, you know,

Will Perry, you can't just take male patients; you're bound to inherit a lot of women like my mother."

"You're that Cooper? Edith's girl? I should have figured—that's where you get your tongue. I *have* inherited them, including her—a pleasure, although I understand she's leaving us. Most of them, women her age—are you interested in this?—have respiratory problems, I suspect from holding their breath for too many decades."

"You can't just take ugly women." I was teasing him.

"I don't have to go looking for trouble."

"What does Spouse Perry think of all this?" I was deciding that she was a lucky woman indeed and that he would be a fine man to be around on a regular basis.

"If it's your business, Spouse Perry decided I had a wandering eye, although she didn't stick around long enough to confirm the hypothesis." He stuck the stethoscope to his own chest and listened. "There might have been a murmur of truth in the idea."

"You could take widows."

"I probably will." He'd grinned back at me.

"Is Nolan Rankin safe in your hands? Should I worry?" In my memory I gathered up my bag and gloves and stood at the door, although surely I hadn't worn gloves. The feel of putting on my proper role was the same.

He'd laughed, taken off his glasses and stuck them in his pocket. "You have my word," he promised.

Once, years later, I'd found him standing in my bedroom looking around, ostensibly putting his coat on the bed at one of our Christmas parties. Nolan and I always had a Christmas party—spruce and mistletoe and wonderful fragrant cherry-wood fires—for bankers, clients, friends. Nolan's physician and attorney were both included. At that time, Will was being paired regularly with a handsome federal judge from Greenville; they were considered a couple. That must have been seven years ago, just after Nolan and I had started sleeping apart. I would have been in my late forties, Will in his early sixties.

"Nice room," he said. "No wallpaper, though. How come?"

"For the same reason you don't give yourself annual checkups."

"This used to be your boy's room."

"George's, yes."

"Last year it was."

"Do you always snoop around?"

"The number of times I've been in your house, Coop, it's not snooping. I noticed, is all."

I'd moved into George's old room because I liked it, I liked the way it looked out at the orchard, the way it angled, forming an L. I'd painted the walls peach, hung Vermeer prints over the high twin beds, covered them with white pillows, taken up the carpet and put a rug with peach cabbage roses on the floor. I'd left the high narrow beds; it felt more like a single girl's room that way.

"You haven't strayed once, have you?" Will asked.

"No." I shrugged, my fidelity a complex matter, not something I intended to discuss. "Why be beholden twice instead of once?" I said.

"No wandering eye?"

I smiled. "That's you."

"I may get married again," he told me.

"Good."

"I thought you didn't like marriage, Coop."

I'd said that to him on one of the twilights we'd found ourselves walking our dogs along the same county road. I'd pointed out, thinking aloud, how glad dogs were to meet up with friends, how different from spouses they were. "You don't care for married life, do you?" he'd asked. "Not a little bit," I'd told him, looking off at the ruddy sunset.

"Married men live longer," I told him that evening in my bedroom. "You know the statistics."

"I wanted to keep you advised."

"Thanks, Will."

But he hadn't married his federal judge after all.

WILL OPENED THE car on Ben's side at one-twenty, gave the lab a nuzzle, and shoved him into the backseat. "Not bad," he said, checking his watch.

"Not bad," I agreed.

I made a U-turn and headed toward Mineral Springs to pick up his dog. I'd asked him, when we were both choosing our pups from the same Sandyland lab litter, why he always named his dogs Missoula. "Because most of the time I'd rather be there than here," he'd said, fresh from a bad case at the hospital. That had been eight years ago, a long spell in canine time.

Will at seventy was still broad through the shoulders, deep-chested, his hair now nearly gone, as if his once too-tight haircut had simply slipped off his head. His skin had age spots, and his teeth were worn and coffee-stained. A most attractive man, and a good friend. It was a bit scarey, moving us into something more. He'd brought a denim shirt to change into, in the color I considered Sarah blue. I had on a T-shirt of the same shade with a white blouse over it, and my dog-walking pants. Not very fancy for a first date.

"Married men," I said, trying to set us both at ease, "get in the car and the first thing they do is look at the gas gauge to see if there's enough gas for the trip. You must be a bachelor."

He reached a broad hand over and patted my leg. "Lucky is what."

Missoula, his lab, was waiting inside the picket fence

near the rose garden at the back of his house. She seemed delighted to see him and Ben at the same time, and climbed happily into the car. Dogs were ready to go with anyone anytime; they were game for a trip to any destination. Dog people never failed to appreciate such an agreeable approach to life.

"Where're we going?" Will asked, when we were settled and on the road.

"To Oconee."

"You get a cabin?"

"I did." I was glad he'd asked; that made it clear what we were doing. I was too old for a pile of coats on a practice-room floor, but not for a bad mattress in a rented park cabin.

"I skipped lunch," he said. "Is there someplace we can get a sandwich later?"

"Rae's Cafe has pear-sweetened pork."

"That's on my diet." He patted his generous middle.

I gestured to the Rooms thermos, which I had filled with coffee for us.

"I could use that," he said, pouring half a mugful and taking a gulp. "When I called your shop, it was to see how you were making it."

"I know."

"I wouldn't have called to ask you out."

"I know. And it would have been all right if you hadn't wanted to go today. I'd have waited. There's no hurry. I'm still getting my bearings; remembering the basics. TGIF."

"Toe Goes In First." He refilled the mug and handed it carefully to me. "Coop's rules for coping." He reached around, putting his hands, familiar and calming, on the labs, talking to them, promising them a romp.

I asked him, "What about the man naked on your table yesterday when I called. What was the good news?"

"That it looked as if the malignancy was contained and could be resected."

"Ouch." I didn't know how he survived his job. Watching close at hand while one man died had been almost more than I could bear—to see it in his eyes, to read it on his face, to watch his body grind to a halt.

"It goes with my line of work," he said. "I was standing there holding the stethoscope, wondering how to broach the news to him, when you called. It caught me unaware, hearing from you. Without thinking, I put the stethoscope to my chest while I was talking. When I hung up, the old man laughed. 'What's the diagnosis, Doc?' he asked. I said, 'Premature excitement.' "

"Did you read about the guy who got his black-and-tan hound back after losing it three years ago?"

"Some patient told me. Lost him on a bear hunt in Canada, went back later and found him near Sudbury. Something like that. They always tell these tales: man puts his hunting jacket down, comes back ten years later, Old Blue is waiting on the jacket." He turned to the backseat. "You hear that, pups? You get lost today, we expect you not to take up with the first passing redneck who throws you a chicken-fried steak."

"My mother always had dogs," I said, after a bit. "Scotties mostly."

"A woman alone could get around better in those days with a dog. My grandmother kept bulldogs. The big ones with the drooping jowls."

We hadn't talked about Nolan's dying, even after Will gave me and then my husband the bad news. Will had talked to me about what I could do to make things easier, when to call him, when to worry. But we'd kept our friendship out of it. I knew Will would try everything to save Nolan; I knew he hated death.

I remembered a party at his place. He always paid his married friends back with an annual midsummer party, because he had the beautiful rose garden, plus a lot of air-conditioned rooms, glassed in, that had been added on the back of the house when it was his grandmother's.

He'd brought me an orange juice and vodka. I didn't drink much, even then, and I didn't like vodka; it was greasy and I could taste the potato. "Pretend it's castor oil," he told me.

"You look under the weather," I said.

"Nobody is getting well." He looked as if he hadn't slept in a week. "I've given up serious reading. You're sailing along on this ship, meeting these people, learning a tad of history, getting a tot of manners and morals, and then—wham—you find out it's the *Titanic*. That's too much like life. I'm sticking to detective novels," he said. "The private eyes who work in some crummy office up a flight of creaking stairs. The man or woman gets beat up or hog-tied, her place is burned down or his car blown up, but they whup the bad guys in the end. I like to read those because you know the PI is going to walk away. They're a series. Real life is not a series."

"You can't think of them collectively," I told him. "You have to take them singly. You have to handle trouble OLAT."

"How's that?"

"One Leg At a Time."

That was when—two pups ago.

When Nolan had died—after such a brief time if you were outside it, such a dreadfully long time if you were in it—we hadn't talked about him then, either. After, we'd sat together a spell in the hospital room.

"I'm sorry, Coop," Will said.

"There's no easy way, is there?" I'd asked. I felt shredded and more angry than tearful, angry at the whole bad idea of mortality. I'd thought of Harriet and Knox, him being there one minute and gone the next, her not able to see him at the last. Was it better or worse, or just a part of the same dreadful scheme?

"That was it," Will said. "That was the easy way."

"I have to let them all know——" I'd got my handbag and put on my shoes. I'd been—it seemed confusing, out of place—in my Rooms jumper. The children, who had visited on the weekend, had gone back. Mother was somewhere in Tanzania. Bess would come when I needed her.

"You want I should make any calls?" Will had asked.

"They're paging you already."

"I can handle that." He had on doctor whites, and looked worn to the bone.

In the end, he'd delivered me to Katie, who took me by the funeral home and then to my house, where I stood for a long time in Nolan's room before making my calls.

But Will and I were not starting there, with someone's death. Rather, we were starting over from that first time in his office when he was the new young doctor and I was a new young wife, from the Christmas party when he stood in my separate bedroom, from the summer party at his house when he talked about his private eyes. We were warming up a friendship of four-dog duration.

I RESISTED THE URGE to swing west off Long Creek Road, to show Will the Wild and Scenic River overlook, with its view of the faraway blue mountains and a four-year-old in shorts and canvas shoes, gathering pine needles with her mother—such a young woman, her center of gravity shifted with her pregnancy—and listening to her daddy, young, too, slim and tanned, call out, "Where's my Sarah?"

Instead, I drove us straight to Oconee's fragrant and near-deserted park and the cabin I'd reserved. Stopping at the lodge, I picked up the key to number 22 and left a check. It was a one-bedroom log cabin, near the picnic table where I'd sat a scant six weeks ago. We let the dogs run a bit, track down smells, mark the bark of a few tall pines, and then we brought them in.

There was a moment, as I unlocked the door, when I hesitated, waiting for some awkwardness. But then Will filled the water pans and unwrapped the Gainesburgers while I found the bathroom, and then, while he did, I got them settled and closed the door. Leaving the dogs by the fireplace that on some later winter day would welcome a blazing cherry-wood fire. Next time, I thought, I'd bring them a blanket to snooze on.

In a practiced motion, Will loosened his tie, unbuttoned his shirt halfway, and slipped them together over his head, the tie still around his collar. I had to smile; there was no chance that this time I was the more experienced lover. Remembering the bold girl I'd been—"We'll do it upstairs on the practice-room floor," "Do it to me here, now"—I decided I could surely take my own clothes off without constraint, and stripped down to my underpants. Then, feeling a bit undressed, added back my white shirt, unbuttoned.

"You're not my first older man," I said.

"First old man, I bet." Will took off his trousers and shorts, seeming to have no embarrassment standing there naked while I pulled back the covers of the sagging bed. His chest hair was white, his broad shoulders covered in age spots. He stood studying me, apparently not self-conscious about his belly or his erection, which hung down heavy as a hammer.

"The last, young or old," I told him, moving to make room for him on the side of the double bed.

"Don't be hasty," he said. "OLAT."

"ABTE." I smiled at him.

"Aim Between The Eyes." He leaned over to kiss me, and that was my only moment of terror. It could go so wrong, kissing someone you knew well. It could inhibit you both, turn out to be the same as kissing your kin. But it was all right. Will took off my white shirt, ran his wide palms over my shoulders, then kissed me again, but not in any urgent way. "The thing about old men," he said, "is we take a long time, but we always get there."

He crossed to the other side of the bed, got in, and for a time held me against him. Doing nothing but holding me, getting us used to touching without our clothes. After a while, when I was almost drowsy, he began to rub my back, saying, "Put your hand on me."

Then, when he was hard again, he bent down and began to kiss my thighs, my stomach, my collarbones; then he turned me over and kissed along my shoulder blades, my neck, my ears. By the time we made love, we were familiar to one another, and I was as aroused as I hadn't been since I was a schoolgirl making love to Mr. Brown. When we'd rested a bit, with me lying on top of him, my wide hips below his belly, a comfortable fit, he got up, opened the door and whistled the dogs in.

Ben and Missoula piled on the bed, turned around, thumped their tails, getting settled. "Nap time," Will said to the lot of us.

We rested maybe fifteen minutes, and then, as if he'd set himself like a clock—which he must have trained himself to do at the hospital—Will brought shirts for himself and me, and we lay against the lumpy pillows and talked.

"What was the trouble?" he asked. "With Nolan."

"You told me that your wife decided in advance you had a wandering eye—"

"She figured it was just a matter of time. She might have been right."

"That was the trouble. He was jealous."

"What for? You gave him no cause."

"Does that ever matter?"

"It should have. It should have meant the world to him," he said with some obvious feeling.

"World enough and time." I looked away. I didn't want to go into all that, go back over trouble I had not been able to remedy. "It didn't," I said. "Let's don't bring him here, Will."

"We're not. We're just clearing the decks, solving the crime after the private eye who's coming back in sequel after sequel gets the good-looking woman in bed."

I slipped a foot from under the cover and rubbed Gentle Ben's head. He was a larger dog than Rogers, my first black lab, but he had the same trustworthy nature. He fit his name.

"Your sidekick get the business if you die?" Will asked.

I nodded. "And I do if Katie does."

"She's got a Huguenot name."

"Pegues? Is that right? I know her people have been around a long time."

"I suppose families don't make trouble with inheritance like that these days. Kin can't make trouble the way they used to."

"My mother's grandmother," I told him, "left her house and furniture to a black woman, here in Carolina, plus the right for her and all present and future children to hire out their own time. Before Emancipation."

"A wonder she got away with it. Her folks must all have been dead."

"Mother says they were probably sisters, the women, and that enough people knew it. She says white men used black women for birth control."

"I'm surprised," Will said, "that a naturalist would take notice of that. Seems like she'd find it hard to shift her sights up to the human level."

I told him, "Any woman who's made it in the field knows exactly which women made what gains and when and which got held up and by whom, back to when we first stood upright on two legs."

"That figures." Will slid us both down until our heads touched.

I put out a hand and began to rub slowly on his chest, careful not to snarl the hair. Much in the same way I was moving my foot back and forth on Ben. Dog people were used to touch. They knew how to hold out a hand for a strange dog to sniff; how not to move too fast. I need not have worried about how Will and I would do. We were dog people after all.

He moved his hand up and down on my leg as if he were stroking Missoula. It was strange how intimate it was, putting our hands on each other, without being erotic. I tried to recall if Will and I had ever touched at parties, had exchanged hugs or cheek kisses, but I knew we had not. That we had always been careful not to.

"Did you have a father?" he asked me.

"I did. For ten years. MacDonald Cooper."

"What did he think of your mother's spiders?"

I had often wondered about that myself. How my daddy— so eager as I remember him, such an outdoors person himself, leading us through the pine forests—would have felt about her becoming a noted naturalist. Who he might have been, older; how that might have affected her, now.

"She was only thirty-three," I answered him. "She'd just begun to study. Who knows? He died editing a collection of records on the WPA in Washington. I sometimes think that's why she's glad to be based back there."

Will moved his hand to my face, then turned me toward him. The dogs began to thump their tails; in a minute we'd have to put them out again. "The good ones don't all make it to the last chapter," he said.

Life Estates

. . .

WE STOPPED OFF at Rae's Cafe on the Long Creek Road on the way back. A truck stop as well as a local hangout, it didn't matter the time of day—there was always a crowd filling the high wooden booths and a lot full of truckers' trucks outside.

We'd driven down the red hills from the state park, past the signs for HOT BOILED PEANUTS, SALMON EGGS, HONEY, CIDER, CHAIRS CANED. Later, in the summer, there would be cars parked bumper to bumper at U-PICK APPLES and U-PICK PEACHES.

The pups, left in the car, were promised a greasy pork-filled doggy bag.

Inside, a young man, who couldn't be over eighteen, was talking to his pregnant wife and her mother (his mother?), explaining his training methods. "I whup that dog with a bullwhip but it don't hurt him. It's not supposed to hurt him; it just scares him, makes him mind. I know for sure he'll be waiting in the road for me next time I get home."

I leaned over and murmured to Will, "I hope that kid's dog gnaws his leg off."

"The mother-in-law's going to," he whispered back.

Across the dining room, an old black man in streaked khakis and heavy boots talked food to his white liver-spotted buddy. Their hair still showed the smooth flattened bands where their hats had been. "I'm going home and fix me up a steak. I like to fry my steak medium well, put it in the skillet with no grease, just flour, till the flour scorches. That makes it brown. Then I drown it in milk, that's the way to make gravy. Not the custardy business they serve in here."

"I understand their sausage isn't all meat, neither," his

companion chimed in. The two of them had six beer bottles on the table and no food in sight.

The heavyset waiter with the tower of hair didn't appear to take offense. Her role seemed to be that of a call-in show deejay: don't pay too much mind to what the customers have to say. Keep them on the line; keep them coming back for more.

She'd seen me in Rae's before, and raised her arched brows at seeing me with a man, then winked. I ordered for both of us: pear-sweetened chopped pork barbeque sandwiches, sugar-sweetened tea and molasses-sweetened apple crisp. "Give up here," I said to Will. "Everything has sugar. This is deep-country food."

"Beer and sweets." Will looked around. He'd ordered himself a Budweiser. "I get a lot of patients been living on this combination. Most of them, I have to say, don't look anywhere near this lively."

At a table in the center of the room, a pair of women with bright yellow curls and a mountain of makeup which did not hide their age smoked and waved long scarlet fingernails. Both wore beige turtlenecks.

Widows, I thought, and then, of Harriet. I took a bite of the sweet-tart-greasy pork, and a swallow of the frosty iced tea to wash it down. "My Texas friend—" I said.

"This the one who goes way back?"

"Harriet. She was here last fall, when Nolan was first sick. Before her husband died."

He shook his bald head. "My mind was on getting him out of that tight spot."

"I got a troublesome call from her, yesterday. Do you mind?"

"Mind what?" He downed a swallow of his cold Bud.

"I don't want to use you—as a doctor."

"Use any and all I've got, Coop." He made a gesture with his hands, as if he were holding a stethoscope to his chest.

Looking at him, I thought it was possible to love someone forever and yet never have to have that awful interlude called "being in love," which made you dumb and sick and foolish.

"She had a cough when I was there, a nasty crouping sound. I said she ought to have someone check it. She's just been and she reported he'd heard a—wheeze. And that, just as a precaution, he was going to do a bronchoscopy."

"Hmm." He knit his hands together, thinking. "She mention anything else?"

"Something odd, I don't remember."

"Fingernails?"

I put my sandwich down. Something in his tone got my attention. "Yes, that was it. Is that important?"

"There's a thickening, called clubbing. Not good."

I felt the pork grease on my tongue and in my throat. "What is not good?" I remembered the man on the table in Will's office about to get the "good news" that his malignancy was operable. *Not good* from Will was a terrifying idea.

"Growth in the lung, possibly."

"Is that—what does that mean—?"

"Can't tell. That's why he's doing the test."

I tugged at my plait, leaning back in the booth. "I had you on my mind and forgot—"

"Having your friend on your mind and losing sleep over it, I hate to tell you, won't make any noticeable difference in what he finds." He nudged my foot under the table. "Drink your tea."

"I should have called her back—"

"Let her call you."

The waiter brought us spicy deep-dish apple crisp, with big scoops of vanilla ice cream on top. "On the house," she said, winking again.

"Sugar diabetes is in our future," I told Will, trying to get a grip on my panic.

"Your children coming to see you Sunday?" He moved us to another subject, tackling his dessert.

"For Mother's Day? Not my daughter. She's going to my sister's." I hesitated; did Will want to get involved with my people? He himself had no family; his parents were dead, his only brother had died in WWII. Naturally, he already knew a great deal about my children, having been around their entire lives. In recent years, he'd followed Fannin's pregnancies, one by one, and the boys' naming. I'd liked talking to him about the babies as they arrived, since he had a way of reassuring me that a woman's having the children she wanted was not a catastrophe. I sometimes wondered if he wished he were stockpiling grandchildren himself. "She's pregnant again," I said.

"This is number five?"

"It is. I'm unglued."

"What's it to be this time? Second Timothy? First Corinthians?"

"Of course everyone is making jokes. Serious Matthew went to school and told his teacher they were going to have a new baby named Revelations." Every time I thought of that, I wanted to wrap my arms around my grandson's small stiff shoulders, and undo the bafflement, the laughter. "How to explain to a kid the joke, without making him, all the boys, feel their names are a joke? Impossible."

"You worried they're coming too fast?"

"She's still worn out from the last one—little Jonathan."

"I've met the husband, right? OB, Johnny McAlester. A bit overdetermined."

"And you've only seen him relaxed at our Christmas parties." I bit my lip. Nothing was gained by blaming my son-in-law, a most likeable, somewhat cowed young man.

"A big family his idea? Or doesn't he know where they come from?"

"He wants six, she says. But she's the one having them. The doctor—a Japanese woman—says this is the last."

"A healthy woman having healthy babies is not the worst case I've ever seen," Will said gently. He studied my face, his ruddy, lined, kind. "How about your boy, George. He coming?"

"Yes, amazingly. To take me to lunch at the Depot. Eat homestyle food he doesn't even like." I'd been touched when my son called to tell me. I thought perhaps he'd decided to drive over from Charleston when he heard his sister was going to be at Bess's. That perhaps he worried that I'd be here by myself the first year without Nolan. Then I wondered if he was coming because his dad wasn't here. "Why don't you go with us?" I asked Will, thinking that a grand idea. "I'd like that. George is comfortable with you. He knows you. His dad's doctor."

"Thanks but no." He pushed away his dessert, as I had already done. "A boy has a hard enough time watching his mother climb into bed with his father for a couple of dozen years. He doesn't need to be hit in the face with the idea that once Dad's dead he could have somebody else to worry about. Wait until I'm eighty, then we'll tell him. Then he'll think we're getting together to rock on the porch and pick ticks off the dogs."

"I hope we are," I told him.

"You can't carry them all," Will said. "You got to remember: they're ambulatory. They walked in; they can walk out."

I nodded, hearing him, finding a smile. "Of their messes, you mean."

"Of their lives." He took my hand in his huge one.

"So." I bent and kissed his fingers. "We're having lunch.

At Rae's Cafe." I drew in my breath and let it out. Looking at him, I remembered that when he'd been dating the attractive judge he'd had a mustache. Maybe he hadn't married her because he'd decided to shave it off. "Why didn't you make it legal with that federal judge with the prodigious chest?"

"That wasn't why."

"I didn't think so."

"We were better lovers than friends." He looked down at his melting ice cream, finished his beer. "Does that bother you?"

"No." I spread my hands. If you'd lived with jealousy, as I had. "It wouldn't have bothered me," I said, "if you'd married her. Do you understand?"

"I do. I did at the time."

"Are people going to talk, our being together so soon after—"

"Not a chance. Age, you'll find out all in good time, is a great alibi. Not to mention that most people spend less time having sex than they do flossing their teeth. Most of them think of sex the way they think of car chases, as something that happens in films, or among kids who ought to know better." He grinned at me. "I imagine they'll consider us quaint."

"Will you mind my twin beds?" I asked. "I've left Nolan's room the way it was until the little boys are older, their granddaddy's room; until George and Fannin don't need it anymore. I remember Mother did that, left Daddy's small home office untouched. I used to go in and look at his old typewriter. I don't know when she packed his things away; when it didn't matter. When I was gone."

"We'll be crowded in one. . . ." Will patted his middle. "But we'll manage. Will you mind that my bed has had a fair number of visitors over the years?"

"No. It's going to be lovely to stay over. I waited thirty-three years for you to take off my clothes."

GEORGE PICKED ME up Sunday and drove me to the Mineral Springs Depot for our Mother's Day lunch.

Looking at him behind the wheel of his fancy imported car, I was pleased he'd cooked up the idea. He didn't look like his father, my son, that broad North Carolina mountain look; rather, he looked more like my father, MacDonald Cooper, the elegant South Carolina bones, the cleft chin and prominent brow. Sometimes, now that he was grown, I could get a glimpse of my daddy as I remembered him. It came as a shock, thinking of that on Mother's Day, to realize that George was now the age Daddy had been when I was born. Somewhere I had a faded photo of a young man holding a baby, or at least holding a bundle in a christening gown and beribboned cap.

The last time I'd seen my son, at the funeral, he'd been heavier, puffy, and I'd worried he was drinking too much. That could happen to an affluent bachelor in lush Charleston; it could also happen to a young man who'd lost his father too soon.

"We're going to have someone else with us," he said. "It's a surprise."

I thought it must be Fannin, since if it were a girlfriend, she'd be with us already. Perhaps they'd cooked up the story that she was going to Bess's, and she was going to show up, to let me make amends for my grudging reception of number five. If that was something they'd worked out, I thought, then that would be fine. That would be good.

"The Depot is definitely the place to go," he'd told me on the phone. "The place to be seen to prove that you produced young."

I'd been amused. "What is all this?" I'd asked him. "We didn't do Mother's Day back when I *was* your mother."

"Are you trying to tell me something?"

"I mean, when we lived in the same house." I'd laughed.

"An interesting concept of kinship you have, Mom."

"Rankin, table for three," he said to the female host when we'd parked and joined a crowd at the Depot. He was looking spiffy in a light gray summer suit, cream shirt, wild tie with black walleyed fish on it.

Spiffy was a word of Mother's—its coming into my mind should have been a clue. Still, I was amazed to see Edith Huntt Cooper appear in the wide doorway, hobbling slightly, her mouth tight with obvious discomfort. She was headed straight for our table.

"Mother!" I rose and helped her to a chair. "I cannot believe this. And what happened to you?"

George looked quite pleased with himself. "I sent her a plane ticket, and arranged a rent-a-car. Happy Mother's Day to you both."

". . . was getting the Hertz car," Mother said, sinking down into the chair, "and I didn't see the step. Somehow I've jammed my hip. Apparently I've plain and simple injured the muscle. I can't lift my leg worth a damn. It didn't matter driving—the left leg these days is like the appendix, left over from another era, in this case when automobiles had clutches. But I'm to leave for Tierra del Fuego Wednesday. I can't hobble down there—"

"Eat, Grandma, then we'll see," George said. He didn't want his party dampened.

"We'll check with Will Perry," I said.

"No need to do that. I'll have to work it through. It's a matter of moving it back into position." She beamed at her grandson. "What have we to eat, then?"

We were in the side dining room, which, like the rest of the restored building, had train timetables framed on the walls—mementos of Mineral Springs in its heyday as a world famous spa. The menu contained familiar staples: chicken with chive dumplings, meat loaf and mashed potatoes, pork loin and sweet potato pie. What they always served here: down-home food for people who never had and were never going to eat like this at home.

The other tables were filling. Looking around, I saw a son alone with his elderly mother, an aging daughter with hers. At the bigger tables—for six or eight—you could spot a mother surrounded by the son and his wife, the daughter and her husband, plus a couple of other grown children, unattached, between alliances. Usually, I saw, the oldest male at the table looked tired, restless, stole a glance at his watch. Usually the youngest female looked withdrawn, angry, off somewhere else. I could feel the rip and tear of kinship in the restored rooms, the air beneath the old timetables rippling with attempts at armistice.

I had to admit what a different meal it would have been at our table if Nolan were here. In fairness, not all of that was his fault, some of it was the nature of the beast, the strain of being father to a son. Nolan would have been fighting the army of feelings he had about George: pride that the boy had followed him into finance, hurt that he never asked his advice, above all envy not just that George was investing in a future his dad wouldn't be around to see (too true, as it turned out) but that he had such a grand time doing it.

I was glad I'd worn my brown linen: Mother had given it to me a few years back, saying, "I saw this and it looked like you." That was unusual, as we seldom bought for one another; more often, we both bought for Bess. It had a square neckline, bell sleeves, and was longish, nice with sandals.

Mother wore a light yellow dress with self buttons and stitched, inverted pleats. Very much a Washington-in-the-spring sort of dress, good from the desk to the Rose Garden. With her hair a cap of white curls, she'd made the transition from looking like a naturalist in loose bloomers, hiking boots, khaki jacket and bobbed hair, to looking like someone of possible importance. I knew this was not a calculated decision; rather, it was my mother's instinct for protective coloration.

George ordered for us, sweet potato biscuits and corn soup all around, the pork, meat loaf and chicken to pass around. For Mother's Day the Depot was serving champagne, since it was after church hours, and he got us each a glass of that.

"What're you working on now, Grandma?" he asked Mother. My son being the only person in the family who really understood what Edith did, why her work took her all over the world, and—his real interest—why the government was willing to finance her trips.

Mother's eyes lit up at his question. "I'm studying a tropical moth which the spider cuts out of her silk net rather than eats." She reached over and patted George's sleeved arm. She had lost weight and now had a certain stringy look, pared down for just such obstacles as her jammed hip.

"What does the moth eat to guarantee he won't be her supper?" He was already a jump ahead, his hazel eyes fastened on his grandmother.

"An alkaloid, which is passed on in his semen to protect his female's eggs from predators." She beamed. "Aren't you the smart one?"

"Would you send me a copy of your report?"

"If I get there. You may notice I'm having parboiled chicken in Mineral Springs, South Carolina, and could hardly walk up the Depot steps. We'll see."

"I want to be in on the ground floor when you perfect an alkaloid-based, disease-resistant vaccine."

"Mercy, George," Mother waved a hand. "Not everything has to have an economic value."

"The United States government is not paying your way to Tierra del Fuego because of its general interest in arachnids. Or to verify that there are over three hundred thousand spiders on the rain forest floor."

"Right you are about that." Edith looked at her heaping plate of food. She buttered a biscuit, then raised her champagne glass to her grandson. "And how about you, George, what are you touting today? I know you've got a pitch. Some new snake oil."

"I invested in my own snake oil, actually," he said, brushing back his flyaway brown hair, adjusting his wire-rimmed glasses. "Quite a bit of money, it happens, which my mother signed over to me in such a cavalier way I had to hear about it from a lawyer." George looked at me, letting his affection show.

I felt myself flush. Was that what this was all about? His arranging this lunch, his flying Mother down? A thank-you for Nolan's money? Amazing. When I didn't hear back from Theo Kenton, the messy fussy hulk of a lawyer in his red suspenders, I'd figured it would take from now until Christmas to snuff out Nolan's offending secretive will. His last word from the afterlife. That meant that both my children had received their inheritance already. Perhaps, I considered, that, and not her father's death, was what had prompted Fannin to become pregnant with number five. The knowledge that there would be funds to rear it.

How different, truly, males were from females. If you gave a son money, he became convinced you loved him. He thought: She parted with money, what more can a mother do? If you gave a daughter money, on the other hand, she thought you were trying to buy her affection, attach strings. She gave me a check: what's going on?

I told George, "I'm glad your father's attorney finally moved his ass," glad to find myself the Good Guy, and on Mother's Day at that.

"To answer," he said to his grandmother, "I'm hot about this substance called elastomer. It's the plastic of the future. Let me give you one example, Grandma. A piece the size of a gumball in a can of car paint makes a permanent impenetrable coating. It's coming out of Belgium; I'm pushing it and I'm buying it."

"Mercy," Edith said, enchanted. She liked nothing better on earth than a good look at vistas well into the twenty-first century. "Elastomers." She made a note on the back of an envelope in her bag.

"Buy in," George said, smiling at her.

She smiled back, but shook her head. "I'd prefer to have invented it."

We stopped to choose dessert. Mother got the bread raisin pudding, George the apple skillet pie, and I the banana pudding with vanilla wafers. Homestyle sweets that were never served at home. We all agreed to share, to taste all around. The coffee came with sugar cubes and real heavy cream.

I acknowledged that it wasn't just his son that Nolan would have been jealous of, it was my mother as well. He'd have suggested she talked too much about herself, thought too much of herself, was, by implication, putting down women like his own mother, who had been—his term— "a simple homemaker." It meant that Mother, answering questions asked by her grandson—out of his nose for news, his knowledge that insects' survival strategies today were tomorrow's chemistry—would have been seen by Nolan as Edith Huntt Cooper's having hogged what would otherwise have been "a pleasant luncheon." In fact, Nolan resented Bess as well. His sister, he said, had been crazy for horses, too, "at that age," but had given them up when she was grown. In truth, what he objected to in the women in my family was their—our—priorities. Our putting something, anything at all, ahead of a home and a man like him. If my mother's and sister's interests were all-consuming, then what did this suggest about me and my wallpaper shop? Jealousy, I thought, not for the first time, was pervasive, systemic. Why did we construe it only sexually?

Unsettled, I looked at the train timetables on the wall, willing myself back into another era. I was dismayed at the anger that still rushed over me when I least expected it; at how married I still clearly was.

"They start so young, now," Edith was saying. "Did you see the girl, Hungarian not Russian, who is a chess grand master at fifteen? Youngest ever, first female. What a way to begin your life. And I saw a TV spot on this tennis-playing ten-year-old—she was Russian—who was already in training, planning to turn pro at twelve. It amazes me, I must admit. At a time when I was playing jacks, riding bikes, trading mysteries, these young women—one can hardly call them girls, with those achievements—are already competing and winning in world class events."

"You haven't done so badly," I said, finding it painful that she should compare herself and find herself wanting.

"But see what it cost me, dear. I'm seventy-eight and may lose my last chance to go into the field because my damn body is misbehaving. Had I started even ten years sooner—"

I didn't answer. What was there to say? I would have preferred to be in my mother's shoes, even with her hip, at her age, than to have had the high point of my life some sixty years in the past when I was a tennis prodigy or a chess luminary. But I could hear my mother's frustration in her voice, could sense that her passion would outdistance her flesh. Having the chance to go for it when you were ready: that was the point.

I could and often did feel guilty that Bess and I had held Mother back. Guilty even that we had not done with our lives what she might have expected. Yet I knew that my mother's loss was personal, her own. That it was her own race, her own best time, her own distance she was measuring and finding wanting. There was no reproach regarding what Bess or I had done with our lives, only regret with what she had not yet done with hers.

Mother said, "Sarah, my grandson enticed me down here with a nonrefundable ticket, knowing I couldn't refuse, even though I'm due to leave in a matter of days. I didn't set out to make this a secret trip, but I didn't call your sister. I know Bess has her hands full with guests this time of year—"

"Fannin and the boys are there for the weekend," I told her.

She shook her head. "Isn't it odd the way we all rally round and think of your sister on Mother's Day? Even your dear daughter does. I had a Vermont cob-smoked ham sent to her—sending coals to Newcastle to send pork to Carolina, I know that. Still, she can have something to carve and set out."

I nodded. "I sent her cow plates and bowls, as if there were still milking sheds at her place."

Edith pushed away her plate of dessert, and looked at both of us, smiling. "I have a war story to tell on myself before we go. I was on a plane, going somewhere, long flight, Africa it was, and I got to talking with the man seated next to me, the way you do when you have time to exchange your entire life stories and you can't see any way out of it. He began by telling me about his combat service and how the war had changed his life. Before I could stop myself, I asked him, 'What war?' " Mother threw back her head and laughed, her white curls bobbing. "Honestly. But, in my defense, my dad had been in WWI, MacDonald in WWII, your Nolan in Korea. . . ." She waved a hand. "Naturally, he was offended and soon turned his attention to the in-flight movie."

" 'What war?' is a fair question, Mother," I said. "I ask it of myself all the time."

"Thank you, dear," she said. "And thank you, George, for the luncheon. I do feel it's quite my day."

MOTHER AND I were sitting on the porch when Will brought the dogs back from their evening walk. She had taken a nap, held on to a chair and tried ever so slowly to raise her left leg front and back, then got on her hands and knees and tried to swing it to the side. We were having an iced tea and watching the strawberry sunset seep across the sky until even the distant trees and hills reddened in the dusk.

He climbed the steps, and reached out a hand. "Edith Cooper, Will Perry. A pleasure to see you. You may not remember me, but I'm the 'young doctor' who took over your old doctor's practice." He indicated his middle with a gesture that suggested he hardly fit the description now.

Mother stood, wincing at the motion. "I remember you well, young doctor." She took his hand and held it in both of hers. "I thought you quite attractive, and hardly enough younger to make a problem. I'd have pursued the matter— but doctors weren't free to travel in those days."

"I'm freer now," he said kindly. "Where did you have in mind?"

"How does Patagonia sound?"

"Like hell, I have to say."

"Sit down, Will." I liked seeing them together. They would have made a good pair, actually. Mother could have done worse than take up with him thirty-odd years ago.

He settled himself, and the dogs did, too, on either side of his chair. "No tea. I've got to get back to the hospital."

"Bad?" I asked him. The hospital on Sunday night, on Mother's Day? It must be.

"Not good. The man on my table the day you called."

"I'm sorry."

Will turned to Edith. "Let's talk about that hip."

"Butt muscle, the one that lifts. Gluteus maximus, to be precise."

"I brought you a little homeopathic remedy. If my memory serves, you have an aversion to pharmaceuticals." He fished in his jacket pocket, handed her a small tin.

"Your memory serves." Mother looked pleased, touched at his recalling her accurately.

"Arnica. It's from a mountain plant, an Indian remedy. Rub it in. It'll heal the tissue from inside. Your hip should feel better. I'm leaving you a large enough sample that you can take it with you."

"That's very kind. . . ." She demonstrated that she could lift her foot only inches from the porch floor. "I'm going down there if I have to crawl."

Will stood. "Is there anything else the young doctor can do for you?"

"As a matter of fact, there is. Could you? I'm accustomed to travelling with three things: aspirin, eugenol, and paregoric. Now the last two are prescription and they're fussy even about giving them."

"Eugenol—that's oil of cloves."

"Yes, for your gums, teeth, when you're out in the heat, eating strange food, nowhere near water clean enough to brush with. Cloves. I've been chewing them, but it is not the same. Paregoric, well, I know that's opium. But for dysentery or pain—the two terrors of the tropics—a teaspoonful is a salvation."

Will nodded, not making notes but getting it all in his head. I had wished for him at lunch, although it was, and rightly, George's occasion—he seemed already to know my family better than my husband of thirty-three years had. At least to have more understanding of them.

"I'll see you have both to take back with you," he said to Mother. "I'll call them in tomorrow, refills guaranteed. Let me know when aspirin requires a prescription, too, and you'll have that."

"I'm much obliged," Mother said.

He gave each of us a cheek kiss, holding Edith's face in his hands for a moment. "I missed a fine chance," he said.

"You'll be good for my daughter," Mother told him.

"She'll do for a consolation prize." He touched my face. "Missoula wants to stay," he said.

"Ben is counting on it."

"Will Perry wants to stay, too."

"I hope your man makes it," I said.

At the bottom of the steps, he stopped. "I lost a boy last night. Just pushing thirty. Kid didn't even make it to the end of the first chapter."

Mother shook her head. "Was that your first?"

"No, but the worst."

I hadn't been with Will long enough to grow accustomed to this, his dealing with death on a daily basis. Mother seemed more comfortable with it.

"Hanging around, waiting for the experts to give me the bad news on my man, I started forming a plan to shake up the medical world here. They think AIDS is a Yankee disease, imported down here to whup us again."

Mother tapped her fingers together. "Tell them it's killed more men already than the Civil War."

"How about the Second Siege of Shiloh?" Will asked. "More soldiers died at Shiloh, if my memory serves, than in all the U.S. battles before it combined." He rubbed his hands across his face, looking tired and his age.

Mother shook her head. "Carolinians like to concentrate on Carolinians. Make it the Second Battle of Fort Sumter."

"I might do that," Will said, and then he was on his way.

We watched him trot out to the county road, while the pups raced around the circular drive under the oak, the smell of night animals in the air.

"That's good fortune for you both," Mother said. She was holding the back of the rocker, making an effort in the dusk to move her offending muscle.

"I didn't mean to take you by surprise," I said. "If he and I had been younger we might have waited a more decent length of time."

"You mentioned his name at lunch," Mother said, as if that was all the announcement she'd needed.

"So I did."

When the red sunset was just a faint line edging the horizon and the sky was dark, we went in. "What would you like to eat?" I asked her.

"Cereal? Fruit?"

Inside, while I set out various brans, oats, wheat, strawberries, bananas, blueberries—wishing my peaches were ripe—Mother worked her hip with her hands. "I used to want," she confessed, "to have a baby by every man I was interested in. I used to get so disgusted with myself. Way past the age of possibility or good sense, I'd think about it, having his baby, as if that were an option. Later, I came to the conclusion that it wasn't really a signal the body rigged up to increase the species, but that what one always wanted was collaboration with a man. What easier way to collaborate than by reproducing part of the world? In my day, it was rare for women and men to work side by side. Now a lot of women do marry the men they work with. Or work with the men they marry." She bent and stretched, holding on to a kitchen chair. "You don't think about that? With Will?"

I considered, surprised at the question, and at the topic. "He never had children," I said. "I do, I suppose, think of that." I'd never asked my mother about men. I'd lost my only father; I imagined as a child I'd assumed my mother had lost her only husband. Children see their parents as their creators and not much more. I'd do well to recall that where Fannin and George were concerned.

"Why did you never remarry?" I asked Mother now.

"At first, the good ones were like your Will, too tied to their jobs to travel. By the time anyone promising had come along, I'd got used to being in charge of myself."

While we fixed ourselves bowls of cereal and fruit, I admitted that I liked living alone already, and told her a story. "The weekend before I went to Harriet's, I was spraying the front flower beds, to keep the chiggers off, and other bugs, with that mess I mix—ammonia, water, flea and tick powder—and I heard this car pull into the drive and looked around to see this stringy-haired man with wild eyes, skin bleached pale as bone, bad teeth. Serial killer, was my first thought. He got out and started over to Nolan's old car— both his cars, as you saw, the old back-roads car and his new one, were still sitting in the drive. He said, 'I want to see the gentleman of the house,' and pointed to the old car. 'I'm the gentleman of the house,' I told him. 'I got this GM,' he said, 'like that one. I want to take out the compressor and see how does it work.' 'You can lift the hood,' I said, 'but don't take it out.' And went right on spraying. After he left, I thought: What difference would it have made if I'd had a husband down at the bank? Whatever comes along on a daily basis that I don't handle myself?"

"That's easier to see when you live alone," Mother said.

"You aren't second-guessing what a man will do." She'd finished eating and was busily rubbing her feet with Vaseline. Then, when they were thoroughly coated, she put on a pair of white socks. "Keeps them from drying out," she explained, "or getting calluses. Sometimes when I'm at home, I'll sleep with my hands greased up in a pair of socks, too." She asked me for a cup of boiling water, then dropped in a tea bag, bent down and breathed the steam. "The tannic acid keeps my sinuses clear," she said.

"What else can I get you?" I asked, thinking that Mother was truly a clean machine, someone who treated her body with the same care another woman might have spent rubbing and waxing an antique.

"Some hot cocoa? Sometimes I have a cup at bedtime when I'm at home. It's something you can never get travelling."

I set out two cups for us. "You always said warm milk tells the system someone is taking care of you."

"It tells you you're taking care of yourself."

THE PHONE RANG while I was in the kitchen slicing strawberries and Will was measuring sugar and cream for home-made ice cream. Our shoes were at the back door—it had been muddy out—and the dogs were still running around outside, chasing the tail end of the day. It was our first night to try out my single bed upstairs.

I reached for the phone out of habit, and then heard myself speak in the still-strange taped sound: "This is Sarah. I'm glad you called. Please leave a message and I'll return it as soon as I can." How odd, to stand and eavesdrop on myself.

There was a silence, then Harriet's hoarse voice came on:

"*You?* With an answering machine? I don't believe it. I don't know which is worse, having to go through the girl at your shop or talk to some wires in a box." Another pause. Then, "The doctor says they won't have to operate. Isn't that great news? He's going to shrink it instead. I think about it like a fat plum they're going to turn into a prune in my chest, if I'm lucky. What do you think? Sarah? Where are you?"

I stood frozen, looking at the machine, while Will reached over and punched the SAVE button.

"Will—" I looked at him. Did this mean what I thought?

"Go take a shower," he said. "Then you can call her. Wash off your walk. Clear your head."

"Not good, then?"

He stroked my arm gently. "Whupped, I'd say. Just off the top of my head."

"Oh, please—"

"Go take a shower. I'll fix us some ice cream."

I stood under the water as hot as I could stand, feeling it hit my scalp, the part in my loosened hair, my upturned face. Just the way it had with Nolan, it felt as if a large black shadow, the wings of some vast condor, had fallen over my world. You walked along, getting on with it, and then something moved across the sky and you were beneath its spread, seized with panic. How much worse it must be for them, the one who feels the claws sink into his side beneath the ribs, the one who feels them sink into her back below the shoulder blades.

I'd not cried when the gnawing pain in Nolan's body was labelled and his chances whittled down to nil. I wasn't crying now. Rather, I felt as if the breath were being squeezed from me, stones piled on my chest. This time, having seen so recently that death is careless, arbitrary, rapid, an X-rated film in which you cannot hide your eyes, I no longer managed even surprise. Only entreaty.

Not again. Not Harriet with her lovely legs and jewelled good cheer. Not her. We'd meant to be great-grannies to-gether, tatting and knitting and rocking and chatting, putting the youngsters in their place, bawdy, familiar. Octo-genarians playing Remember When. Clinging together, grieving for Doll and Edith when their times came, putting the old country place with its hogs and hickory nuts on the market, conveying the intricate web of Edith Huntt Cooper's work to the designated library. Listening to the tape, made by the young oral historian, of Nat Sloane telling one last time the final score: Notre Dame 27, Stanford 10.

I turned and bowed my head, letting the water beat down on my back, pressing my palms against my breasts, then moving them down my ribs to my flanks. Flesh and bones, so fragile. So frangible, so frail. I knelt under the pelting water with my face in my hands. Not Harriet, I pleaded until the water turned cold.

When I slid back the glass, soaked, chilled, Will was waiting with a bath towel. "Here," he said, "I'm going to dry you off." He wrapped me in the towel and in his arms and led me, still damp, to the high narrow bed. "You need to be reminded that nothing's wrong here at home." He had on his trousers and shirt, unbuttoned and flapping, and while he got me under the bedcovers, he undressed himself.

"We may be too much for this cot on stilts," he said, "but we might as well find out now." He dried my body with the soft much-washed blue towel; then, more slowly, he dried the moist hollow of my throat and under my arms, and the back of my neck under my wet hair, which he wrapped in the towel as he kissed my wet face. Still standing by the bed, he kissed my skin, above my navel, on my temples, where the pulse beat in my neck and at my wrists, as if marking all the vital spots.

Had I ever told him of my old schoolgirl fantasy of being

led from the shower to the bed? Or did he know that because he understood women, or because he understood me to my bones? No matter. In long years past I'd longed for such erotic handling, for years after the time it had been refused me in this house, and I reached for Will, made room for him beside me. I shut my eyes, letting the room go dark, and took him inside me with a desire, a greed, that stunned me. Then held on to him afterwards with my hands, my mouth, my locked legs.

"How did you know?" I asked him, letting my hair spread wet on the pillow, my face still flushed.

"When I've been up all night," he said, lying on his side against me, "when I've lost one or come up to that stone wall where there's nothing more to be done, I could hump a sheep. I get this empathy for those cases you read about: some poor pig farmer's lost his crops, his home, plus half his kin and he wants the nearest thing that's warm and moving."

"And do the dying feel that way?"

"I couldn't say."

I thought of Nolan then, and our final unsatisfactory couplings. Him angry in his denial, taking me as if in revenge for something, slamming my door on his way out. Or, later, unable, unsatisfied, telling me to get out of his room and close the door. "I think not," I said.

Will pulled on his pants and buckled his brown belt. "Make your call, Coop. I'll clean up the pooches and bring us up some ice cream."

"Yes." I sat and let him hand me my blue cotton robe.

"You got paper and pen?"

I nodded, indicating the drawer of the night table.

"Take notes. We'll go over them in the light of day."

My fingers, shaky, dialled a wrong number twice before I heard Harriet's voice say, "Is that you?"

Listening, I wrote: Tumor a small-cell carcinoma in the left mainstem bronchus. No metastasis. Some paresis of the left vocal cord, some invasion of the nerve. Adjacent to the heart, in the mediastinum. Harriet, clearly, was reading from notes as well.

She said it had been dreadful afterwards: she couldn't swallow or cough, couldn't eat or drink. But she was fine now. The best thing, Oh, Sarah, she said, the very best thing was that there was no need for an operation. She wasn't going to have a nasty scar, like a crime victim or something. She'd been terrified of that. She knew that cutting through the breastbone, whatever they had to do, hurt like old billy hell, but mostly it was the scar she'd been terrified about.

David McCord, her young man, she said, had been a dear. He'd called her lots—and they were definitely planning a trip, after she'd had her thing shrunk up like a sundried tomato. After it was just a flake in her chest. She'd set the trip as her goal: not one single cigarette after she got on that plane. They were thinking about Aspen—she had had that great time with Knox there, one of the best times. Wouldn't it be grand to go back and pick up where she left off? Wouldn't it be wonderful to start over there with someone else? David, she reported, was almost finished with his recordings of old-timers. He said he could go anywhere she wanted. That was the advantage of her having grown children and his having none; they could just pick up and go, wherever.

I listened, drawing a small chest on the writing pad, a tiny little dried tomato inside. I was having trouble breathing, and finally opened my mouth and gulped air.

"How do you feel now?" I asked. I drew a little plum in the chest, and then wrinkled it like a prune. I drew a heart, putting a bow on a sprouting valve.

"Relieved, honestly. Thrilled—I can't tell you how scared

I was—that this isn't going to mean being laid up in the hospital, being sawed in half like some magician's lady friend." Her voice sounded strained, like someone recovering from laryngitis. "I was the most scared—I mean, having just met David and everything, and him such a hunk— of having this scar right here by my bosoms, you know, something he couldn't help but see or, worse, have to touch. If we—when we—when he gets this chastity business out of his system, I don't want to be a mess. My spirits really took a nose dive down there while I waited on that lab in Houston to locate my records and the doctor to see me. You know how long it takes at those big places."

"Did you have anyone to keep you company?" I didn't want to bring up the sore subject of Harriet's children. Or ask whether she'd let her parents know. Would Doll have sat in a waiting room at M. D. Anderson Cancer Center? It was hard to guess. I drew little tendrils from the prune to the heart. I'd covered half a dozen pads while Nolan was ill, filling pages with tiny pancreases shaped like elongated bunches of grapes, each with a worm inside. Toward the last, the cluster of grapes shrank, drying to raisins.

"Birthday Club has been great, really. Honestly, they've all had one thing after another, and this is just one more to add to it. I think secretly they were glad to find out that I wasn't the only one with no problems, since most of them, you know, are in lots worse shape. So shrinking this thing, like a fibroid or goiter or something, doesn't seem so bad. You know those pictures in our biology books at Pritchard's? Of the old men with goiters on their necks from not eating Morton's salt? I imagine it like that—the thing going to go down the way a sprained ankle does or a toothache— awful and then the swelling disappearing until you can't even remember how the hell it hurt so bad or why it put you on the blink for so long."

I stared at my pen. "When do you start the—treatment?"

I couldn't think of what else to call it, the radiation. Harriet hadn't used that word. Perhaps it was too frightening. What should I have said? The procedure?

Harriet said, sounding uneasy, "He said to get back on my feet. I guess he means feeling better and able to eat something. Next week, I guess I'll tell the kids, and get that over with. 'Hey, kids—' "

I thought of our planned October reunion; October, tonight, seemed light-miles away. "Why don't you come see me this summer?" I asked. "Why do we have to stick to the old routine? Who's to care? Who's to be inconvenienced? We're footloose. Come for the Fourth of July. You know how you hate East Texas in the middle of summer with the air too thick to breathe. It's pleasant here. We can have picnics in the Blue Ridge." I knew Bess would coax Fannin and the boys back to William of Orange over the Fourth; foxhound pups and fox cubs would be big enough to handle, and there were splendid fireworks.

"I think," Harriet said, nervous, "I'll still be—going in, you know, for treatment. I have to be through for Birthday Club's Midsummer Night's Party for husbands. I have to show the Turtlenecks just how good a widow can look."

"The next-to-last week in August, then," I suggested. "Come for the Mineral Springs Summer Fair. You've never seen our little town pretend it looks the way it did in its old and famous days. We get crafts from Georgia and all over the Carolinas. And every church tries to outdo the others with home-cooked food. Even our small St. Andrew's has a booth. Do come. My peaches will be ripe by then and we'll have peach cobblers and peach turnovers and peach pancakes. . . ." I could hear the pleading in my voice. Was I that worried that time would run out? Was I right to be?

"How about chocolate cake?" Harriet asked, laughing a raw laugh.

"The best."

"I don't know why not. You're right. Why do we have to stick to the old schedule? We don't have children to get to school or husbands to stash at the bank. Besides, in August I can wear my short shorts, can't I?"

"Everywhere you go," I told her.

"Promise."

"I promise."

After a pause, she said, "If we can visit back and forth anytime we feel like it, you can even come hold my hand this fall if the shrinking doesn't work, I mean, if I have to take that bad stuff that makes you sick as two big hogs."

"I will," I said. "Meanwhile, call me anytime you want to talk about it. Let me know when they set up the— schedule. And when you and your David decide on your trip." I didn't know what to say; I felt far away and of no help. "We had that slumber party," I said, "and now I'm five states away."

"You're taking the southern route." Harriet's laugh turned into a cough and she covered the phone. "If you go through Arkansas and Tennessee, you're only three states away."

Off the phone, I went to the dresser and slowly began to brush my hair. I looked around the room with its peach-painted walls, its rug with cabbage roses, the Vermeer prints over the high beds. Harriet and I had been rearranging our marriages when I did this bedroom over. Now we were rearranging our very lives.

When I was steady, I tucked my notes in the bedside drawer, tightened the belt on my robe, put color on my lips, and piled extra pillows against the fruitwood headboard. At the top of the stairs, I called down, "Where's my ice cream?"

"I fed it to the dogs," Will called back.

In a bit, he came up the stairs and through the doorway, an outsized bowl of strawberries and homemade ice cream in each hand, a paperback under his arm. Ben and Missoula padded along behind him.

"Move over," he said, shifting himself up onto the narrow bed beside me. "They're making mincemeat of my private eye."

FOUR

I LET MYSELF INTO Rooms of One's Own. I was thinking of Harriet; everything reminded me of Harriet. I remembered her being hurt that I hadn't named my shop Prints Charming. Her being shocked the first time she saw the sign SARAH COOPER AND KATIE PEGUES, PROPRIETORS. Saying, "But you've been Rankin now for almost twenty years. How can you call yourself Cooper, as if you never got married? Has Nolan seen this? What does he say? Why, Knox would have kitten fits if I suddenly dumped the Calhoun name and went back to Sloane. He'd give birth to cats." And all the years of Harriet referring to "that girl" and Katie to "that woman" in the same tone of voice, neither understanding the other.

While I was having my breakfast on the porch, the mail carrier had brought August's Potato of the Month. SHEPODY, the tag on the burlap bag said. And I had to stop and close my eyes, thinking that the damn potatoes would still be arriving when Harriet was gone.

I looked around the shop. The room, a corner space on Mineral Springs's main street in the brief downtown, was large and light. It had two walls of windows, one that contained the counter where Katie and I sat, and one that was papered and covered in color photographs of all the rooms Katie and I had done. In the corner, where the windows met, we'd set out a round table, covered in sample books, with two armchairs for browsing. Even the ceiling made me think of Harriet, the old tin squares a reminder that we both lived in locations left over from yesterday.

I was eager for her visit, yet dreading it at the same time. I was afraid of what I would see when she stepped off the plane in the Greenville airport, fatigued from transferring in Atlanta. Afraid I would see what I did not want to see.

Will had talked with me about her. He'd looked at my notes, and then had tucked my drawing of the chest with its dried tomato and bowed heart into his wallet. That was in May. Since then, we had not said much about the small-celled tumor. I'd asked him why radiation and not chemotherapy; he'd said because my friend was not going to make it anyway, and radiation didn't make you as sick. There was little else to ask.

I knew Harriet would also arrive angry or, more likely, hurt, and that was my fault. I'd had to ask her to delay her trip for two days, to get her nonrefundable ticket reissued. It had been a harrowing month already, and it wasn't over yet. First Fannin lost the baby, and then Rooms lost a client, which Katie had had to deal with all alone.

Will and I saw each other as often as possible, and talked on the phone as little as necessary, and then logistics only. He calling to say he'd see me late or not at all. Me calling with news of some new crisis, to ask him to walk the dogs. We'd not even mentioned living together; it seemed too complex even to imagine. Requiring time and attention neither of us was ever going to have. But we'd each got familiar with the other's already familiar home; we'd found corners, spots, spaces that could be moved into without crowding. When we were together, I let my answering machine intervene for me, surprised at how my callers resented it. Sometimes we'd be on the bed at my house, reading, in our robes, and Will would get a call on his beeper at the same time that my machine was speaking. These are the robots for Sarah and Will, we'd say. The new guard dogs of the age of technology.

When Katie came in, I filled us each a mug of coffee from the thermos. I'd not only arrived early, I'd brought us donuts. We leaned over and bumped heads, saying "Knock on wood," a new routine. Silly, a sign of stress.

"What time does your friend arrive?" Katie asked. She wasn't in her jumper and T-shirt, but instead was all dressed up in a brown suit with shoulder pads, a cream silk shirt, heels, and a pocket watch on a gold chain around her neck. She consulted her fancy timepiece.

"Just before noon."

"We'll have to close up; I can't stay."

"I have the feeling you're not headed for the country in those clothes."

"You're right." She rubbed her slender hands together as if warming them over her coffee cup. "I have a lunch date with a certain contractor."

I smiled. This was the last man in Katie's life. This must be good news, I thought, or else she wouldn't go. "So?"

"So I don't know, but I'm giving him a try. We invested close to ten years."

"Will it be hard to see him again?" I knew she'd had a difficult time when he'd opted for someone with less muscle, someone less enterprising.

"I expect so." Katie shrugged.

"You don't have to hang around." I wanted to let her be on her way.

"I have time."

We talked about my new client in Greer, a pretty Victorian town on the other side of Greenville. I'd been by the woman's house last week and was going again after Harriet was gone. I'd found a nice print already of white morning glories twining across a dark blue background, very 1920s floral print, yet very contemporary. If she didn't like it—the client, Thomason—we agreed I'd start again. There were metallic papers from the Twenties; that was a possibility.

We finished the coffee and then talked about what was still on our minds, the client we'd lost.

"Do you think Morrison really killed herself?" Katie asked me.

"She did kill herself," I said. We'd been so shocked. Her son, who told us, said she'd gone to sleep after taking an undisclosed amount of an unnamed brand of sleeping pill and not waked up.

"I mean, intended to do it?"

"I don't know," I said, trying to sort it out. "I think people get into binds, straits they can't get out of. They can't see their way clear. So they throw themselves on the odds. Let chance decide. Perhaps, Morrison might have thought, Dexter Junior will check on me, maybe they'll pump my stomach, maybe I'll throw up the pills. Maybe I'll sleep through eternity. I think people cast themselves on fate. I don't know what to call that. Is that intention?"

"Hey, are you talking about Morrison?" Katie asked, looking at me closely. "Sounds to me like you're talking about that woman's husband."

"Knox?" I shook my head at the idea. Surely not Knox, such a dandy, such a ladies' man. Always a handkerchief in his pocket, always smelling of after-shave and barbershop. Surely a man light-years from depression. Still, he had that other woman. Could he have got drunk and called it close taking the curve, letting fate make the choice? God, what a thought.

"Morrison was doing so much better than she had been," Katie said, sad at losing a successful client, and a friend.

"She was tickled to pieces with that upstairs sitting room with its cocoa-and-rose zigzag paper. And she had a big time with having a nice roomy space her son couldn't invade." She looked glum. "I can't figure it."

"Harriet said Knox had made that curve every day for years, sometimes more than once. And he always drank." I couldn't bear to think of someone letting go of a life when hanging on to one was so difficult.

Katie looked at her watch and stood. "I got to go." She looked at me and said, "You know, we never got Morrison's last payment."

"Is that right?" I thought that if Nolan had died in a crash, I'd have been sure there was some unacknowledged intent. He'd been so difficult at the last, snapping at the children on the phone. Flaring up at every crime report on TV. "They ought to be shot," he'd say, or "strung up," of someone who'd robbed a convenience store. "They ought to be deported," of someone of a different nationality. "That's what you get for letting everybody think this is a free country. Where do they get off? I paid my way; they can, too." But that was after he'd been diagnosed, after he knew that something was eating his insides.

I ran my hand over the pleasing matte finish of a white-and-coral wallpaper sample, wondering if Katie's seeing her man again had anything to do with the recent loss of her client. Wanting to salvage something? "If you have lunch with your contractor," I asked, not wanting to pry, "does this mean negotiations will reopen?"

"Could be," Katie said. "Could be it's too late. There's a statute of limitations on caring. Both ways, I'm talking about. You can't just relight it like a pilot light. It's more like a brushfire. When the brush gets all burned up, there's nothing left to light."

I watched through the windows as a man got out of an

Olds in front of the shop. He looked up at the Rooms sign before he opened the door. A slim, nice-looking man, he had razor-cut fair hair and an expensive tailored suit.

"I found this, Ms. Pegues," he said, stopping Katie at the door. "In Mother's checkbook. I'm trying to get everything paid off as best I can. . . ."

Katie made the introductions. "Sarah Cooper, this is Dexter Morrison, Junior."

So this was Maisie Morrison's boy, the one who'd been having all his friends over downstairs, the indirect cause of the lovely upstairs sitting room. Not, I hoped, of Maisie's dreadful end. I held out my hand. "We were so sorry about your mother."

"It's a shock." He had a square jaw and wore one gold earring. "I haven't started to recover. Do you think she— meant to? But how could you possibly have an idea. You hardly knew her. Who did?" He reached out and handed Katie a check. "Here—I guess she still owed you something? It's made out to you. To this place, I mean. I couldn't find a bill anywhere—"

"Yes," Katie told him. "It's for us. Thanks."

"Sure," he said, looking around.

"Sorry we drank up all the coffee," Katie said.

"No, I can't stay, really, Ms. Pegues. I just wanted to drop this off. I guess she owed it to you? There wasn't a bill. There's a lot of things you have to do when someone dies. You probably don't know that, but there is—"

"Thanks, Dexter, for bringing it by."

When he was gone, Katie handed me the check. "She wanted us to see this," she said.

I saw the neatly printed MAISIE B. MORRISON on the gray bank check and felt tears start in my eyes. It was almost like a message for us. Even after Morrison had lost her husband, when she came in as our client, she refused to take his name off her checks, insisting on signing them *Mrs. Poindexter P. Morrison, Sr.* She must have wanted Katie, wanted Rooms of One's Own, to see that she had finally got her own account. "Ouch," I said, looking at the signature.

"I know. It gets to me." Katie put the check down and then picked it up. "I don't want to keep this, okay?" She endorsed it and slipped it in a printed envelope for EMILY'S List, an acronym for Early Money Is Like Yeast—a women's political action group Mother had got her interested in.

"Why do you think Dexter brought it by instead of mailing it?" I asked her. "Do you think he thought we'd give it back to him?"

Katie said, her hand on the doorknob, "I expect he wanted to see somebody who knew his mother."

I was thinking about Harriet's children, seeing them arrive somewhere, as Junior Morrison had done, stunned, puzzled, caught by surprise. I wondered if they were in any way prepared for what was coming.

AT ELEVEN, I CLOSED the shop and aimed my car for the airport.

When Fannin lost her baby and Harriet was due to arrive, I'd said to Will, "I can't be with both of them."

He'd said, "Don't try to think it out. Leave it to the bottom of your feet. In the war," he told me, "the medics talked about triage. Sometimes you hear it still from old-timers like myself. Some are going to get well without you; some aren't going to get well even if you try your damndest. Some can go either way; they're the ones to work on.

"In civilian life—I'm not going to call it real life, the comparison works the other way—but in civilian life, with plenty of anaesthesia and clean operating theatres and state-of-the-art pain-killers, you don't think that way. Maybe when push came to shove we didn't in the army either. You get a gut feel where you need to be. At whose bedside. Sometimes I'll be standing there staring down at some face in ICU and I'm asking myself, What are you doing here? And then I'm reminding myself who's around the corner and down the hall, and who's on another floor. But there I am, talking to what seem to me to be deaf ears, nobody at home, eyes rolled back in the head. Then the patient will open his eyes and say, 'You'll get fallen arches standing on your feet all night, Doc,' or she'll raise her head, put on a flirty smile, and say, 'You're putting on weight, Will,' and I'll know I'm where I ought to be."

We'd been in Will's downstairs bedroom on the four-poster, which made me feel as if we were in some grandparent's room, which we were, in fact. It had been his grandmother's house, just as I lived in what had been my grandmother's. I was going to keep a flannel gown there when it was winter, a granny gown, for when the wind came down out of the mountains. There was even a mud room off the kitchen for wet galoshes (where had they and the word gone? with those grandmothers?) and mittens and scratchy outer clothing. I liked his house. I had never seen the secret side of it, the private rooms, its past, back when Nolan and I had come for the summer parties to which Will invited his married friends. I'd asked him about the judge; how she'd liked his house. "She didn't care for the livestock," was all he said.

There was even a sauna, which he'd had installed in what had originally been an oversized cedar closet. A sauna? I'd been amazed. "Umm," he said. "Why not? Dog people are Sybarites, didn't you know?" So I'd learned to shower and go wet into the square fragrant hot dry room with its two benches, stretch out and cook my bones, and then let him wrap me in a towel and lead me to the four-poster. "Come winter," he said, "you can warm the sheets for us."

In the end, I went to my daughter.

I'd just come in from picking peaches when Bess called me. Out at seven in the morning in the pouring rain in my scruffiest clothes, a scarf over my head, getting drenched. I loved it when all the trees ripened in turn, and loved sinking my teeth into the juiciest fruit as I picked and tasted: the O'Henry, a sweet yellow eating peach; the white tart Georgia Belle; the dark luscious Monroe; the Indian pickling peach, fuzzy and white outside, red inside; the creamy Loring's rosy pulp. I'd filled one basket and then another, watching the chill rain soak the throats around the trees, the branches overhead growing outward like raised arms.

My feet squishing in the wet ground, I remembered when the children were little and I used to send them out with rolled-up newspapers to beat the trunks of the fruit trees, to massage them and get their sap running. How much fun they'd had as youngsters, two rowdy kids, pelting the bark, the dog (Rogers? No, Hardy it would have been) running at their feet. A few times Harriet's two had been here also, all of them out together. Then all of them deciding when they reached middle school that they looked like dunces and weren't going to be caught beating tree trunks anymore. But trees were like people: they grew tired.

"She lost the baby, Sis," Bess said. "She's scared to tell you."

I sank down in the wicker chair, still wet, my feet going right out from under me. I felt like an ogre. "She was scared to tell me when she got pregnant."

How far along was my daughter? Four months, surely. The summer was a blur. Recalling it, all I could bring to mind had to do with Harriet. Tracking the radiation, listening to the reports with a sinking heart. Will sometimes rubbing my back while I talked late at night on the phone, the dogs on the rag rug by the window in my bedroom, their new favorite spot, where they could catch the first crack of daylight.

"She's pretty upset. She bled all over the floor."

"Has she been having trouble?" How could it have happened so suddenly?

Bess's voice had wavered. "I feel so guilty. She was spotting when she came to visit on the Fourth. But I didn't know what to do. If it only has two legs, you know me, I'm lost."

"It's not your fault," I told my sister. Wondering who I was to be passing out pardon. I who should have told my grandmother that if she didn't take care of little Bess I'd put ten of mother's spiders in her bed. But I knew that all of us longed to shoulder blame; it implied we had at least some control over our lives. No one wanted to think that events or bodies simply went haywire. If you couldn't blame yourself, then you blamed someone else. Was Harriet doing this? Saying to herself, If Knox hadn't run around with that tacky size-ten woman then I wouldn't be gasping for air? It was too unbearable to think that it didn't matter what you did, that your body could betray you for no reason, a random attack, a derailed train. No wonder people went nuts over vitamins, exercise, cutting out fats, cutting out salt, all the regimes. It was an effort to prove you retained some responsibility for what happened to you.

"She wants to see you," Bess said, sounding just slightly left out. "I said I'd stay at the house with the boys if you came."

"Of course I'll come," I said. "I'll work it out."

Later, I called Harriet, who was, as I feared, hurt and mad at having her long-planned trip postponed. "Can't your sister take a break from romancing the roan to look after your daughter? Fannin practically lives with her anyway. I don't see what you can do—"

"Be there," I said as gently as I could.

I called my son-in-law, who said that Fannin would be in the hospital a day or two more, to make sure the flow had stopped and to get her strength back. He also said that since he spent all his waking hours there, he wanted his wife close at hand. He sounded unnerved and young.

Will flew down the evening of Bess's call and went straight to the hospital to have a talk with Johnny. "One medicine man to another," he said.

I called Mother, trying to picture her in her work clothes and boots, somewhere south of the 38th meridian in a locale known as Patagonia, which straddled parts of Chile and Argentina and had rain forests, tablelands, mountains and—spiders.

"Shall I come home?" she asked.

"Don't even think of it." My remorse over Time Lost for my mother made my words almost a shout. I heard her laugh lightly, as if reading my mind.

"See if you can find some nice tropical lilies to send her from me. It's impossible from down here—I'll check with you in a day or two. And thank you, dear."

The next day, I got to my daughter's door at the start of visitors' hours. "Fannin?" I called, stepping into her room.

"Mom?"

"I'm so sorry," I said.

"You are not, don't say you are." My daughter wept.

Drying her eyes with a Kleenex, I studied her. Such a thin stalk of a girl, long legs, thick dark hair around her thin face, blue eyes freshly wet. Peaked—if that word was still in use—she looked like a runner who had used up her last wind and was still making slow laps around the field, her muscles moving in reflex. Tensile—that was another

word. She had the shoulders, the carriage of her North
Carolina daddy, the softer features of her aunt and my own
daddy.

"I did worry," I said, pulling up a chair by her bed, "that
you were not strong enough to have another. I didn't wish
this. . . ."

Fannin squeezed her eyes shut and then opened them.
"You know what Matthew did, Mom? He told his Sunday
School teacher that our baby Rankin had died in his
mommy's tummy and she sent him home with a sympathy
note and an extra lamb on his shepherd's poster. Poor Matt.
He has to tell everybody everything he knows."

"She sounds like a good teacher. Better than the one he
had in second grade."

"Don't be mad, Mom. I guess I mean, don't be glad."
She wiped her eyes with the back of her hand. She was in
a loose blue nightie, one that looked familiar. Maybe she'd
worn it after she delivered Jonathan.

"How could I possibly be either?"

But a nurse came before she could answer; it was time
for a shot.

I thought about my grandsons, whom I loved far more
than I got credit for. Stalwart Matthew; jolly Mack, now
nearly a first grader; kindly Lucas, who liked to push his
youngest brother around in his yellow dump truck; baby
Jon, who wasn't a baby anymore, a big boy now, in training
pants and black baseball cap, talking at the top of his voice,
wearing a whistle around his neck so he could get everyone's attention. My daughter was good with them, her boys.
Easy. Come on, scouts. Let's go, fellows. Hey, gang. Yo,
guys.

I did not know how to do that. I had treated my two as
separately as possible from the start, just as Bess and I had
been treated. Had that seemed lonely to my children? So

much so that George had elected to have none, and Fannin, a team? Neither replicating the sharp focus of parent on child, one on one. I tried to imagine Edith calling out, Hey, girls, get a move on. Come on, kidlets, hop to. Not possible. I had to laugh at the idea.

"Daddy's doctor came all the way to Atlanta," Fannin said, a spot of color on her cheeks, when the nurse had gone. "Can you believe it? Dr. Perry. I didn't really talk to him much while Daddy was—I mean, he was just the old doctor who came in and out with that stethoscope hanging down, the kind that makes you wonder why doctors are always heavy yet they fuss at their patients about gaining weight. He was really neat to do that. He sat right down here and talked to us about the baby. He'd talked to Eiko— you know, my doctor—and she'd told him she'd said for me to wait, not to get pregnant again so soon. And I admitted that she had and that I'd promised, but that I'd wanted, we'd wanted—" Fannin looked at me, tears welling up.

I nodded for her to go on.

"—that Johnny wanted six, that we'd said all along we wanted six. I told Dr. Perry that I guess I was missing Daddy. I said I guess I'd got pregnant knowing he was dying, and wanting to have another baby and name it after him."

"What did Will say?"

"He said the nicest thing." Fannin looked up, rosy. "I asked him were you doing all right about Daddy's death, and he said, Well, he didn't know, but that if you'd produced such a sensible and pretty daughter, maybe he ought to look into it. Wasn't that neat? I don't think anything has ever been as flattering. Me, sensible? Not hardly. Not exactly what I'm used to hearing." She looked at me, flushed with the compliment.

I smiled. "I trust his judgment, so it must be accurate."

"Anyway," she said, sitting up and swinging her legs off

the side of the bed, looking much the way she had when she'd got her tonsils out, shaky but ready to go, "I promised Dr. Perry and Johnny, too. He sort of put Johnny on the spot, a little bit, saying that four should be enough for any man, that he'd made his point and what was my health worth? Johnny looked offended, but then he got embarrassed. I mean, coming from who was saying it, what else could he do but say that, sure, maybe we should take a few years off."

God bless Will. How good he was with them. No one else could have collared Johnny that way, no one. My son-in-law and Nolan had got into a grudge match from day one. Nolan thought he was uppity, a smart aleck, not a real man. No doubt Johnny thought his wife's daddy a redneck in disguise, a cracker in a banker's suit.

"I don't know, Mom," Fannin said, lying back down. "I want a houseful of kids, that's the thing. For their sake. I want them to have each other no matter what happens to us, Johnny and me. I want them to have a big close family even if one of us—you know. I just think that you and Aunt Bess had such a lonesome miserable life growing up, with your daddy dying and your mother abandoning you to that old woman who didn't know a thing about kids. It must've been awful. I don't want to do that to my kids; I want them to have a gang of siblings. Half a dozen—" She wiped her eyes, which had filled again, even the lids wet. "*I* wanted six, *I* did, no use putting it off on Johnny."

Oh, Bess, I thought, with some vexation, what a sad story you've handed my daughter. What a picture of our growing up, poor little match girls, the Coopers. I could see Bess with her dark curly hair, fat cheeks, and big grin that could crumple into sobs in thirty seconds. I tried the light approach. "Your aunt likes to dramatize," I said. "Edith Huntt Cooper is a hard act to follow." I scooted my chair closer as if for a confidence. "Did you ever hear how Bess used to joke about her marriage?"

"She never talks about him. Randy?" Fannin sat up, at once interested.

"Randy, Randy. He was a glamorous polo player from Camden, a fable, better than good-looking. She went to all his matches, just out of school she was then. She saw him get all his silver championship cups. When they married, all his teammates were in attendance. Then, she used to say, it dawned on her on her wedding day that she'd ended up with the rider instead of the horse."

Fannin looked shocked but joined me in a laugh. "Really?"

"She used to tell them when she was at the Redfield Academy that she was an orphan. That she'd been raised in an orphanage."

"Aunt Bess?"

I felt my irritation at my younger sister ebb away. I liked recalling Bess's stories, her good nature, her funny way of dealing with growing up with horse posters instead of parents.

"I have to go home today," I told my daughter. "Will you be all right?"

"Sure. I'm going to stay another night; Johnny said it was okay." She looked as if she could use the rest. "Mom, guess who came to see me while I was here yesterday, did he tell you? My brother."

George, being a help to all of us. "I'm glad."

"He came in here and then went out to the house to see the boys. I don't think they even remembered they had an Uncle George. I haven't, honestly, I don't think, Mom, seen him since Daddy's funeral. We all went to Aunt Bess's for Mother's Day—I hope you didn't get mad—and then—it seems like forever. He was great about my losing the baby, really upset. Imagine, my brother."

"I haven't seen you two in the same location since your father died either."

"Yeah," Fannin said. "Gosh. What if I have all these boys and then they grow up and live in different places? In Timbuktu and the Klondike and the Andes and Borneo, and never even write to each other." Fannin looked at me, her mother, appalled. "I guess you don't think about how it's going to be from a parent's point of view."

"Or from your child's. . . ." And with that I enveloped her in a serious South Carolina hug, my daughter, whose slim arms wound around me fiercely.

I HEAVED HARRIET'S HEAVY garment bag into the trunk and maneuvered us along the tree-lined airport streets, turning right, west, at the clay embankment. I'd got to the airport with thirty minutes to spare, but it had taken time to park my generic Toyota among the Hondas and Hyundais. Soon, when the BMW plant opened in Greenville, we were going to think we were seeing a foreign car when we saw a Dodge or Chevrolet.

Harriet leaned back in her seat. "I'm going to savor the scenery," she said. "When you come from the swamps, this already seems like being in the Alps." She was taking short breaths but her color was grand, as if she'd just come back from a stay at the shore.

She was complaining about her flights. "Every seat on the plane was taken from Houston to Atlanta. I got stuck next to two women who were carrying on one of those reinforcement conversations that drive you up the wall. 'I know, I know, I know,' 'You're right, you're right, you're right.' If echolalia is repeating everything twice, what is three times? 'Sure, sure, sure.' 'I get it, I get it, I get it.' And if that wasn't enough, on the quickie from Atlanta to here, we hit some turbulence, and a woman near the front begins to see her life—her death actually—flash before her eyes. She starts screaming and hollering—I've never heard that before in my life—to be let off the plane. The flight attendant—we could hear her—called in 'distressed passenger' as we were landing. That applied to all of us by that time. It was one of those little DH-7s."

"You look wonderful," I told her. I'd been so relieved when she came out of the gate, jaunty in a short skirt inches above her knee, her prize legs in sheer hose with a sheen to them, green high heels. Her face had that honey tan that blonds get, and was less drawn than the last time I saw her. What if Will was wrong? What if it really had shrunk away, the small-cell tumor, the currents radiating it to a tiny dried prune of no consequence?

Harriet said, "I've got an amazing story, Sarah. That's one reason I couldn't stand it when you postponed my visit. My big news is, I found out whose blouse that was supposed to be."

Blouse? I had to think. The bow-tied gift Knox had so foolishly left behind on his closet shelf. "You did?"

"I did. At Birthday Club, of awful places to find her. Let me start at the beginning. It was the Midsummer Night's Party for husbands. I've known all that time, but I guess I wanted to tell you in person. Some things you just can't say on the phone."

Besides, I thought, she'd been on radiation since that time. Perhaps this story was what she'd held on to, something saved back, something that was left to tell in her old style of arriving with a surprise.

"It took forever to decide what to wear. I was scared to look in my closet, afraid I'd find turtlenecks cloning on the hangers. I ended up getting out everything I owned, and finally decided on the boat-neck amethyst-and-white Albert

Nipon that's as old as the Thicket, and I knew it was a smidge too bare and short, but the main thing was, it wasn't new. I didn't want to look like I'd bought a brand-new dress to try to vamp their flabby, bald, tiresome red-faced husbands."

"You got that dress for your fiftieth-birthday party."

"I did. And I decided, what the hell, I was going to add my pearl choker; I was sick of vandals deciding what I could and couldn't wear. Besides, I had my .22 tucked in my evening bag already."

I listened as she re-created the evening of more than a month ago, her own jewel, mounted in its elaborate setting. I knew the Stagecoach Inn, so I could picture the event. Wagon wheels on the wall, heavy gilt chandeliers and Victorian flocked ruby wallpaper. And the requisite game dinner—rabbit terrine, venison medallions moutarde, duck breast suprême with walnuts, quail with watercress puree. Dishes no real hunter ever ate—much as the Depot here served homestyle meals never cooked at home.

"Then—the most amazing thing, Sarah—when I got in the special party room, I saw that every single woman in Birthday Club had worn jewelry, too. As if we were all sick and tired of being scared out of our wits every time we left the house. They had dinner rings—how long since you've seen a dinner ring?—in aquamarines, tourmalines, moonstones, citrines, those big beautiful stones we used to wear. And pieces that had belonged to their grandmothers, old heirlooms: an opal brooch, a rose cameo, a topaz butterfly, a heart made of rubies that looked like red-hots, a bow of diamond baguettes. And, just for one minute, I wished that Knox had figured out that an emerald was my dearest wish. We could have posted a Brink's guard at the door. I mean it."

I conjured up a military ball from boarding school days,

Harriet and the other girls looking the same except their faces were forty years older, and their long formals had gems instead of corsages at the shoulder. The boys, in their military haircuts and glossy patent shoes, now with grandfather jowls and bellies. And myself, upstairs in the practice room on a pile of overcoats, getting out of my dog-walking trousers, my hair graying in a plait. Ned still pale and tubercular but having grown bald and looking strangely like Will. I had to smile.

"Everything was going wonderfully," Harriet was saying, "and I was actually having a terrific time. A redheaded dentist had given me the high sign that we were going to dance later, and I forgot that I'd ever been worried about coming alone. The Turtlenecks were off in some corner, talking to each other in their high-necked gray taffetas, and I was sitting with this realtor, Madge, and her stump-dumb spouse, who I've never been able to stand. And I was thinking, He's the test case: is any man better than no man at all?"

"And the answer?"

"You bet. At a dance anyway."

I laughed.

"They'd just put out the chocolate mousse with whipped cream when I found myself studying Madge's outfit. She and her plank-brained mate had always sat with Knox and me at Midsummer's, it was a sort of tradition. And she used to be so pretty, in a top-heavy kind of way, until she fell apart this fall. But I hadn't put all that together."

It took me a few miles to register that Harriet wasn't smoking. It took a few minutes to notice the absence of motion, the cigarette pack appearing from her handbag, the automatic flick of her lighter. It must be hard, I thought, listening to her, to lose such a long-time habit when she most needed it.

"Anyway, Sarah, she was wearing this dress that had a white bib and faux man's tie—with a red-dotted background and tiny black-dotted bow ties on it. And something just clicked. The bow ties, how much Knox and I used to see of her, the way she'd had the collapse this fall. And I remembered Knox saying to her last year at the table, 'You look fit to be tied,' making a joke, and how she'd looked back at him. I guess I didn't want to see it, so I hadn't. The same way I wanted to believe that Knox had bought that stupid thing for me in the wrong size.

"Before I knew what I was doing, I leaned over and said to her, 'I think I have a present that was intended for you. The tie that binds.' I don't even know where the words came from. And she looked at me funny, burst into tears and ran out of the room. When I went after her, all the rest of Birthday Club came, too, thinking it was time to duck into the powder room before the dancing started.

"And, Sarah, I followed her into the bathroom and I reached into my purse, ready to point my gun at her stall. I actually did that. I was actually about to pull a gun on this woman." She turned and looked at me, stricken. "I'm ashamed to tell it. I could die remembering. But I guess you don't know what you'll do. . . ."

Or how scared you can get, I thought.

"I stood there, looking down at the damn .22, too shocked to move, and then it turned comic, in a way. One of the Turtlenecks, named Jo, spied the gun in my bag and she said in her timid voice, 'Me, too,' and pulled out a big .38 from her satin purse. And then every single member of Birthday Club opened her bag and all of us had guns! We had ourselves an arsenal—five .38s, six .22s and one Tec-9. And when Madge came out someone shouted, making a joke, 'Present arms,' and we all raised ours in the air. And I looked around at them, these women that I see every day, and I thought, What difference does it make if Knox bought one of them a blouse? We're all of us in the same boat, fighting for our lives."

"We are," I agreed.

"Well, that's all water under the dam now," Harriet said, quoting Doll's old line for ending a story.

"You had a fright," I told her, thinking of several things, the gun, her health.

"The only thing is—how *could* Knox have picked some-one with such short legs?"

I laughed as I was meant to. She never stayed down long. Then I slowed the car and turned in a horseshoe off the highway—a blue line of hills, a glimpse of Georgia to the west, and fruit trees close at hand on either side of the narrow state road.

"Madge moved to Houston, and I figure what the hell. One of these days I'm either going to hang that blouse out on the line and shoot every single bitty bow tie out, or I'm going to rewrap it and mail it to her, and she can cry her eyes out over that tacky size ten. Anyway, who knows? I may need her to sell my house for me one of these days. If I should become Mrs. Young Man's Wife and decide to move."

I could hear a squeak in Harriet's voice. I told myself to stop. Be with your friend. Leave the medicine to Will. I reminded myself that even he left it behind him off duty. That he walked the dogs, read his mysteries, towelled me dry. He didn't try to diagnose everybody he ran into at the dairy counter at BiLo or having supper at the Depot.

I felt a lurch in my midsection when the road curved past the cemetery, through it really, the old part sloping up a low hill on one side of the road, the new part stretching out flat on the other. On previous visits, I had mentioned that there were more people underground in Mineral Springs than aboveground. On previous visits, Harriet and I had sometimes stopped to walk around the sprawling burial grounds so different from the family plot in East Texas with its all-day grave-cleaning and sociable covered-dish dinners. Here each family was fenced off from the next by ornate ironwork or low stone walls overgrown with kudzu, honeysuckle, Virginia creeper, until there was so much vegetation you could hardly see the monuments until you were right on them.

Nolan's grave was there, in the old Huntt-Cooper plot. There was no one left in his family to care: his parents were dead and his sister off in California. I had memories of going with Edith when I was young, us careful not to let our shoes sink in the clayey soil, careful not to stain our clothes on the bushes and vines. Memories of running my fingers along the iron filigree, the path a sort of treasure hunt with my daddy's grave at the end. Our plot began with a stone baby on a stone bier on which was carved, faint now, all but rained away, the words PRECIOUS IN HIS SIGHT. And a six-foot granite cross entwined with granite Easter lilies and flowering vines, the COOPER etched at the base.

"Doesn't it give you the creeps?" Harriet asked, making a shudder. "I mean, having to drive right through here every day of the world. Well, I guess you don't come this way; you go into town, to your shop. But still, every time you go into Greenville. It would give me the creeps. I haven't been out to the Sloane plot since you were there. When I was scared out of my wits, about this trouble, the last thing in this world I wanted to see was that vacant chunk of soggy land just waiting for me."

I PULLED THE CAR into the drive, under the big oak, which curved toward the white-painted brick house with its four chimneys. Ben was racing back and forth in the fenced yard, happy to see my car. He had thought he was getting a drive when I stopped back by the house on my way to the airport to change out of my jumper into a brown skirt and sandals. And had looked heartbroken when I drove off again without him.

There'd always been a dog waiting, I realized. When Harriet first started the annual visits, so many years ago, with her children in those early years, it had been Tracy, then Hardy, then Rogers, the first of my black labs. We had got together every year since all four of our children were babies still in cribs, still in diapers, still using strollers and playpens. (Where had playpens gone? I wondered. Now young parents got jumping chairs and bouncing swings and crawly walkers that even infants could scoot around in, shoving with their fat legs. Fannin's boys had all of them, those robotic locomotions. Fannin's home looked like a vast extension of Equipment "R" Us.)

"Come on, Ben," I said, getting the garment bag out of the trunk. "Calm down. Where's your pal, hmmm? There she is, good girl." I opened the gate.

Harriet stepped back. She never liked to get too close to the pups, had always been uneasy with them, afraid they'd jump on her or try to lick her. Now, perhaps, it was just as well; certainly she didn't need to be breathing dog hairs.

"It always seems odd to me, Famous Edith's girls having all these domestic animals." She brushed at her short skirt. "Dogs, horses. Don't naturalists make this big point of going out there in the wild and leaving things the way they find them?"

"Mother always had dogs," I reminded her, taking her in the front way.

"That's right. Boy dogs. I remember." She caught her breath on the porch. "My, look at your trees. Even I can tell one from the other, or at least the plum from the peaches. And the apple trees, they don't look the same at all." She turned toward the road. "He's got the apple trees, doesn't he, your neighbor?"

"We sometimes trade fruit," I said.

"It's strange to be here this time of year instead of in the fall. I can't get used to the trees with all the peaches on them. Remember how you used to make us all help you, when the kids came with me, back in the Dark Ages? Mix up those awful vats of beer, tea, Ivory soap, Epsom salts, and what all else. Tobacco, was it? Ammonia—I remember that because it stunk. And how the four kids would run around like idiots out here in their shorts, smashing those paper bats against the tree trunks, whooping like Indians." Harriet turned and put her hand on my arm, breathing heavily. "Whatever happened to those kids, Sarah? However did they turn out the way they did?"

I patted the dogs, nuzzling them, promising they could come in later, and took Harriet's bag into the kitchen. "I sent off for some seeds this year," I said, watching her, trying to gauge how she was doing. "From Seeds Blum, B-L-U-M, and Seeds of Change. Don't you like the names? Yellow sugar snap peas, sweet potatoes of an older variety, tomatoes. I thought I'd make a try at a vegetable garden. I spend more time outside now; I have more time to spend. I get out there in my old sneakers, heavy red socks—folk wisdom says they keep the bugs off—khaki pants with ten years of stains, an old cotton belt to keep my shirt out of the way, a scarf. I'm a sight! That's the best thing about living in the country—I'm sure Doll would agree with me—nobody circulates a petition to lock you up as the Madwoman of Chaillot."

"You like it," Harriet said, stepping out of her heels and leaning against the counter. She was still out of breath. "You do all that stuff because you like it. It's your escape."

"I do. I must. It's satisfying work. The trees seem grateful to be looked after, protected against insects in the summer. And in the fall, the roots send up messages that they are direly in need of feeding before they have their snooze through the winter. I feel honored to tend them. The trees and the gardens give me so much more every year than I could ever give them. All but the weeding. . . . Sometimes I think I'm better at tending my life than weeding it." I was talking on, to give Harriet a chance to regroup. Now I held her at arm's length. "Let me get a good look at you. You look wonderful, honestly."

She smiled as if she had a secret. "I could use a little lift. How about a Bloody Mary? Or sherry. Even white wine is fine."

"Anything."

"Gin. Make me something with gin. Gin and a jigger of juice." She watched me mix her drink, flexing her feet and looking sly. "You didn't even guess, did you? I can't believe that you didn't figure it out."

"What?" I stood by her, drinking orange juice, glad to see her perk up for whatever reason.

"I got an eye tuck." She opened her eyes wide, then relaxed them, looking delighted with herself.

"You didn't." How amazing. I couldn't tell.

"I did. Right in the middle of that ghastly radiation. I was going three times a week, and not worth shooting. When I asked the doctor if I could have one, he said that was the silliest thing he'd ever heard of. I said, 'I don't care whether you think it's dumb, I just want to know: *Can I?* Will it make things worse?' I mean, it's a local they do it under. You sit up and you're zombied out of your mind, but you're awake. It's not like I was going to get a general anaesthetic, you know, put that stuff in my lungs. When you kept saying I looked good, I wanted to crow. So it really worked. And the tan"—she stopped to swallow half her drink—"well, the tan comes out of a tube. What they can do now, with self-tanning cream, makes the sun seem puny. I slathered it on before I came. I thought, By God, for all this misery I've been through, I'm going to look like a million, a hundred thou anyway."

"You do." I reached out a finger and gently touched the skin along Harriet's lid and beside her eye. I couldn't tell a thing.

"State of the art," she said. "The best in the entire country. I was going to do it when I turned fifty, but Knox . . ." She stuck out her tongue. "Let's don't even mention his name—"

"Amazing," I said. "I want to hear every detail. Let's get you settled, then we can have lunch. You must be worn out. . . ." I didn't want to exhaust her further.

"Quick refill? A little less juice?" Harriet held out her glass. When she had another swallow of gin under her belt, she said, "I'm lucky you made me go to the doctor for that cough. If I'd waited until I started hurting . . ." She left it unfinished.

"You had a scare." I tried to pick up my cue.

"You don't know the half." She wrapped her arms around her chest, as if around an injured friend.

"I'm glad the doctor let you come visit—"

"He was glad to be rid of me, I think. I'd nagged him so bad about the Aspen trip, but he wouldn't back down. He said trying to take in enough of that thin air might tear something loose and undo all the nasty work they'd done. I said, 'Forget that idea.' But when he said I could come here, I asked him, 'How come South Carolina? They've got mountains, too.' 'Short ones,' he said. 'Midget mountains.' " She started to laugh, then stopped when it seemed to hurt. "He's young and cute, to tell the truth, the doctor.

That helps. Who wants a doddering old type getting familiar with your chest. No offense to your friend."

"I won't tell Will." I smiled at her feelings about a man of seventy. Where did that come from?

She patted my hand, setting her empty glass on the counter. "I honestly think it's good that you've got somebody who comes around and who can dog-sit when you're out of town. Not just that, but someone you don't have to hide your feelings from. We have to put on such a cheerful face for everybody, you know, the children, and our friends. But somebody who was there by Nolan's bedside in the hospital, who must have seen you at your worst, your tiredest, that must be great. I didn't have that. Not just didn't I have the warning, the chance to mourn in advance, but I didn't have anybody who was with me when I went through it. Knox took that away, breaking his damn neck so carelessly. So tell your Dr. Perry, your Will, that I didn't mean him. There's something to be said for fatherly types."

I put an arm around her shoulder. I hadn't used Will for that, but she was right; I never hid my feelings from him. And she was right, he was there. What anger she had, what a sense of betrayal. And no way to speak to Knox about it. Sudden death was cruel in a way I'd not seen before. "I'm sorry your trip to Colorado was cancelled," I said.

"David has been wonderful." She leaned against my arm. "Calling me, and sending me flowers when I looked a mess and felt like hell and didn't want him to see me that way. We've moved our trip to the fall. We're going to go somewhere flat. Sea level. I teased my doctor about that. I asked him, 'How about Port Aransas?' 'How about South Padre?' 'How about Galveston?' 'Can I canoe down the bayous of the Big Thicket?' But when you think about it, they didn't go to the shore to recuperate, in books. They went to the mountains. For TB. I reminded him of that. I said that in

all the novels you read in school, they're up there at the
sanatorium in the Alps recovering in the sunshine, eating
that crusty bread and drinking that goat's milk. 'What do
you think about that?' I asked him. But he's so young, my
doctor, he probably thinks that *The Magic Mountain* is the
name of one of Disney's theme parks."

"I should have asked if you wanted to bring David—"

"No, goodness. I just want us to have a real visit, like old
times."

I picked up her bag and started upstairs. At the landing,
she paused to catch her breath. "I brought us something. . . ." She was winded.

I set the bag down, not wanting to seem in a hurry.

"I brought you—us really—something darling, Sarah. A
hostess gift." Her voice had taken on a slight squeak. "David wanted to go back out to Mom's—he's going to put her
and Dad in his book on oral histories of East Texas, and
I'm really proud of that, whether Mom is or not. He wanted
pictures of them, so we were looking through that old album, which mostly has photos of you and me. Anyway, I
sneaked one of us, for a surprise." She reached down toward her bag, then straightened up. "You look, there, in
that outside pocket."

I pulled out two hot-pink T-shirts, each printed with a
picture of the two of us in shorts, taken in front of the main
hall at Pritchard's, with a blooming dogwood beside us.

"See?" Harriet reached for one, struggling for breath,
and held it against her chest.

I held mine up, too, noticing that it was a couple of sizes
larger than Harriet's. They were cute, the sort of things
schoolgirls might sleep in. I put it over my arm and picked
up her bag.

At the top of the stairs, out of habit, Harriet turned left
toward Nolan's old room. It was a reflex, turning to go into

the room where she'd stayed when she came to visit. Staring in confusion through the open doorway, she let out a yelp. "What on earth? Sarah, it's a damn mausoleum!"

I bit my knuckle. I hadn't thought, not for a minute, how his room, just as he left it (or just as I had restored it after his illness), would hit Harriet. I'd grown so used to it. I had remembered as a child slipping in and touching my daddy's shirts, his ties, even looking under the bed he'd shared with Edith. I remembered looking in the medicine cabinet that hung in one of those metal boxes on the wall to see if his shaving cream and brush were still there. The tangible objects had meant a lot to me. I'd wanted that for my grandsons. You couldn't tell who remembered what at what age.

I'd wanted that for my children, too. For George. Boys and their fathers were a complex labyrinth you couldn't fathom. Whatever he needed of Nolan's, I wanted it to be there for him. And for Fannin, too. It was hard, as I knew, as Bess showed, for a girl to lose her daddy. (When had Edith moved MacDonald's stacks of papers, modest half-closet of clothes, old Underwood upright typewriter? I couldn't recall. By the time I went off to boarding school, only the typewriter remained.)

"I'm so sorry," I said. I dropped the bags and gingerly threw my arms around Harriet. "Poor thing. First a trip through the cemetery and then the Nolan Rankin memorial bedroom. I should have said something to you on the way. . . ."

I led Harriet into my room and helped her up on one of my high twin beds. "Are you all right?"

"I never thought you, of all people—it's like those ghastly rooms you read about where the kid has died and all the stuffed animals and his little pajamas with the feet in them are still on the bed. Jesus, Sarah, how can you stand it? I moved everything out of Knox's room the very next weekend after the funeral. How long do you plan to leave it like that?"

"I thought a year," I said, stroking Harriet's back lightly, afraid of hurting her. "You have to go by your instincts on these things." I moved to hang her bag in the closet. "Of course the stupid side effect is that Will and I have to pile up on one of these single beds whenever he stays over."

"You're sleeping with him? The old doctor? I don't believe it. Don't I know anything at all about *anybody*?" Harriet's wail turned into a cough which shook her body until tears coursed down her cheeks.

WE ATE LUNCH ON the porch. The peach-washing rains had chilled the air, and it was pleasant, cool for early August. I'd fixed open-faced ham sandwiches on salt-rising bread with green mustard, then worried, as I carried the plates out, that the fare was too heavy. Maybe I should have done a salad. But Harriet said, no, she had an appetite. She'd taken two pain-killers after a coughing attack which had left her hurting dreadfully. "Distressed passenger," she'd managed to say. "Bring me a glass of water."

On the way outside, she had stopped in the living room, looking at the burled end table which held my grandmother's collection of shoes, which I treasured. There was something about women and shoes, women and feet. The bound Chinese feet, high heels, pointed toes, nail polish, pedicures. (Whoever heard of a man getting a pedicure?) Most of these were salesman's samples: a wedged sandal, a buckled pump, high vamped lace-ups. Some were actual size, some miniatures. There were a pair of cancan dancer's legs in ankle-strap shoes, made of wood, a German porcelain lady's boot no bigger than a doll's.

Life Estates

"I always forget how good you are at *house*," Harriet said. "I mean, mostly I see *you*, and we're somewhere else, and you don't—no offense—take all that much interest in how you look. But this room . . ." She gestured to the rusty-red-and-gold paper, the rusty wood trim the color of the clay the pines grew from. The heavy draperies that came to the floor and spread out like a fan on the waxed planks.

I looked about the room myself, seeing it mostly through the eyes of two younger women—myself and Katie, fifteen years ago—who used to clean it for parties, who knew every inch of the walls and wood. I saw it also as where I'd come *from*—like an attic where I'd stored those trunks of old velvets and watermarked taffetas, and hats with ostrich feathers. From another era.

"Thanks," I said. "I don't really see it anymore. I'm afraid I only go past here on my way out to have breakfast or to watch the sunsets." It's time, I thought, I used this room.

When we were seated in the porch rockers, Harriet said, "You're so lucky, having your shop. I envy you that. Not that I'd actually want to have to be somewhere every day of the world, or to be a businesswoman myself, but, you know . . . I still get mad when I think about going to fat Freddy the accountant and getting the brush-off. As if nothing I'd done in my whole life counted for anything, because it didn't make money. But that's the way men think. . . ."

I couldn't argue with that.

Harriet had stopped talking to catch her breath. She pinched off a bite of ham and popped it into her mouth. "They don't understand—men don't—that women simply aren't used to charging each other. You know? I mean, isn't that hard for you, with all those women who come into your shop? Men bill one another all the time: lawyers bill their doctors who bill their accountants who bill their bankers who bill their lawyers. But women don't." She looked up.

"I'd think that having your job would feel the same as if I asked Birthday Club to chip in every time I set out refreshments when it was my month for them to come over."

She was right in a way; Katie and I didn't bill. I hadn't thought of that before. "We don't actually," I said, "send bills, now that you say it. We keep a ledger; our clients are responsible for paying what's due."

"I wouldn't mind that. Having a service, say, to tell widows how to put their best foot, their best leg, forward. Provided they just mailed me a check and we didn't have to talk about money." She kicked off her shoes. We had both pulled on the pink T-shirts with our schoolgirl likenesses on the front, but she'd left on her short skirt and hose and heels, and I'd left on my brown skirt and sandals. She rubbed her ankles, then tucked her feet under her in the rocker. "Not Betty Grable legs today," she said ruefully, sounding hoarse again. "First I missed my morning walk— I'm still going half the distance with them—and then I had to cram myself into those airplane seats."

I asked, "What would you like? A glass of wine, a little more gin? Or something sweet?" I stooped to pick up our plates, not wanting to remark on the fact that Harriet's lunch was almost untouched.

"Something chocolate?"

I brought out what I had, a Hershey's chocolate almond bar. "I didn't have time to make anything. This is from the airport," I told her.

"Yum," Harriet said. "Aren't you an angel. The best I can ever get from Mom is chocolate sauce on top of whatever she's serving. Last week it was tapioca. Really. Sauce with glue: Mom's specialty."

What I heard as she complained was that she had been to Doll's a lot recently—that was the implication—with or without her handsome young David. Perhaps she wanted to go back to a time when her mother had worried over her; perhaps she felt that only her mother would know whether this was really something to fear or not. "Anything Doll fixed was fine with me," I said.

"So, Fan lost this one—baby Revelations."

"Yes. I think she was worn out."

"There's no book named for a woman in the New Testament. Did you know that? The Gospel Quartet and Salome? Ruth? Esther?"

I was tired of the joking about my grandsons' names. "Rankin, she was going to call it."

"For her daddy, I remember. At least she wanted to see you when she was in trouble."

"She wanted me to be sorry," I said. "To admit it was a loss for her." I sighed. "I don't know how well I did, but I went anyway." I made a gesture with my hands, indicating that I was sorry it had meant postponing Harriet's trip.

"I guess that's why I got mad. Because she asked for you. I finally got the story on why my daughter decided not to have children in the foreseeable future. Apparently I am the last to know."

I watched her break off squares of chocolate and melt them on her tongue. We always got around to daughters, I thought, sooner or later. And wondered if our daughters got around to us, with their friends. How hard both our girls had worked not to repeat the lives of their mothers and grandmothers. Fannin acting out of what she perceived it cost women—Edith, me—to leave home, to work; Pammy, out of what she judged it cost the women in her life—Doll, Harriet—to stay at home and not to work.

"Good or bad?" I asked, wondering if Pammy had made partner, and also wondering what if anything Harriet would have considered reason enough not to have children.

"What do you think?" She crossed her slim legs out in

front of her and finished the last bite of almond Hershey. "I couldn't bear to tell you on the phone, particularly after you told me about Fan and the lost lamb. I figured we'd be grieving in different directions. You know. But she chopped me with the ultimate ax Wednesday. I'd finished my treatments and got my strength back. I'd had my eye tuck. I thought I was looking pretty fine, and was up to standing the bombardment of my children, a worse beam, as we know well, than what the labs hand out. I'd survived the Midsummer Night's Party and finding myself about to pull a gun, and I was on my way to see you. I felt ready to handle whatever they could dish out.

"We were going to have dinner, paid for by me, needless to say, at The Bayou, their favorite small, intime cafe not remotely accessible off the loop or the interstate. So I'd braved the five o'clock plague of lotus-eaters in their Japanese cars bumper to bumper. When I arrived, there was Pammy, early, checking her watch, with no sign of her brother, late as usual."

I looked out across the deep oak-shaded yard. It felt strange to be out here in the afternoon. I felt I should be shelling peas, as my grandmother had done. "I'm listening," I told my friend. Women must have sat here and talked about their children since the early days of the spa.

"We were at the table." She was talking in spurts, short of breath. "We'd ordered our summer greens and a bit of fish with puree of something; we weren't going to wait for Dwayne. We weren't saying a word."

I hadn't seen Pammy in years. Not since she became a lawyer, really. Surely she was shaken by her dad's death; they were very close, or seemed to be to someone on the outside. It was hard to think of her in the way Harriet described. She'd been a total charmer: Miss Congeniality and Best All Around at summer camp, Class Favorite every year in school. She'd been everybody's favorite. When she was small and they came to visit as a family, she'd coax Nolan into taking her on his lap; she'd call him Fan's Man right to his face. She used to tell me I was the best cook in the world, and then whisper to her mother that Aunt Sarah, as she called me, wasn't "near as pretty as you, Mom." She had those big dimples and the square jaw of her daddy, and that same thousand-watt smile, which she turned on everyone.

She used to charm circles around her big brother's friends, her daddy's friends, too, or so Harriet said. When she graduated, she'd turned down Harriet's offer to go away to school, saying as far back as I could remember, certainly as far back as sixth grade, that she was going to be a Texas lawyer so she would have to go to school in Texas. An Outstanding Student and Bluebonnet Belle at the university, she had refused to get pinned or engaged, being everybody's prize date but nobody's catch. That was about the time, when her senior year came and went with no ring on her finger, that she and Harriet began to be at odds. She was small-boned like her dad, with his brown eyes and hair, but her mother's creamy skin. And legs. A single-minded ambition behind an easygoing style. But sitting at the table not speaking? Being unresponsive? It didn't fit the old Pammy, the Pammy Calhoun I had known.

"By the time Dwayne joined us," Harriet was saying, "I felt tomahawked. Scalped. Tied to the wagon. Pammy and I had been sitting in stony silence; even our small talk had blown out to the Gulf. Dwayne, being Dwayne, didn't seem to notice. He was just there, looking scrawny and under-nourished in some basic way. And I was thinking, as we do, Is it my fault?

"He started right in, as usual, about how I ought to have a computer. And for once, I didn't even mind. He went on and on about hard drive and ram, and about slots and floppies, and the more he talked, the more sexual it sounded. I almost had to laugh; he sounded just like some boy entering puberty. Do they know how it sounds when they use those terms? He was all excited because Apple had a new division called 'personal interactive electronics'—do I have that right?—which they were calling Apple PIE. 'Get it, Mom?' he said."

I remembered Dwayne as a boy, and Harriet was right, he had been scrawny, tense but also inventive, talky and full of ideas. I'd always thought he had his granddad's mind. Electronics came easily to him, in whole chunks, in concepts that translated up and down into the smallest details. I used to think he'd have been at home back in the Twenties, building that super-heterodyne radio receiver, grounding it to the garage's water pipes, getting it completed in time for the first-ever Rose Bowl broadcast. Or with the modern equivalent: somebody in his own garage tinkering with microchips and daydreaming while he designed. He would have done well to marry an engineer, some female computer whiz herself who thought scrawny guys with horn-rims were cool. But trapped in the financial set, without his daddy's womanizing charm, he was a fish out of water. Another version of the sad saga of boys and their fathers.

As if reading my mind, Harriet said, "I like to blame it on Knox, them never having two consecutive words to say to one another, even though they were both in money. And whether you call it banking, investments, brokering, bond trading, you're still talking about spending your life making money out of money. You're not even spinning flax into gold like in the old stories; you're just spinning gold into gold." She had been talking in jerks and now stopped, held back a cough and washed down another pill. "Maybe it's not his fault," she continued after a minute, "maybe it's mine." She wrapped her arms around her pink T-shirt. "How can you not take it personally when you have two children in their thirties and neither one is married?"

"Maybe that's not the worst thing," I suggested. I could remember Edith's dismay at my going with Nolan all through school, at my marrying him forthwith upon graduation. What hopes had she had for me? What reservations about the life I was entering into? How we do plunge headlong into our lives without giving a thought to our elders. We did; ours had.

"No fair," Harriet said, making a bitter laugh. "You're stealing my punch line." She wadded up the Hershey wrapper and tossed it over the porch rail. "Anyway, that was the moment Pammy picked. Picture her in those horrid worker's shoes and a casket-black dress almost to her ankles, with her hair chopped off shorter than her brother's. A onetime Bluebonnet Belle, this daughter of mine. She leaned forward and said in her now nearly inaudible voice, 'I had lunch with Madge yesterday, Mom. I hope you don't mind. I didn't think it mattered now, since Daddy's dead and she's moved to Houston and all.'

"It was like one of those movies where a platform in the floor falls away and you see someone drop right out of sight into the dungeon. That was me. Me, who had barely put two and two together over the weekend. I asked her, 'Did you call her or did she call you?' 'What difference does that make?' she asked. She might as well have driven a butcher knife through my—chest.'' Tears sprang to Harriet's eyes. She grasped the arms of the rocker and sucked in air.

I took away the iced tea glass I'd brought with the candy bar and fetched her another gin and juice.

"And then, Sarah, I knew. I *knew*. I don't know why it hadn't occurred to me before. I'd gone over every single reason in the universe why a girl of thirty as pretty as she is, as smart, didn't have a boyfriend and wasn't even interested in finding one. I'd even—don't laugh, please—wondered if maybe she didn't like *men.* I had; I had even wondered that. And never once had I thought she might be carrying on with someone who already had a wife and more than likely children. 'Pammy, are you seeing a married man?' I asked her, right there in front of her brother and his hard drive. 'What if I am?' she said to me, bold as you please."

I felt my heart go out to both of them. To my old friend, but to her daughter also. What was it with these girls of ours that they had to tear themselves to pieces one way or another? In their effort to be grown-up and better at it than their mothers. "Did she talk about him?"

"Not who he was, if that's what you mean. I didn't care. I don't care about that at all; it doesn't matter. She is obviously in love with the impossibility of him, the inevitable destruction of going with him. What was there for me to ask or her to tell?" Harriet leaned her head back and drained her glass. "What I did ask, all I wanted to know, was, 'Did your dad tell you about Madge? Did he know about your—man?' 'I don't have to answer that,' she said. 'Yes, you do, Pammy,' I told her. 'Yes, you do.'

"Then we all had mousse au chocolat, at five times what it was worth, I picked up the bill and we all climbed into our separate cars. That's Houston: a city of two million and every single person has a car." She put on her heels and held on to her knees with both hands. "I don't think Pammy and I will ever mend this."

"I'm sorry. . . ." I said, and I was. It was too painful to think about, this new estrangement at which families were so skilled. Part of me was wishing I wasn't here on my porch but was wandering around one of the old historic homes in Clemson or Pendleton. What could I say to Harriet? The fault lay in the institution, not in us. Marriage was a fence that invited leaping. How else could people agree to being penned?

With a groan, Harriet asked, "What on earth could we have done to prepare for having children?"

WITH GREAT PLEASURE I had invited the three of them, those friends closest to me, to my table for supper. And although all three had been at my home many times through the course of many years, it seemed to me a first in some way with each of them.

Harriet was here for the first time without my having a family or husband to juggle. Without my having to say good night to her, in her robe, in the hall, settle her (or, in the early years, her and her children or her and Knox) and close the door on whatever room Nolan and I were sharing when company was in the house. I could recall the strain of our lying there in the dark, in one bed and later in two, exchanging heated words—Nolan having had a great deal to drink and needing to comment on Harriet, how she talked too much or to inquire how long she was staying this time. Words that caused the tightening in the stomach which went with the divided loyalties of a married woman's life: husband and children, husband and friends.

Will, too, had been at our house as often, for almost as long as she, but in a different context. There was the strain of keeping us dog-friends only, with an occasional off-the-record comment, the unveiling of some private part of our lives. My revealing the confining nature of the married state; his confessing that he was close to trying it again. But with us both aware at all times that he was a guest in Nolan's home, invited at Nolan's behest; that he was Nolan's doctor.

The greatest joy was in having Katie at what was now *my* house for a company meal. Katie, who had helped me prepare for more than a dozen parties but who had never attended one at my home before.

Inviting her had been a bitter point between Nolan and me.

"How can I not have my partner?" I'd asked him.

"This is in no way racist, Sarah," he'd responded, on the defensive, "not with today's tricolored bank employees. You can hardly say I'm prejudiced. But right there's the key word: *employee*. This is a party for our friends, for clients."

"Katie Pegues is not an employee," I'd countered, deeply angry. "Our Rooms account is with your bank; half of our clients are yours as well."

"No and no," he said. "For the people who remember— we're talking long memories here—she used to be an employee here. I'm talking maid. Do her a favor, your friend, okay? Do her a favor so some drunk vice-president doesn't hand her his empty glass, okay?" He'd been proud of that line of reasoning—standing knotting his rep tie, checking his Swiss watch. It was to spare Katie. Katie, whom he would not have recognized if he'd seen her on the street.

It did no good to say she'd never been a maid, she'd been a party service. Did he ask the bank caterers to come? Did I include the German woman who cooked for parties? He would not budge.

In the long run, it had had one good result. Katie and I had got into the habit, which we liked immensely, of having all our clients for a sherry party at the shop on the day after Christmas. It was a way of offering them someplace to go after they'd showed off their newly papered rooms in their refurbished homes to all their kith and kin. After they'd hung all the holly and evergreens, and filled all their kitchens with food, they were ready to get together with Sarah and Katie at Rooms of One's Own, for this one evening truly a room of their own, and let down their hair.

Sometimes literally. One woman had done it the first year: Jameson, who wore her hair in a large, tight bun, was never without her three strands of pearls, and who came all the way from Athens, Georgia. She'd come with her graying hair long and loose, held back with two old tortoiseshell combs that had been her mother's. She'd also come in jeans and a heavy cable-knit gray sweater. "You said to let down our hair," she'd reminded us, looking around at the mostly Carolina people who were there. "What's with this getting all dressed up?"

After that year, a number of other women had done the same, those with short hair wearing it wash-and-wear, not straight from the salon all poked and sprayed. The second year, I had let mine down, too, unbraided it and worn barrettes the way I'd done as a girl. That had pleased them, the clients, seeing me off duty, informal. It had freed them to be comfortable, commenting on Katie's hair, the changes she'd gone through, the scalp-tight cut, the cornrows, now the current rooster-comb style. What was more intimate for women than hair?

And of course shoes. I had decided earlier today before our lunch, watching Harriet stop to look at the old collection of salesman's samples, that they would go nicely in the shop. I could set up a table in front of the wall of house photos. Women in their homes; women in their shoes. Those little enclosures, those mobile homes.

The next year Jameson had showed up in walking shoes. And by this past Christmas—something of a blur for me, with Nolan going downhill—they'd all come in serious shoes. I'd worn my dog-walking shoes; Katie her Doc Martens. Some had paid designer prices, some had bought theirs in the boys' department at Sears, and some from athletic shoe outlets. If it hadn't been for Harriet's sore feelings about Pammy, when she first mentioned her daughter's awful "killer shoes," I would have said that seemed to me to speak well for the law firm's attitude.

Getting ready for my company, I'd braided my hair loosely and left the plait hanging down. I'd put on a long blue gored skirt which I liked a lot, two smudged shades of smoky blue, a V-necked blouse and sandals. I felt festive; blessed because of the evening ahead. I reddened my cheeks and lips, realizing that I could have my friends over every week if I liked. On the spur of the moment. For great formal banquets. For fresh peaches on the front porch. At least I could have Katie and Will, who were already in my life every day. What a marvel that would be: to meld the parts of my life. Home, work, sex, friendship. How marriage did compartmentalize. How it did foster gender-distinct, function-distinct, affection-distinct divisions. And to what end? I darkened my brows. To perpetuate itself.

I could have done well back in farming days, running commercial orchards—all the hands pruning and feeding, picking and marketing, family members and hands sitting down to meals together, at the groaning board, for green beans and pork, cornbread and biscuits, cobblers and vats of sun-made tea. But why did I have to think of that as something I had forgone, that belonged to a time past? Why not think of it as a glimpse of my future? I liked that idea: seeing myself the age of my mother now, waxing enthusiastic, as Edith did, about the possibilities of the seventies, declaring it a good decade for a woman. Me supervising my fruit trees, looking over acres of them, perhaps on that good climbing land north toward the lakes. Me managing Cooper Crops.

Harriet came out in her panties and bra, and I saw that she was a good bit thinner than when we'd dressed together in Texas in April.

She wanted me to help her decide what to wear. "I bought

these two-tone slingbacks. Look." She held them up. "What do they remind you of? Aren't they absolutely an echo of the saddle oxfords we wore at Pritchard's? I couldn't resist them even though they cost an arm and a leg—well, okay, an elbow and a knee. I thought I'd wear them and this white piqué." She glanced at me. "I see you're bare-legged; maybe I will do that, too. See, I've belted the dress in the same caramel color as is on the shoes. What do you think?" She held up a short sleeveless dress, almost a tennis dress.

"I like that," I said from across the room at my dressing table.

"Sorry I parboiled myself in there so long." Harriet looked almost too thin, her ribs outlined beneath her breasts. "I can't resist those deep tubs. I wanted us to get dressed together, the way we used to. Of course nowadays nobody has anything that zips up the back or has to be hooked at the neck. Remember all those clothes? They go back before panty hose, which to today's generation is probably like saying before the combustion engine. I think panty hose and television arrived the same year. Has anyone done a study of legwear and communications? The radio and silk stockings?"

"Radar and leg makeup?" I tried to go along. I knew such talk was her way of gathering herself together. Her skin seemed unusually pale, and I realized that in addition to her tanning cream she must have worn a lot of makeup on the plane.

Harriet made an imaginary check mark in the air. "Very good. The microchip and seamless hose?" She pushed me off the slipper chair in front of the mirror and sat down to do her face.

I stood watching as the roses returned to Harriet's cheeks, the flush to her brow, her lips became pink and her lashes thick. It was misleading; my friend now looked so glowing, so rested, so *well*.

"I was remembering," Harriet said, brushing her shiny hair, "all those parties you and Nolan used to have. Remember? When did we quit doing that? Coming to the big anniversaries, five, ten, fifteen? The big birthdays, thirty, forty? Wasn't that the last? Ye gods, that was ages, eons, ago, and it seems like weeks. Forty. I can hardly believe I'm *that* old, even. Thirty-seven, that's a nice age for a blond; old enough, not too old."

I recalled those parties, too. After we'd stopped trooping the children along, instead leaving them with friends here, mine; leaving hers with Doll and Nat in their old house past the Thicket. I remember Harriet and me dressing together like girls waiting for our dates. Skirts up or down, it didn't matter the fashion, Harriet always wore something that did justice to her legs. When hemlines were long, she'd worn her highest heels and sheerest hose, and a slit in the skirt if that was allowed, or, if not, simply hiked her skirt when she sat down. She used to say she couldn't have endured living in the days when women's clothing, heavy and layered, came all the way down to their shoetops, where the most you could hope to show was a "well-turned" ankle.

Nolan had enjoyed having Harriet and Knox visit in those days. He'd used it as an excuse to fix something fancy to drink. He was still a fraternity boy at heart, the kind who'd thrown parties with a keg of beer in the backyard in high school. Whatever the time of year, he'd have something special. In the summer—that would have been for our anniversaries—he'd set a Waring blender of frozen daiquiris on the counter in the kitchen. Icy snow cones of rum and lime juice that we drank on the porch while Nolan talked banking with Knox, and "we girls" caught up with our news. In those days, we didn't worry about drinking too much; it wasn't part of our thinking. There might be pitchers of Bloody Marys, hot with Nolan's secret mix of pepper and spices, cold from the refrigerator, or maybe Tequila Sunrises or Margaritas, in homage to our Texas visitors. When had all that festive drinking turned serious for the men, when had it turned worrisome and damaging?

"I think it's great of you to have your friends over to meet me," Harriet said, standing and turning to see how she looked from the back, "but next time I think we ought to do something just us, to celebrate that we are single now, you know? Maybe something with just women? That's what I'm going to do—I've already decided—when you come to Texas next spring. I've already got it all worked out.

"I'm going to invite all of Birthday Club—whoever's left by then—and have an old-timey luncheon with flowers and cloth napkins at card tables. And maybe even little prizes. A number under your plate and the package wrapped and placed under the table? The way we did when we were first married, remember? Back when we were trying to be grown-up women having bridge parties. The absolute Dark Ages. Antebellum, several bellum for that matter."

I wanted to tell her about our all-women clients' party, but the disparity between what she was imagining and the reality of our gathering stopped me. Sometimes it was hard to translate her life into mine or mine into hers. Yet, if you looked at it with a clear eye, we after all had simply moved into a new stage together: the all-women party having come around again with the same purpose but in a very different form.

Harriet slipped into her short white dress and raised her arms to clip a white velvet bow on her smooth hair. But the gesture of lifting her arms to secure the ribbon seemed to hurt, and for a moment she froze, sucking in her breath.

She'd taken a handful of pills with a little orange juice as she'd climbed into the tub. Since then she hadn't been coughing and her voice sounded more the way it used to.

"Ouch," she said. "Damn. Damn." She finished fixing the bow and hugged her rib cage. "I think these coughing fits tear something loose. They're bound to. I imagine it like"—she winced, paused, taking a shallow breath—"the inside of some sound system with a couple of wires pulled loose. Not that they have wires anymore. But, then, I was made in the old days."

"Are you all right?" I stood nearby, not sure what to do.

"Fine. It goes away." She sat back down and checked her lipstick. "I didn't mean to be telling you who to invite to your house," she said, looking at me reflected in the mirror. "It's just—you don't have somebody over who took care of your husband, not at something like this, a little dinner. I don't care what's going on with you two, you and the old doctor. It's like asking the rector, who, at lowly old St. Bart's now suddenly calls himself Father. Really. I mean, it looks like you're asking for special treatment." She turned around on the stool. "And her, your partner. You just don't have somebody you work with. They're like The Odd Couple Who Came to Dinner, is how it looks to me."

I expected a bit of a skirmish between "that girl" and "that woman," some resistance on both their parts to being lumped together, each so threatening to the other on general principles. But I trusted to their affection for me, and mine for them, to smooth things out. And I knew that Will would welcome the chance to look after us all, and would not mind being outnumbered three to one. "You're my friends," I told her.

"Besides," Harriet added, anxious, "being a doctor, he'll spend the whole evening staring at my chest."

I laughed. "That would hardly be a first, now would it?"

WILL CAME IN THE back way, leaving the dogs in the fenced yard to run about. He kissed me on the mouth and ran his hands down my back. "What's for supper?" he said.

"I haven't seen you two going at it before," Katie told him. "You look right nice."

Will took off his jacket and hung it on the back of a chair, giving Katie a pat on the shoulder by way of greeting. "Man comes in the kitchen, I've read the literature, he's supposed to kiss the woman and ask, 'What's for supper?' " He helped himself to a beer.

I told him, "The woman's supposed to lift the lid off the iron skillet and say, 'Stew.' " I was flushed from the heat of the stove—and the joy of having these two mingling with the smell of supper.

Katie asked, "Where's your friend got to?"

I put my spoon down and looked at Will. "Harriet had a bad spell, just as we were getting ready. She was laughing at something I said, and then—"

"You holding up?" he asked me.

I nodded. "I made three peach desserts for dinner." In truth, I was feeling guilty about Harriet. I wanted it to be a nice party for her, after the trauma of having to drive through the cemetery and then stumble into Nolan's room. And I'd been thinking mostly about what the evening meant to me, my pleasure in the preparing of it.

"That's a good enough answer," Will said. He gestured toward the front of the house. "I'm headed for a rocker. Want to join me, Pegues?"

"In a minute," Katie said. "I've some news for Sarah."

I'd made my favorite stew, glad the weather had turned cooler. I'd baked a pork roast with cumin and thyme and black pepper, soaked red, white and black beans, and then thrown them in, adding potatoes (I'd used the shepodys, Harriet's Potato of the Month), red and yellow bell peppers, and a turnip for flavor. While Harriet had napped earlier, propped on three pillows, the sound of her breathing filling the bedroom, I'd cut up the meat and potatoes, added the juice and beans and peppers, tasted the stew, chopped in fresh tomatoes, added a little red wine and left it to simmer down.

It was such a satisfaction not to have to fix party food for people more interested in the bar: thin sliced beef, shrimp on beds of ice, vegetables presented as works of art. Just a skillet of stew, some spoon bread and washed salad greens. I'd been unable to decide which peaches to use or which dessert to make, and, suffused with delight at the bounty, had made three. I'd put tart Georgia Belles and Cortland apple slices on a French pie dough, then made a cobbler with the rich Monroes, mixing in vanilla and heavy cream, and was going to pile the sweet yellow O'Henry eating peaches on a shortcake. What a feast. How well my trees had provided for me.

"Junior came by the shop late this afternoon," Katie was telling me. She was on a stool, watching the cooking, in a long black-and-brown wraparound skirt tied up on one hip like a sarong, high wedge sandals and a black T.

"Did he want his check back?" I stirred and listened.

"He wants to be a client."

"Junior?" Imagine that.

"He says he'd like to do the downstairs in the same Calhoun-style I used in the upstairs sitting room for his mother. He wants to use different papers but get the same effect." Katie looked pleased. "Sounds to me like he wants to do over the entire house, room by room."

"Did you tell him how we do things?"

"I did. I think it was finding that check that cinched it. He liked his mother writing it out and the fact she kept track of what was owed all by herself. I expect that Dexter Senior kept a close fist around the money."

"Our first male client." I turned and raised a wooden spoon in toast.

"We never had a policy against it," she said.

Just then Harriet came down the stairs and into view. "It's me at last," she called out in a squeaking voice. She'd reapplied her makeup; small gold balls hung from her ears. She'd put on jewelry for my party. I was touched, knowing what that meant to her.

"Hey, don't you look pretty!" Katie stood holding out a hand, making an effort on my behalf.

"Don't *you*." Harriet thrust hers out as well. "Can I help you, Sarah? I'm sorry I took—so long."

I put the lid on the stew. "This has to simmer. Let's go out on the porch."

Outside, Harriet offered her hand again. "Will, isn't it?"

"Most of the time," he said amiably, enveloping my friend in a hug. Seating her in a rocker, he asked, "What'll you have? I've got myself a beer, the other ladies are having lemonade. I can get you Old Corn Cob or whatever the house-brand whiskey is, you name it. What's your pleasure?"

Harriet looked up at him. "I'll take a lemonade, too, Will, if you don't mind. With a little something to sweeten it?" She made it a question, a furrow between her brows.

"How does gin sound?"

"Just fine. Fine." She seemed clearly relieved.

He didn't go right in the house, however, but stood by her chair. "Let me get this out of the way first," he said, "then we can get to visiting."

He was in a white shirt and suit pants, his coat and tie left in the kitchen after making rounds. He had deep wrinkles, I could see when I looked at him objectively, and too much weight around his middle. But the sight of him here, as a lover, as more than a physician or a friend, filled me with happiness. How fine it was to have things be in public the way they were in private.

"I was mighty sorry to lose Sarah's husband," Will said. "I'm sure you don't recall me all that well from the gaggle of specialists attending Nolan Rankin from head to toe, but I was there. He was a good man; I looked after him the best I knew how."

Harriet looked embarrassed. "I know you did. There was nothing anybody . . ."

He went to fetch her drink, touching my cheek with his hand as he passed.

"Imagine Sarah and me becoming widows the same year," Harriet said to Katie, being friendly. "I guess you knew my husband, Knox, died in a car accident only last November."

I looked at Katie, wondering how she would answer. She was sitting on the porch floor, her back to the railing, her long legs folded yoga-style. I knew her thinking: that if someone you loved died, that was bad news and you were entitled to have a bad time. But you weren't entitled to make a big deal out of whatever name the world gave your particular version of living without a man—widowed, divorced, single. I'd heard her hold forth on that, pointing out that, in fact, if you took into account girlhood, widowhood, those who divorced, those who never married, most women didn't live with men, and the women who did did so for less than half their lives. I also knew that Harriet would get her back up once they were on that subject. Considering her feelings about Doll having left Nat and Pammy being unmarried, living without men was a topic wild horses couldn't get her to discuss in public.

But Katie didn't make her speech. "I was sorry about

your man," she said. "It was a bad year all around in that department."

Harriet nodded. "I'm seeing somebody new," she confided, a bit tentative, in case this wasn't all right to say to a feminist.

"I may join you in that," Katie replied, sighing. "I had lunch today with a long-time steady, but the sparks didn't fly." She twisted her gold bracelet. "You give a chunk of your life to somebody and it leaves a big gap when he goes. But then when he comes back, it doesn't seem possible that he can fill that big a hole, not him, just a normal guy."

Harriet said, "I bet," and then, "I guess I'm just at the stage where he's starting to take up that—chunk." She repeated Katie's word.

I relaxed. The two women might be miles apart in their thinking about women, but they were clearly close enough in their attitude toward men.

Will brought Harriet's drink, a jigger of lemonade in gin, he said, in a highball glass with a lemon slice on the rim. After handing it over and making sure it was to her liking, he settled himself in the rocker next to me. I leaned back, my arms behind my head. How fine, I thought, to be at home in my home. The dogs, making contented noises, settled at my feet.

"I found a new private eye for you, Will," Katie said.

"A series? I like a series."

"He's just starting out but he's done colors in the titles so far: blue, red, white. The PI's named Easy Rawlins. He's black. They're set in the Fifties."

"Fine," Will said. "John D. MacDonald did colors with his Travis McGees. I get queasy when they pick too short a list, say the days of the week. In seven days the PI could get snuffed. I like that gal who's doing the letters of the alphabet. I figure by the time she makes it to *Z is for Zealot* I'll be"—he counted on his fingers—"on my way to ninety, staring down the road to it."

"I don't know those—books," Harriet said, stopping to swallow part of her drink. "Knox never read anything but his Civil War histories."

I realized she was feeling outside the conversation. I'd been looking at Will as he talked, hoping when he did get to be ninety we'd be rocking right here, supper simmering on the stove, new frisky dogs thumping their tails.

Will picked up on her tone and changed the topic. "Sarah's got me hooked on these radio call-in shows," he said. "Do you have them out your way?"

Harriet hesitated, then found her voice. "Most people listen to tapes, I imagine," she said. "I mean, I've been going to Houston every week. . . ." She looked upset, as if she'd given away her secret, then hurried on. "My children are there. I can't believe I have grown children running the financial and legal world, but I do. Anyway, I like to put on some familiar music and that helps when I'm fighting that hellish traffic. . . ."

Will put a hand on my arm and sat a bit. Then he said to me, "Did you see that the sheriff's office has decided to train hounds to track down criminals? The trail gets cold quick, he said."

Tracking criminals in our neck of the woods? Traffic violators? Tourists from Chattanooga? "What kind of dogs?" I asked him.

"Redbone hunting dogs." Will held up two fingers. "The first pair are named Bonnie and Clyde. Figure that: naming canine crime fighters Bonnie and Clyde. The sheriff said they were just starting the hounds on the basics. TGIF."

"Toe Goes In First," I supplied.

"At home," Harriet said brightly, "our sheriff is concerned about crime, too. He's got a program that puts habit-

ual offenders to work fixing highway right-of-ways. It's a
rehabilitation program. I don't know if they use dogs—"

"That's not rehab, that's a chain gang," Katie snapped,
then looked at me and shook her head as if she couldn't
help herself.

"I don't think that's its purpose," Harriet replied stiffly.

"Sorry," Katie said.

"Do you know why men never ask directions?" Will said.
"They never ask directions because they have an aversion
to finding out they're lost. We tell ourselves we're in this
dark alley with no exit and the bad guys are heaving toward
us, aiming to put our lights out, because that's where we
mean to be."

Suddenly Harriet rose, seizing her white dress.

I reached out a hand but the sounds of a racking cough
stopped me in my tracks.

She clutched at her chest, but shook her head, as if to
say, Don't notice, it's nothing, it will pass. But she couldn't
seem to stop, her eyes wide with pain.

"I'll do the honors," Will said. He bent to pick up her
glass as if to get a refill and remained standing inches from
her. To Katie and me he said, "Why don't you two serve up
our supper? We'll join you in a spell." Then, just as the
screen door swung shut, he called, "Get my bag, Coop. On
the floor of the car."

WE ATE AT what my grandmother used to call the candle-
light hour, in the dining room, the wall lights dimmed. The
large room had the heavy flocked brown and rust paper that
was a favorite of mine, English about 1890, the original in
silk, peonies if you looked closely, but the whole seeming
only a variation in color. The floor was bare, the high ceiling

papered also. I was glad to reclaim for my own this room which had once been saved for company.

Katie ran her hand over the waxed surface of the gate-leg table and smiled at me. "Nice place you got here," she said.

"Glad you could come," I replied.

I ladled out the stew, which gave off steam as it reached our plates, and scooped up mounds of spoon bread swimming in butter. Will had brought us each a sweating bottle of cold Grolsch beer and glasses. I'd tossed dandelion greens, arugula, Boston lettuce and endive with a buttermilk dressing to have after the heavy dish.

Katie told that she'd been given a recipe by Patterson, a client of Rooms from Asheville. "I think she took one look at me and her mind shifted right onto Brown Betty, and she didn't even know where the idea came from."

"And did you make it?" I asked her.

"Sure I did. A little mace, a lot of vanilla in the crumbs. I'm going to do another room for her. Hey, maybe I'll get brown-butter cookies this time."

I laughed at that; Patterson was a new client, still on trial. I saw that Harriet was stirring her stew, picking her fork up and putting it down. She looked uncomfortable, but Will had eased her, done something that seemed to give her temporary relief, a respite from the coughing.

Dessert, I thought, would help. Harriet could be counted on to perk up. She had a sweet tooth.

"A largesse of peaches," I promised them, bringing in the cobbler and the pie with apple slices. How grand both smelled to me. I brought in the shortcake and whipped cream while Will poured coffee for us and decaffeinated for Katie and Harriet. As an extra, he brought sugar cubes and brandy to splash.

"You understand," he said, loosening his belt at the sight

of the three treats, "this has got to be a quick fling between us, Coop. A one-decade stand. I can't be around this much food on a regular basis."

"We can order takeout from Rae's Cafe, next time," I told him.

I heaped the plates—old china ones with paintings of fruit glazed in the center—with a sampling of each dessert, trailing whipped cream across the top of all of them. It made me happy to taste the difference in the peaches, to wonder if I would have known, if someone else had made them, which peach was in which dish. But of course I would have. I could even smell the difference as the steam from the cobbler and pie mingled with the cold fresh-peach aroma of the shortcake slices.

"When on *earth*," Harriet asked, amazed, "did you find time to make all these?"

"While you were napping." I hoped that was all right, to mention a nap. I tried to make it sound natural. "While you were sleeping off the trauma caused by the distressed passenger."

Harriet, reminded, told us the story of her plane flights, making much of the screaming woman whose death had passed before her and everyone else's eyes, and the seatmates who drove her nuts with their repetitions. She was enjoying her performance as someone upset by such episodes. It charmed and it also disarmed. How, the implication was, could this tanned blond woman with the gold ear globes be in real trouble, how could she be dying, if she could make such a fuss over trifles? Clearly she must be fine, or we'd be hearing about it. And even though it went against what we all knew, it worked. We laughed with her, relaxed and easy.

(Perhaps the boy had cried "Wolf" again and again so that when the real wolf came no one would believe it, no one would panic or freeze with terror or rush to his side to see the carnage. But would instead say, Oh, him, and go on about their lives.)

Harriet accepted a little brandy and flirted a bit with Will, coaxing out of him stories about his bachelor days, about the judge he almost married, going on in her thin squeaky voice about how she was going to take lessons from him. She was not going to tie herself down too soon, but was going to wait for the right one to come along. She mentioned that she had a young man now, "young enough to be your son as a matter of fact," but she was not making any commitments.

"If he's young enough to be my grandson," Will said, "don't tell me."

"Well, let's see now." Harriet pretended to count on her fingers. "Not even if you were precocious," she said.

"Most like the opposite," he told her. "It's taken me thirty-three years here to get this one even to invite me to a sit-down dinner."

I licked the last of the whipped cream on my plate with my finger. "Let's leave all this," I suggested, gesturing to the dishes, "and catch the sunset."

We were pushing back our chairs and putting down our napkins when the phone rang.

I looked at Will and hurried to the kitchen. I couldn't let the machine get it and ever after have Harriet imagining me at home screening my calls and choosing not to answer. I had to show that whenever I was home I picked it up on the second ring.

I'd called Fannin while Harriet slept. She said she was going home tomorrow; she missed the boys too much. She was going to make them promise to stay close to home when they were grown.

It was Edith on the phone. "Mother." I was delighted.

"Everyone's here." What a pleasant evening to share. "How nice of you to call."

The others followed me into the kitchen.

I heard Harriet whisper, "I thought the Spider Lady was off in the jungle."

"I hope nothing's wrong with her bum hip," Katie said, pulling out a stool and sitting at the counter.

"She's just trying to reach her drug supplier," Will told them. "We've got a little smuggling going." He poured me half a cup of coffee to wet my whistle while I talked.

Mother sounded no farther away than Greenville. It was amazing that she could place a call from such a distance, a trunk call, to use Edith's term.

"I wanted to ask about my granddaughter," she said.

"She's fine. I talked to her this afternoon; she's on her way home tomorrow." I could see Harriet adjust her belt, square the small buckle under the buttons of the white piqué. Was she irritated that I'd called my daughter while she napped?

"Will is there?" Mother asked.

"They all are," I said. "We just ate."

"Put him on."

"Mother wants you to join her in Tierra del Fuego, Will. How do you feel about that?"

"Lukewarm," he said, taking the phone, obviously pleased. "Edith. We miss you." He shook his head. "No thanks required. I'm sending you a further trio of medications that for all I know have also become controlled substances. Argyrol, iodine and ipecac. Add those to your store and you can handle anything." He smiled, rubbed a hand over his eyes. "It went fine, as well as could be expected. It got their attention at least. I decided to go with calling it the Siege of Shiloh—the message being: our war, our boys, but not our yard. How's the hip?" He listened, grinned, looked at me. "I don't know, I'll ask her. Edith wants to know, are you getting serious about me?"

"Tell her OLAT."

"She says don't rush it, please, one leg at a time." He paused, then handed the phone over to Katie. "She has a message for Ms. Pegues."

"Hello, E-dith," Katie stretched Mother's name out. She was standing with one wedged heel on the rung of the stool, her hand on her hip. "I will do that. I think that's more than fitting. You take care now. The tropics are hazardous to your health." She handed me back the phone. "She says she's taking the money she'd put away for baby Rankin's nest egg and is sending it to me for EMILY'S List. Where, she says, it will probably do her granddaughter more good in the long run. I expect she's right about that."

I told Mother I'd sent Fannin lilies in her name and would be getting bulletins from Bess to pass along. She said, speaking of my sister, she'd ordered a hammock for her for her birthday before she left and did I think she'd ever use it?

"You didn't?" I was amused at the duplication. "I did, too. I bet we're sending the exact same one. Crate and Barrel's Pawleys Island natural cotton hammock extra wide." I laughed when she said that was the one. "At least she can pile up with the little boys when they come visit. What will she think of us?" I asked.

"That we had her on our minds," Mother said, ringing off, as was her style, without a goodbye.

Still holding the phone, sensitive to a possible slight, I said, "Harriet's here, too." Waited a bit, then said, "I will, I'll tell her." Off the line, I turned and told my old friend, "Mother says she's so glad you're on the mend." Putting my arm around Harriet's shoulders, I said, "Let's go watch the last of the sunset."

But she wanted to fix herself another splash of brandy, she said, and headed for the dining room.

Katie took her decaf out onto the porch.

I was feeling relieved. We'd all helped Harriet along, making conversation. There'd been that one flare-up, but I felt the two women had both hurried back to the one safe topic between them—men—and the meal had gone fine.

Walking down the hall with Will, I asked him, "What about that doctor's bag? Where did that appear from? It looked like a stage prop from a Fifties film."

"I thought I might be making a house call," he said.

Harriet, catching up with us, told him, "Thanks a lot, Will. You worked a miracle." Then, hesitantly, dropping her voice, she said, "I guess you know what's wrong with me, don't you?"

"I do," he told her. "I have a picture of it right here somewhere." He fished in his wallet while Harriet took a sip of her brandy, looking anxious, afraid she was going to get a diagnosis. "Here we go." Will unfolded a small sheet of notepad paper.

I was touched. It was the drawing I'd made on the phone to Harriet, when I got the bad news: the lung with the tiny dried tomato in it, the heart with the vine growing from it, the flower. Imagine. He had saved my sketch for her.

"What is this?" Harriet asked, relieved.

"My partner's illustration of your lovely chest," Will told her.

"Sarah"—she looked at me, surprised—"did you do this?"

"I did, sure enough."

Outside, Will whistled up the pups who were running around under the trees in the dusk. I took the rocker beside him, swinging my feet, content to be sitting here on my porch watching night arrive with the three of them. The women might jostle between each other a bit, but perhaps there was no more to it than Ben and Missoula scuffling in the grass, chasing the same scent; perhaps it was a way of getting acquainted. At least I was not headed upstairs to a night of recriminations such as had always followed having company when Nolan was alive.

"I wonder," I asked them, "if any place on earth has sunsets so grand as ours. Cherry sunsets in autumn, persimmon sunsets in winter, strawberry sunsets in spring, watermelon sunsets in summer."

As the whole horizon grew blood red against the darkening sky, Katie put her back to the rail, Will took my hand and Harriet caught her breath.

WHEN I GOT upstairs after finishing up in the kitchen, Harriet was on a rampage. She was throwing her clothes off the hangers onto the bed, had dragged her garment bag out and was stuffing shoes in the side pockets. Her face was angry and she wouldn't look at me.

"Distressed passenger is catching the next flight out," she yelled over her shoulder. "You needn't have bothered to ask me to come, but you did, so you have. So I'm going home."

At first, walking through the door and seeing her packing, I assumed she'd taken a bad turn. That maybe it had begun to hurt too much. That it had become the punching pain, front and back, Will had said it might. But she wasn't coughing, although her voice had a strained, scraping sound.

"What is it?" I asked her, not comprehending what had gone wrong. "What?"

"If you don't know, I can't tell you." Her mascara was streaked, but she wasn't crying.

"I don't, and you must tell me. What is it? I thought

everything went so well; it was a special evening for me." I moved into the room and stopped, hesitant to come too close.

"And a perfectly dreadful evening for me, if you want to know." She was almost shouting, her face red. "I don't understand why you bothered to have me. The three of you talked all around me the whole time as if I wasn't even there, as if I didn't exist. It reminded me of how it is with your children, the ultimate in feeling totally invisible." She took the two-tone slingback shoes off her feet and crammed them into her bag. The motion caused a crushing cough which she got under control. "Dumb me, bringing us those T-shirts, thinking it was going to be old times, really old times, before we even had husbands, when it was just us, talking our heads off. I might as well have been in a foreign country. I couldn't understand anything anybody was saying. You and your doctor with all those initials—TGIF— and your partner going on about EMILY's List as if everybody in the whole world knew who Emily was, and all those detective stories you'd all read, going on as if I was an illiterate. I could have evaporated on the spot and none of you would have cared."

"But the dinner was for you," I protested. I didn't know what to say. Had she been fretting all through the evening? All through the meal? "You were the guest of honor. I'd never had them both here before. It was a celebration."

"The dinner was for *you*—to show off how many different desserts you could make out of your old peaches, that's what it was for. I mean, when you handed me the Hershey from the airport—*airport*—you said you didn't have time to make any chocolate dessert for me. Who would rather have chocolate to eat than shoes on her feet, and you know that. We kid about that. Even Mom, who's stone deaf and mole blind and can't even fix an egg without putting a cream sauce on it, melts me some chocolate on her puddings." She began to wail.

I tugged at my plait and sat on the side of the nearest bed. I felt as if I'd been kicked all the way to Georgia. Stunned and dispirited, too. That an evening I'd so looked forward to and so enjoyed had been so differently perceived. Had it always been that way with Harriet? Her grand times at cadet dances had hardly been mine, I knew that. Had we, standing in our wedding gowns and maid-of-honor dresses, been of different minds about what was beginning and what was coming to an end? Posing with our babies for Doll's photo album, had we been worlds apart on what a new generation promised?

My mind kept going back to similar fights with Nolan, after evenings with company, that I had attributed to him, to me, to the nature of the beast called marriage. I had to rethink that. It might be that no two people ever shared the same evening. But where did their anger come from, his and now hers? Where does anyone's anger come from? When we perceive we have not been given our due.

The chocolate—to Harriet's mind, the least she could have expected from me—must have seemed the last straw. Piled on a series of hurts, gratuitous and arbitrary, that her family and her body had hurled at her. Well, that, at least, I could redress.

"It was," I agreed, "a treat for me. Pure and simple. Let me make amends. Come on. You'll find worse company than your echolalia ladies at this hour of the night on a late flight, even if there is one. Come down, and I'll make the richest darkest chocolate dessert I know how to fix, and you won't have to share a bite of it with anyone else."

Harriet wiped her streaked face. She'd taken off her belt, and, barefoot, in her piqué dress, she looked like a camper in Sunday whites, waiting for her parents to arrive. She'd taken off her velvet bow as well and her glossy yellow hair fell across both cheekbones. She looked thin, in the way of a young girl.

Down in the kitchen, I gave her a juice glass of brandy, then tended to the melting of chocolate and butter on the stove. I'd decided on fudgies—the double chocolate butter-laden flour-scarce brownies frosted in double chocolate icing I used to make for George and his buddies. Squares Harriet could pile on a plate and carry upstairs to bed.

"What really did it," she said, still pushing at her hair, still agitated, "was the phone call from the Spider Lady. I mean, I've seen Famous Edith maybe five times in my entire life, five times since we've been grown at least, if that. She's some sort of myth, not a real parent anybody ever saw, not even you and Black Beauty Bess. I always thought she had to reintroduce herself to you and your sister every time she happened back in this country."

I stirred and poured, seeing what was coming and wishing I could stop it.

"But, no, here she calls from God Knows Where, South America, and is big chums with everybody but me. She has some Battle-of-Shiloh gag going with Will, when I'm the one who practically reenacted the Civil War with Knox." She tore out her words, loud and rasping. "Then she says she's sending your Katie this money she was saving for Fannin's miscarried number five, the Gospelette." She beat her fists on the kitchen table. "But what really took the cake, what really wiped me out, was both of them, these nobodys-come-lately in your life, calling her *Edith*. I never called her Edith in my entire life. 'Harriet's here,' you said, and she probably said, 'Who?' I could have sunk right through the floor on the spot. I mean, at Doll's there are more pictures of you in that damn album than there are of me. My mom doesn't even know I ever had another friend;

she hardly knew I had a husband. She thinks Birthday Club is one of those things I order over the phone like Potato of the Month or Fifty Designer Day Lilies—"

"Speaking of which," I said, slipping the greased glass pan into the oven, setting a timer and sinking into the chair opposite Harriet, "the stew tonight had your August potato, the shepody, in it. A long white potato with a fine flavor."

She sulked, "You didn't happen to mention that."

"I didn't." I felt myself wish for a cigarette and then bit my lip at the thought. How much harder it must be for Harriet every moment. "I suppose," I said, "I didn't want to mention Nolan tonight. The potatoes, his present, seemed to be a present to me; I built the stew around them."

"You could have said—" She picked at her nail polish.

"I should have." Had we carried on this way in boarding school days? The anger I remembered most clearly was my own. Flashes of white rage that I was cooped up with not even a bedroom of my own, no place that was mine alone. The frustration of never being by myself. Except for the times with Ned on that drafty wood floor, I'd done everything as part of a group, including showering in that vast bathroom of stalls and tubs.

What Harriet had said about her and Edith was true. My mother did feel closer to Katie and that was a fact. Part of it was because she saw in Katie someone who'd made it the hard way and she related to that. But, more, she kept up with Katie because she was in my life on a daily basis. She was someone whose voice Edith knew on the phone; she was someone in the present. Harriet my mother dismissed as someone I'd known at boarding school, someone on a page she'd turned. The way Bess had known Nolan's sister when they were horse-crazy girls together at Redfield's: not in her frame of reference today.

My mother tended to shed the past as a locust did its

shell. Periodically bursting forth into her new projects, her wings green and slick and ready to fly, she thought the past and its people encased your options, held you clinging to that old bark with outgrown arms.

"My mother," I said, wanting to be truthful and to deal with what had hurt Harriet, "does not like the past. It seems a baggage she doesn't want to carry. I think you remind her of old times and she doesn't wish to be reminded of old times. Whereas your mother, whereas Doll, loves old times. She likes to have that childhood again and again, that daddy who shot the squirrel down in the creek bed. They're just two different ways of getting to the same fork in the road: old age. Look at them. How many women make it to their eighties in such fine shape?" I stopped. I'd almost said: How many women make it to their eighties? How careful we must be. How much of our language deals with the future.

Harriet drained her brandy. "I guess I'm feeling rejected," she said. She leaned forward and let her hair cover her face. "You know?"

I asked her, "By—?" wanting to let her talk.

"Who not? Knox, nothing like being rejected posthumously when you can't carve the guy's throat out. David, the fact that he didn't try to ravish me over the game dinner the first time we went out. I'm kidding, but not really. And let's don't forget my daughter, although we've had enough of that for one visit."

I went to the back door, then remembered that Will had taken Ben home for the night. I'd promised to call him if Harriet had any more trouble, but I didn't think he meant of this nature. I sat back down. "I can see that," I said.

Harriet started to speak, choked, started again. "By my body."

"Yes," I said.

"That was really cute, that little picture you did. Of my

lung and heart. I'm going to show that to my doctor. Or maybe carry it with me, and if any nosy ninnies ask me what's wrong when I'm coughing up the soles of my feet, I'm going to show it to them." She looked across the table, her eyes filling. "You drew that because you were worried about me."

"I guess I did," I admitted.

And then it was time to frost the fudgies.

"Do you think all men have names for their dicks?" Harriet had scooted down under the covers of the twin bed the way she used to at Pritchard's, so that only her face was visible. She used to say it was easier to tell secrets if you were just peeking out.

We'd sat on the stairs with the plate of fudgies, our shoes off, and I'd tried to re-create the forbidden feel of sitting on the floor after lights out, indulging in a chocolate feast. When she'd had her fill and licked her fingers, I sent her upstairs to take what Will had left for her and get herself ready for bed. For our slumber party.

Winded in some essential way, as if after a marathon, I took a moment before locking up to stand on the front porch in the cool air. Last night had been the dark of the moon, and a faint waxing sliver slipped from behind a cloud. I missed Ben, and felt the need to call him in to bed. I missed Will as well.

Now Harriet and I were piled up on the high single beds, back in our hot-pink T-shirts with the schoolgirl pictures of us on the front. I had unbraided my hair and left it loose, hanging straight to my shoulders. Harriet had left off her bow and hers fell across her cheeks a shiny gold. We could have been back in school—that was how it felt—sleeping in men's shirts and our panties, our faces scrubbed, our hair brushed, whispering past our bedtimes.

"I haven't had a very large sample," I answered, glad that she was in good spirits again, wanting to keep my tone light, my answers right.

"I think they do. I think they all have secret names for their dicks—Charlie, Big Ed, Roscoe."

"Richard?"

We laughed.

"Do you remember," Harriet asked, her voice faint over the top of the white spread, "those books we read years ago when we were trying to be good liberated wives? All of us, not just you and me. I mean, women were doing that then. *The Ploy of Sex, Hardly Anything You Ever Wanted to Know About Sex*. One of them—I forget which—said to think of it as if there were three of you in bed: you, him, his thingamabob. A ménage à trois. You, him and—Old Blue?"

"That's a dog," I said.

And we laughed again.

"I bet they do. I bet Nolan did. Something he called it to his horseshoe buddies, that you never heard. I bet Knox did, too. I bet he had some name he never told me and never even told his stump-legged lady friend, some name he used to joke around with his golfing chums."

"Ringer? Putter?" I was getting silly, straining to sustain the mood.

"Think about it, Sarah," she said. "All those years we were married—and if you add them together we had sixty-five married years between us—we never talked about sex to each other, not the nitty-gritty. I mean, we talked about absolutely everything else. I bet I know the kind of toilet paper you use and the details of your dental work—but zip about you and your broad-shouldered North Carolina man in bed. I'm saying if Nolan had a problem, if he couldn't get it up, or had a prosthesis, or had some weird fetish—like coming on your feet"—she giggled—"I'd have been the last person to know it."

I said, "You read about boys who half hang themselves with nooses to get it off. Do you suppose there are women who marry and find out that's what they've got?"

"And we didn't even tell the whole truth when we did say something," Harriet went on. "I bragged, 'Things are romantic now that we're in separate rooms.' I'm sure I told you that a dozen times. When what really happened was that we had started sleeping across the hall from each other and I didn't know what that meant except that I was fixing up my room like a bordello and putting on my satin scanties—and waiting."

I said, "I don't think women in general talk about sex. I mean, even to themselves. It isn't a matter of not sharing so much as not—voicing." I knew that it had taken me years before I'd admitted to myself my anger at Nolan for never pleasuring my body, for never thinking of my need for arousal and satisfaction. I surely wasn't the only female who tended herself and resented the fact. Women complained about being sex objects—but wasn't the real problem, I thought, that you weren't an object at all to them, but an appendage, an extension, something slightly better than their hand to facilitate orgasm? An object is *out there*: you see it, you wax/tune/adjust/play with/listen to/send messages on/implement/fix/tend it. It doesn't tend you.

I began to brush my hair slowly, something I had often done in bed at school. I didn't want to think about Nolan in that way, not now, not anymore.

"You're right," Harriet agreed, sitting up and propping herself with pillows. "Women don't talk to other women about sex, period. It's hammered into us that it's disloyal. We don't call each other up after the honeymoon to say, Do you know how many times we did it? Or didn't do it? We see it as our duty, covering for men, protecting men, not saying anything that would in any way let anybody think their performance wasn't the best. Men don't want to share their dicks with you, that's the truth, because they feel vulnerable; you might pass judgment on their wienies. I mean, have you ever once asked Famous Edith about Spider Sex?"

"I have never asked her about sex, no. Since my dad died, I don't have a clue about her private life. . . ." I said, thinking that the same thing applied to my sister, Bess, for that matter. Perhaps with family members you are especially reticent.

"You think I knew what Doll and Nat did under the covers? Except that Mom seemed mighty glad to get out from under them." She made a face.

"We'll never know," I said, seeing that the breakup still bothered her. It was a shame about Nat and Doll. She was such a generous, ample woman in several senses, and he would have made someone a fine lover, observant, good with his hands, his head always buzzing along trying to figure out how things worked. Something about them reminded me of Nolan and me, despite my resolve not to think of him: their going from good to bad, from helpful to hurtful, and not knowing when or how it happened.

Harriet asked, "You think most women our age still want it?"

"Most women? Any age? I don't know," I told her. "You read about how they say, Hurrah, it's over. Or you hear men going on as if they've tried to get some for years or to warm her up or that they can't get enough. But none of that fits my observation." Or my experience, it would have been more accurate to say. I had the conviction that most women wanted a lot more sex than they got, that most women would be limitless in their enthusiasm if they had the opportunity.

Harriet began to cough, and put another pillow behind her back. "Damn. Damn," she said, holding herself and rocking while I brought her a glass of water and two more of Will's pills. When she'd stopped, she pulled up the covers and said, "We should have had a half dozen years of wild affairs before we got married. Boys did that back then, or pretended they did."

I stayed sitting on the edge of my bed, waiting to see if she was all right. After a minute, deciding she was, I nodded. "Back in our day you were fast if you were kissing two boys at the same time."

"Do I remember." Harriet rolled her eyes. "It was considered fickle not to go steady. It was absolutely promiscuous to see three Stus at once. And if you let more than one of them unhook your bra, you practically had to wear a scarlet letter." She drew one on her T-shirt.

I could see the Harriet of those days so clearly in my mind: popular, pretty, in her saddle shoes and ponytail, talking about how some cadet had wanted to get his hands in her panties, how he'd wanted to feel her treasure. How she'd let him French-kiss her twice but that was all.

"Then's when it starts," she said, bending forward as if to make her point, "when they begin to train us not to get in any situation where we can compare them. Making sure we won't ever talk about who is the best kisser, or compare whose Jimbo is the longest."

I relaxed and leaned back on my own stack of pillows. She was looking fine, her color good. She was enjoying our talk. "I knew a man who called his Henry Adams," I said slyly. ("You're agitating my Henry Adams, Cooper," Ned had said.)

Harriet sat bolt upright. "Who? Tell. Not Nolan Rankin. No way. He could not possibly have had a Henry Adams. A Rambo, maybe, a Lone Ranger. But not a Henry Adams.

Who? You don't mean the old doctor? I don't believe this, you have to tell. Whisper it, the way we used to, you know, the way we'd pretend that whispering didn't count?"

I'd sworn never to tell, not ever, even on my death bed. "Swear in blood," I'd said to Ned, ready to open a vein if he asked.

"Never say never," he'd told me. "Your lips are sealed for forty years."

Young, black-haired, consumptive, kindly Ned had looked down the road forty years and that had seemed an eternity then, a lifetime. Now we were almost there. I hoped he was still around somewhere, getting ready to confess also. To his trustworthy wife of thirty years, or, more likely, to some youngish post-doc who had lured him to her papered rooms. I wished him well, and, in my mind, freed him to tell. What possible difference could it make after all this time? What harm could it do?

Harriet wanted some secret, some confidence, that no one else had had, not Katie or Bess or my children or my mother. Not even Will, who was, as I was, content to have what we had now and not fret over who'd been where before.

What could it matter now to tell?

"Do you remember," I asked Harriet, in a teasing tone, "our history teacher, junior year? The one who left at the end of the spring term to go back for his Ph.D.?"

Titillated, she sucked in her breath. "The one who looked like Heathcliff?"

"That one. He's the one."

She pulled up her knees and hugged them. "Really? Mr. Brown? How did you know? You eavesdropped on him? You read his letters? You caught him with someone? Oh, tell me, Sarah." She swung her feet out of the covers, toes painted, ready to climb into my bed for every whispered detail.

I shook my head. I leaned back against the pile of pillows, arms behind my head, just the way I'd done at school. "I heard it from the horse's mouth."

"He *told* you that?"

I smiled. Would that sex had been that way for nearly forty years. Enough, I thought, it was again with Will. "He showed me."

"He did what?" Harriet gasped. "Exposed himself? Mr. Brown? I don't believe it. We used to say he must be dying of tuberculosis, and when he didn't come back we pretended he'd gone to a sanatorium. You remember?" Her voice higher, squeaking slightly with excitement, she sounded no more than fifteen.

What I could never have told in those old days, I told now. "We were lovers, Mr. Brown and I. Ned."

Harriet slid till her feet touched the floor. She stood very still between the two beds. Her impulse to climb onto my bed to hear the juicy news had stopped. She stared at me. "Did Nolan know?"

"Not who, just that." I felt suddenly on the defensive. "I was afraid he could tell I wasn't a virgin; in those days we thought it was so obvious. Besides, he had to know I was on birth control already."

"When did you tell him? On your wedding night? Before? I'm going to absolutely die of shock." She climbed back on the side of her bed and sat looking at me, her legs hanging down.

"I told him the summer after Ned left, before my senior year. Nolan and I met then, when his family came to visit mine. Our sisters were friends from Redfield Academy." I made a gesture that meant she knew all that.

"You and Nolan had *sex*? Is that what you're saying? When you came back to school in the fall, you'd had sex with Nolan?"

"In those days," I said, "it was such a deep dark secret—"
I was pleading silently for her not to be angry.

"I can't believe it." Her voice had become a hoarse whisper. Her face had grown pale and silent tears rolled down her cheeks. "You'd had two lovers by the time you got out of Pritchard's, you, *who weren't even interested in boys*, and I haven't had one yet. Stupid me. The last to know. Dumb me, thinking that you were just chums with that old medic when he'd been sleeping in this very room. You've probably been lovers with him, too, since the day you met. How many more?" She ground her fists in her eyes.

"No, there was no one while I was married—"

She turned her back on me, her shoulders hunched, her breathing labored. "I've been on the outside of everybody's life all along, haven't I? I could understand Knox—a man doesn't tell his wife he's cheating on her. But Pammy—to tell him about her man, to know about her daddy's woman. I thought that was the worst thing that could ever happen to me in my whole entire life."

I sat on the bed, not knowing what to say. Or, rather, how to undo what I'd said.

Harriet walked around, her shoulders thrust back, her hands on her hips. "I thought at least you, *you*, were someone I knew. We always did everything together. Every step of the way. Boarding school, our weddings, our babies, even losing our men. All of it." She sobbed. "I thought we were the longest-running buddy movie in history."

"Please, I'm so sorry." I pressed my palms on my knees. What could I say?

Harriet grabbed the foot of my bed and began to ram it against the wall, screaming, "And none of it was true. Not ever. We never did anything the same way; we never did anything at the same time. The two of us never were the two of us, were we?"

I got down and took Harriet in my arms. She was weeping and doubling over coughing, unable to get her breath. Her arms still pushing and shoving.

"Come downstairs," I pleaded. "We'll have hot chocolate. Mother says warm milk cures everything. I've upset you. I got carried away. That was all such a long, long time ago."

She jerked loose and slapped my face. "Keep your hugging hands off me. I'm going to sleep across the hall in that mausoleum, where I belong. And don't come knocking on the door with any of Famous Edith's cures. Because I don't want anything else from you ever."

WILL APPEARED AT my kitchen door for early morning coffee, bringing Ben and Missoula back. "I'm on duty at the Middle School until midmorning," he said. "They've got cancer-screening booths set up. Health is this year's theme at the fair. How about meeting me at the apple fritters at ten-thirty?"

I was in a wicker chair at the windows, gazing out at my peaches, still in the pink T-shirt and a cotton robe, my hair still down, a sleepless night's fatigue in my bones and doubtless on my face, too. I'd been clearing my mind. I held the idea that the iron-laden soil in our part of the world was the source of the special flavor of the county's fruit, and was grateful this morning that the primordial ore had settled beneath my orchards.

I shook my head, too wrung out even to worry that I must appear a wreck. "I don't think I can make it," I said. "It was a—rough night."

Will poured himself half a cup, eyeing me. He had on scruffy sweat pants of a faded gray and a sweatshirt nearly as old as he was. He didn't appear to be in much better shape than I did. I was exceedingly glad to see him, although too bone-tired and frazzled by last night's fight to do much but motion to him to pull up a chair.

"Didn't my pharmaceuticals work?" He stayed by the door.

"They did," I said, not knowing where to begin. Or quite where the blowup had begun. When Will had exited out that same door last night, whistling up the dogs, it had seemed an almost perfect evening to me. I stared down at my pale legs in their dog-walking shoes, then at the pups, still frisky from an early morning run. "But by the time she took them . . ." I started again. "She got upset, it was my fault, and ended up sleeping half the night in . . ." I could hardly bear to go over it all again, even to Will. "In Nolan's room. I moved her toward morning; she was groggy and I wanted to have her where I could hear her."

Will rubbed a hand over his eyes. Maybe he'd made a call to intensive care in the night himself; he seemed wrung out. "Let me get this straight. You're saying here that Harriet is not going to make it to the fair this morning. Well, fine, let her have her rest; the shape she's in, she's entitled to come unglued from time to time. I'm saying I'll see you at the apple fritters at ten-thirty."

"I can't go off and leave her. . . ." I pushed my hair back behind my ears. If I wasn't going to sleep I ought to eat something. I thought of last night's cobbler.

Will poured himself a refill, watching me. He took my cup, warmed it under the hot water tap, and filled it halfway. "Here," he said. Then, "If you're going to pal around with a doctor, Coop, you've got to toughen your hide. We've got a nice day planned: see the crafts fair, buy handmade toys, listen to the Crawdaddy boys tune up their banjo, ukulele, fiddle, harmonica and spoons, eat a catfish plate and a barbeque plate. I traded weekends. You've got Harriet to worry about—she's the good news compared to what I've got in ICU. If I worried about each of them in direct proportion to how bad they're doing, I couldn't get out of bed in the morning. And I barely did."

"I don't see how I can leave her—"

"Fix yourself up pretty," he said. "You look like you're trying out for the part of a nurse in the *Gone With the Wind* hospital scene."

I flared up, "You planning to distribute information on preventing cancer looking like some great gray unshaved bear? You're a fine one to talk."

"There," he said, approving. "That's more like it."

"Smooch." I went to the door. And we did, for a minute, with the puddle of dogs at our feet. We kissed and nuzzled and reminded each other what it was all about.

"Say TGIF," he said, on the back steps.

"Toe Goes—"

"Thank God I'm Fine."

"Yes," I agreed.

Will bent to stroke behind Missoula's ears and tell her he was leaving. "Eat her out of house and home, girl. Make her add an egg to that chow."

I watched him trot out of sight, then washed our cups and sank back into the chair by the window, feeling iron-laden myself. I couldn't make sense of the scene with Harriet. It felt quite similar to old scenes with Nolan, and that made it all the more painful and all the more bewildering. How could they have been so disappointed? Wasn't being friends for life or being married simply an agreement to *be there*? If you took away the trappings of similarity or sex that drew you together, wasn't it just a promise to remain? Perhaps what they saw as entitlement I saw as covenant.

Well, it was too late to right old wrongs with Nolan. But not with Harriet. So as not to wake her, I showered in my husband's old room, steeling myself against the sense of trespass and the almost physical impact of absence. I braided my hair loosely and then slipped across the hall into my room for a dress to wear to the fair. Harriet was sleeping heavily, her breathing labored but steady.

Downstairs, still listening for her with one ear, I formulated in my mind what I would do. Something she would see and even smell as soon as she walked into the kitchen looking for me, before she had time to be angered afresh or to feel once again betrayed—by her husband, one of her own in Birthday Club, her daughter and, now, her oldest friend.

I made a batch of biscuits, cutting the shortening into the flour as if I'd done it every morning for a dozen years (the hands remembering such matters—separating eggs, beating batter, kneading dough—just as they recalled the smooth feel of piano keys or the heft and pull of a hairbrush). I made cream gravy to pour over them, hot and split, something I had never done before. But I'd seen many times in old country homes and cafes the look and texture of it, white, thick, slightly browned. I mixed melted butter and flour, then some of last night's cream, plus black pepper and a spoon of coffee for color. Then, trying to picture in my mind's eye Doll's plump white hands, I dredged short strips of bacon in flour and fried them in butter and their own grease (having no wild-hog fat handy in my larder). After I put the breakfast where it would stay warm until Doll's daughter woke, I spread the pink T-shirt with our picture on it out on the kitchen table.

From a sheet of paper I cut a large white balloon, and from my teenage mouth put the words:

> Harriet,
> > I'm at the Fair. See you later.
> > I'm so sorry.
>
> > Love,
> > Sarah

. . .

CARS WERE PARKED for blocks in the residential neighborhoods around the fairgrounds, and couples with small children, and teenagers, hurried along the cracked sidewalks in front of old pink brick homes which had sunk a foot a century into the red Carolina clay.

Little was left in the shady sprawling park of the famous spa: a wooden covered bridge, a rickety old springhouse, a few foundation stones from the grand hotel, the railroad trestle past the creek. I thought that if both Harriet and I lived in such once-fine forgotten towns, then surely there were millions more of them across America. Places that everyone came from and no one was going back to.

Will was waiting where he'd said, at St. Andrew's Apple Fritters under a blue-and-white-striped awning, leaning against a chest-high wooden counter. The smell of the pastries was so enticing, I had to close my eyes to breathe it in.

"Made with tart green Golden Delicious," he said. "Not Granny Smiths, as you might think."

"How do you know that?" I held out my hand for a plate of six steaming fritters dusted with powdered sugar, and left a dollar in the jar.

"I'm getting into fruit," he said. He looked pleased with himself.

I tasted a sample, assessing its texture and flavor. "I wouldn't have guessed Golden Delicious," I admitted.

"I asked the first good Episcopal lady I saw what kind of apple, and she said 'Green.' But the one slicing them into circles on the machine back there, she gave me the lowdown. How come you're not back there dipping slices? This is your congregation—"

"I don't do much for them," I said. I looked across the counter toward the clump of women in the back. "A couple of our clients worked on this." I didn't see them there; perhaps they had a later shift.

He put a hand on the shoulder of my blue cotton dress. "You look mighty nice. You doing better?"

"Some," I said. I'd also tied a blue ribbon on my plait. He was in a fresh shirt and tie, a dark suit, and I said, "You're an improvement, too."

He led me a few steps away and said, "I guess it's not telling tales out of school, but the woman slicing the apples—"

I looked. "I know her. I understand her husband's been sick."

"That's what I was about to tell you. He's the man who was on the table in my office the day you called."

"Oh, Will, that's awful."

"Good fritters she's making."

"Yes." I looked back again at her busy bent head, reminded that our world was smaller than most.

Will took my elbow and turned me to greet a trio of men wearing big felt hats, their bellies hanging over their belts and their shirtsleeves rolled up. They were the husbands of the church women.

"You know Emmett, here—" Will said, "and Otis and Dawson."

"I do." I shook hands all around.

"The wife comes to your shop, correct me if I'm wrong," the one named Otis said.

"She does." I was glad he made the connection.

"Your girl fixed up our dining room real nice. Looks just like, I said to my wife, the one I grew up in, it's got that molding and what I call bird paper."

"I'm glad," I told him. "Katie's good."

After they'd moved on, Will took my hand and kneaded the fingers. "I guess you need to know what's what," he said. "Dawson's boy is one of my Siege of Shiloh patients."

"How is he?"

"Still here."

"How hard that must be for a man like that."

"It's harder for the boy," Will said grimly, more a reminder than a reprimand.

I had a long way to go before I could hear his stories without my legs going wobbly on me. How on earth had he learned to deal with such bad news daily?

At the First Baptist Pork Barbeque stall, he said, "I got us pig tickets already; that'll save us standing in line."

"I thought we were going to eat catfish." I was still looking after the three men in felt hats, who were now standing at the apple fritter booth, chatting with their wives.

"That's lagniappe."

At the Mt. Zion Bakery booth, I stopped. "Why don't I get two slices of chocolate cake to take Harriet, before they're gone." I remembered this cake from last year—so rich and moist that it sold in about ten minutes after people had finished their dinner plates.

Will took a finger and rubbed away a line between my eyes. My worry line. He studied my face. "Don't do that," he said. "Ask the nice lady there, Mrs. Thompson, to put you back a couple of slices. But your friend Harriet made this trip to see the Springs Summer Fair. She's going to want to see the fair. Don't deny her that."

A lot of things Will had said about Nolan toward the last came back to me, things I'd let get beyond my recall when I was coping and mourning. "He hasn't been a baby for nearly sixty years," he'd said, "and he's not one now." "He's a man as long as he's got breath. Treat him like one." "He came into this world alone and he's got to go out that way. I'm not saying you have to open the door for him, Coop, but you can't bolt it either. You stand to one side while he makes up his own mind when to go through it."

I nodded, shut my eyes for a minute, and then negotiated for the slices of chocolate cake.

"Let's go hear a little music." Will put an arm around my waist and led me past the springhouse up the slope of the hill toward the street.

We stood by the bleachers, which had been set up for the crowd's favorite band, the Crawdaddy Brothers. They were playing the first of four hour-long gigs for the day. The fiddle and ukulele players were singing into the mikes, carrying the melody, while the harmonica and banjo did the backup and an impossibly tall man with a red beard played "drums" with a couple of spoons on his blue jeans.

"Who's gonna shoe her pretty little feet, who's gonna glove her hand? . . ." The crowd was singing along and we did, as well.

On the way back down the hill we listened to hand puppets "singing" gospel songs to a tape, and passed a sign-up table with a placard reading PUT THE TEN COMMANDMENTS BACK IN THE SCHOOLS near clusters of black and white school kids in designer T-shirts drinking from quart-size paper cups. Will bought a bag of boiled peanuts and I tasted one, the hot salty water still inside the shell. Fat free, they advertised, this year's theme being health. We had a ceremonial cup of the cold bubbling spring water, which tasted of iron and like my memory of well water.

I was taking lessons in how to walk around and mingle and not let myself be pulled back home to the thought of Harriet straining for breath in the upstairs bed, or the memory of Nolan in an earlier bed. Taking lessons in how to eat the apple fritter or boiled peanut when I was eating it, and listen to the country songs while I was hearing them. I wasn't the best student, but I had a good instructor.

We wandered up and down the rows of craft tents which had been set up near the old railroad tracks, where eight trains a day once stopped. Artisans were selling handmade aprons, toys, furniture, rugs, rag dolls, baby dresses, pot-pourri, pottery, blackberry jam and watermelon rind pick-les. Most were from the Carolinas and Georgia, a few were from Tennessee, Virginia and north Florida.

"Would you look at that?" Will pointed to a red-and-white-striped tent, below which two tables covered in white cloths held cow crafts: cow shoeshine kits, cow wastebas-kets, cow bread boxes, cow hat racks and towel holders. But the winner was a wooden footstool painted like cowhide with pink wooden udders hanging down under the seat.

"For Bess," I said, clapping my hands. "I have to get it." I was thinking of her guest quarters, former milking sheds, and the milking stool in the kitchen, where she kept her riding boots. I knew when I called her on her birthday, she'd be a good sport about the two hammocks and say each had room for two small boys and that she'd leave them up until Labor Day. But I thought she might not mind just once getting something that wasn't from a mail-order catalogue.

"I might have to get myself one of those things, too," Will said, holding it up and admiring it. "Prop my feet up on it and clean my shoes."

Stools in hand, we stopped at a tent under a banner for MOUNTAIN MADE TOYS. "Model T," Will said, picking up a wood replica of a car, painted bright blue. "Is that a fine piece of work." He asked the man sitting at a table in the back, "You got a big sack?"

"Sure I have." The man was in overalls that looked to be bought just for the fair, and had short white neatly parted hair.

Will wandered around, finally settling on the Model T, a large dump truck made of the same sanded wood, this painted bright yellow, a smaller truck, a pickup, in cherry red, and a grasshopper pull toy whose legs moved up and down, in apple green. "I'm practicing to be a grandpa," he told the man, who appeared to be in his seventies. "Got boys from not yet three to not yet nine."

"That seems about right to me." The man gestured to his choices with a large hand.

"How'd you get started making these?" Will asked, after he'd written out a check. "You look to be my vintage, same model I'd say."

"More than likely," the man agreed. "More history than coming attractions."

"This is the boys' grandma," Will said, calling me over to make introductions.

Shaking hands, I thought I would have known the man was from North Carolina—the broad shoulders, that mountain voice, the brow ridge—even if the sign hadn't said so.

"My pleasure." He stood to answer Will's question. "I started modelling these toys because"—he scratched his head and then smoothed his white hair—"I used to make them for my boy, when he was small. I modelled that dump truck there on a real truck he used to get a kick out of watching that worked at a quarry near us." He spent a minute examining the wheels of the truck, making them turn. "My boy was killed about a hundred years ago by some drunk punk son of a bitch. I spent a couple of years deciding I'd go around with my shotgun and blow the heads off drunk drivers, but then I figured they'd lock me up and that would be an end to that.

"My wife, the boy's mother, she didn't cotton to that idea anyway, me and that shotgun. She said it was too much an-eye-for-an-eye for her taste. So then I was at loose ends, and I thought, Well, I'd make myself a truck and give it to the church for their Christmas bazaar, and I did, and one thing led to a few more. I got to liking it." He picked up a version of the pull toy in blue. "This is a first, the grasshopper. My granddaughter was pulling some duck around after her, a toy, and having herself a big time with it. But the wheels kept falling off, and the metal sprong that held them, it wasn't safe, not for two-year-olds. So I thought I'd try my hand. If the grasshopper takes hold, I'm going to try a rabbit next year. Another pull toy. I'll make its ears flopping, I reckon."

"I guess we'll be back to check that out," Will said. "Boys'll be a year older."

"You want my card?" The man fished in his overall pocket.

"Your wife around?" Will looked toward the back of the tent.

"She died two weeks ago. She said for me not to think I didn't have to get my butt down here just because it was going to be twice the work without her."

It was too much. I looked at the man's weathered face, at the still way he stood there, saying those things about his losses, and I turned and buried my face against Will's chest, cow stools and wooden toys poking out in all directions. "I can't bear it," I said in a near whisper. "I can't bear that it happens to all of us."

ON SUNDAY MORNING, Harriet said, "I'd like to go to church."

"That would be good." I checked the clock.

"That's what they say about religion."

We made a small laugh together.

"St. Andrew's starts at ten-thirty now, not eleven."

"St. Bart's does that at home. I have no idea why."

We were eating heated-up biscuits and scrambled eggs at the kitchen table, and being fairly gingerly with one another.

Harriet had gone to the fair with me Saturday in the late

afternoon. She had eaten her dark rich cake slices on the spot, had asked the woman at the Mt. Zion booth for the recipe and been disappointed to find it was a secret. "I could have taken a cake next time to the Sloane covered-dish dinner," she said, "and knocked their socks off." We had listened to a set by the Crawdaddy Brothers, this time with a Patsy Cline sound-alike vocalist. But Harriet had grown winded quickly; her legs had tired. The vast park was hilly, the pathways steep except in the crafts area, and the crowd was jostling and noisy—with smokers on every hand.

When I came back from the time with Will, carrying my milking stool and sending the dogs home with him, I'd found her at the table, wearing the short shorts I'd promised would go anywhere in western Carolina in August, ready to go.

"I'm so sorry about last night." I stood across the room, uncertain what to do.

But she'd brushed it aside with Doll's old line. "That's water under the dam," she said.

At the park and back home after an early supper of left-over stew, she'd been full of plans. What she was going to do at her lunch party on my visit next spring, the trip she and David were going to take to the coast in the fall. How she was going to duplicate that fantastic cake. How she thought she might fix up the panelled downstairs room that had been Knox's library, make it into a green and white sitting room, a more intimate place to invite a man than the living room but not as bold as upstairs. "It never was a 'study' anyway," she said. "You know, it was one of those rooms men claim in houses and all but never set foot in."

It was as if the present were uncomfortable, the past had proved painful, and so she had set her sights on the future— which she willed to be a better time.

Now, as we arrived at the church, she asked, "What do you call him?"

"Vicar," I said.

"I mean, what do *you* call him?"

"I call him Reg. It's Reginald. He refers to himself as Father Neill in the bulletin, but I can't go along with *Father.* Anyway, he's younger than my children." I thought of our new clergyman, tall as a beanstalk, who appeared barely old enough to shave.

St. Andrew's was a simple gray-painted frame building, with no stained glass windows—although the congregation was quite proud of the old leaded glass panes. It was not only Mineral Springs's sole Episcopal church, it was also the oldest in our part of the state. A church with a history tended to reassure: some things endured; some things did not fall away, were not forgotten.

Harriet wore a white suit with caramel blouse to match her new slingback spectators, her best pearl choker, hose and gloves. I wore my brown linen, the present from Edith I'd worn on Mother's Day.

The last time we'd been to church together we'd stood, young mothers in roll-brim straw hats, having our infants christened. When we'd visited each other with our families, back when the children were young, Sunday had been reserved for an outing, a trip into the Big Thicket to glimpse the marsh's water snakes and colored birds, or a drive into the Blue Ridge for a day of white-water rafting. Later, when we got together just as couples, we'd lazed on Sundays, eating pancakes, just the four of us, or had friends over for brunch, pouring them pitchers of fancy drinks.

In St. Andrew's, I let Harriet sit on the aisle, in case she wanted to leave, in case she began to cough. We were directly behind the two eldest women in the congregation, both in their nineties. Widowed since Lee met Grant, they always came together, Miss Ima and Miss Lucille. They shared the old Book of Common Prayer between them, and moved their lips along with the vicar even when it was not time to respond aloud. The new prayer book had hardly made a ripple in our congregation anyway; everyone recited what she already knew. Visitors said the new words at the same time. It made a sort of responsive reading.

Seeing the old faithfuls, I wished I'd picked a different pew, one that might have been less painful—seeing friends older than us by a quarter of a century, still here and still together. But I'd sat here from habit, where I always had, where Mother and Bess and I, and later Nolan and I and the children, had sat.

He had never warmed to St. Andrew's; in fact, he had never warmed to Episcopal ways. There was too much bowing and scraping, he'd said, having come from another denomination. "Scraping is just another word for bowing," I'd told him, "and kneeling is hardly bowing." Besides, I liked to see grown men come in and get down on their knees. I liked to see old women, older by a dozen years than my mother, come in with their well-shod feet and proud air and sink to their knees. Had Nolan been devout about, or even truly attentive to another church, I might have compromised. But going mostly alone, I preferred one with a history—mine, my mother's and grandmother's, a whole people's history on this one spot in this one gray frame church.

Rising from the kneeler, Harriet pointed to the program. "Oh, no," she whispered, "a *baptism*."

I wondered if she fretted that she might not be able to keep her cough at bay at an extra-long service, with both baptism and communion. I could have reassured her that this would only mean a shorter sermon—Reg Neill was careful never to run over his time—but the organ music began and with it the service. It was the eleventh Sunday after Pentecost (the old Jewish Harvest Festival). The baptism was to be of twins, James and Jeremy Bywater. The

Bywaters were sitting conspicuously at the front, armed with bottles, pacifiers, diaper bags and receiving blankets. The parents looked to be about fifteen. Such an impossibly rosy-faced young woman with a wealth of light hair, and an earnest clear-faced young man, who had, you could see when he craned his neck to check out who had come, the typical South Carolina face, thick brows and cleft chin. A local boy, Bywater, perhaps new to this congregation but not to the state.

I found I was looking forward to taking communion; it had been too long since I'd been to church. I liked the feel of the paper-thin wafer on my tongue, the sip of wine from the chalice. It took me back to school days, to the drama of communion at Pritchard's, with half the girls fasting, becoming dizzy with the combination of low blood sugar and piety, with someone always fainting, with at least one girl having to be helped from chapel. It was a wonder we didn't have visitations or levitate from the ground before the dazed eyes of our rapt classmates. Our youth, our readiness for sex, menstruation, hunger, awe, all combining to make a very real transubstantiation of the eucharist—if not the one intended.

I saw several of the women from the apple fritter booth sitting in the front, wearing silk, but none of the younger members had dressed up—that was part of the new man's influence. Come as you are. There were young men in shirtsleeves—it was August after all, though coolish—and young women bare-legged in cotton dresses or skirts and shirts. Their children wore rompers and playclothes, depending on the age.

I watched the vicar's assistant, Doris, mount to the lectern and give the First Reading. Dark, ethereal, skinny as a rail with a viselike handshake, she would get her training here and then take over her own congregation somewhere else.

I was reminded, watching her, of the two youth leaders at boarding school who'd been in training to be DREs, directors of religious education, the highest church post in those days that a woman could aspire to. Had they gone on to divinity schools when the opportunity arose? Had they lived long enough to have churches of their own?

It was a moment before fragments of the lesson reached my ears; I'd been back in time. I'd been recalling Pritchard's, and those days, no doubt because of my fight with Harriet, wondering if we'd been after all even at the same school. It was from a new translation of Isaiah: "We have made a covenant with death. . . . When the overwhelming scourge passes through you will be beaten down by it. As often as it passes through, it will take you. . . . For the bed is too short to stretch oneself on it, and the covering too narrow to wrap oneself in it." But if Harriet, hands clasped tightly in her lap, heard or was disturbed, she gave no sign. Perhaps she was also, in her own mind, back, a girl again, attending chapel.

The Bywater boys did a fine job. James bellowed lustily while Jeremy was being sprinkled; Jeremy wailed when it was James's turn to get attention. After, each could be heard gulping and sobbing, then settling down in their parents' arms. Reg had come down to the front row, bringing the silver cup of water with him, handling the whole thing in a young, easy way. Chatting with the babies, gazing at the congregation, encouraging them to join in, to feel in their bones the sense of support and welcome which went with the familiar words. I half thought he might pass the babies around a bit or have everyone come up and do a mild laying on of hands, all the friends of the Bywaters in their shirtsleeves and summer dresses.

It was hard to know how much of this old church had rubbed off on my children. I knew George had been going sporadically to the Huguenot church in Charleston. And that Fannin had taken the boys to Sunday School, because Matthew had mentioned stories about baby Jesus. Which, I suspected, he'd mixed up with baby Revelations in his mind. Wondering if, in some tangled theology, I had no doubt, Jesus had died in his mommy's tummy. I could picture my son here clearly, a small boy riffling through the Book of Common Prayer, finding all those passages I'd never seen in all my years of reading from it (for example, the Circumcision of Christ According to Luke). How did the fingers of the young find unerringly anything in any way titillating? I thought of today's infants, somewhere down the road, becoming two men, James and Jeremy, the Bywater boys, grown with families of their own. Their fresh-faced parents grown also, into other people. I thought of mortality.

Harriet had wept quietly, wadding up a white hanky, during the baptism, but was not seized with coughing until she was standing at the rail waiting her turn to receive the wafer and wine. I was already on my knees, my palm held out before me, when I heard her racked with a cough which seemed to tear her lungs loose from her chest. I didn't know if I should rise and follow her when she left. But Harriet did not go; she stood, clutching her white suit jacket with one hand, the handkerchief held to her lips with the other. When it passed, she knelt beside me and took the wafer. No one had moved to walk around her; no one had moved out of line. At the rail, Miss Ima and Miss Lucille turned and exchanged glances.

After the service, Reg found us in the rose garden, a large plot of blooms in St. Andrew's deep front yard, planted in the shape of a cross. He was in a suit and clerical collar. He didn't like to stand outside in his robes; this was the wrong community for that, he'd said; it gave the wrong idea. Often he dispensed with his jacket. He must, I thought, in his boyhood, long after the time young girls fasted to fainting, have served his own apprenticeship; been an acolyte, a crucifer, given up treasures for Lent, committed the Scriptures to memory. He must have indulged in some necessary excess at an early age that left him now comfortable with himself, not distressed by small matters. No doubt he would grow into someone with a steady nature, able to comfort. That would be at a larger church in a larger community. We got the young ones, our old churches in this iron-laden part of the world.

"Oh, those precious babies," Harriet was saying, wiping her eyes. "Those precious little babies."

She had exited the church looking back at the cluster of friends around the Bywaters. She'd hesitated, as if she wished to press through the crowd and see the infants for herself. I recalled her from when our own children were christened at those joint ceremonies, our boys in Texas, our girls in Carolina. I could see her beaming proudly, holding out the fat offering of her young to the sprinkle of blessed water. What had that represented to her that she wished so fervently to repeat it?

If it had been her Dwayne, his head full of electronics, or her Pammy, her mind stuffed with appellate briefs, presenting their descendants, what role would Harriet have played? The grandmother with the terrific legs; the grandmother sitting in the front row out of the picture. Where had I been when Fannin's boys were named? Twice there with Nolan, twice there with Mother. Nor could I recall now which grandson had got which two of us. It had not been my occasion; it had been each child's in turn. Harriet wanted not grandbabies, I guessed, but rather to be the young Mrs. Bywater in the crowd of parishioners, her cheeks flushed and her prospects stretching far into the new century.

I made the introductions.

"We're always glad to have visitors swell our ranks," Reg said in a welcoming tone.

"I was admiring your roses." Harriet held out a gloved hand.

"Twenty-two varieties," he told her, as if he'd be tickled to tick them off for her if she was interested.

"Does your wife look after them?" She was imagining him half of a pastoral couple.

"When I have procured a wife, will she tend my roses?" Reg smiled down from the heights. "I think not. I feel certain that because of my love of being their sole caretaker, I will select a woman who perceives them as a collection of thorns and busies herself with her brain surgery—but one mustn't be classist, must one?—or perhaps her auto mechanics."

"I hope," Harriet said apologetically, "I didn't disturb your service."

"Not a bit of it. We get some objections to our use of the common cup—although Doris turns it, as you saw."

"She did a good job, the—woman who helped you." Harriet did not say *black*, faltering only for a moment. She seemed subdued, as if all the wind had been knocked from her.

"She'll make a fine member of the clergy," Reg agreed, a beanpole in a turnaround collar. He bent and selected a peach rosebud and presented it to Harriet.

"Those babies." She turned her sallow face away.

With the sure instincts of the young, Reg Neill reached out and put his hands on Harriet's head. "Bless you," he said.

With that her eyes filled again. Looking up at him, she whispered, "I wish I had had grandchildren."

It was the only time I heard her speak of her own death.

FIVE

WILL AND I WERE on the front porch looking out at the oak and the dogs chasing the start of fall when the mail carrier brought an overnight delivery from Harriet's Uncle Bob with her obituary. Doll had called me two days earlier with the news. "She's gone," she said, her voice shaky and faint. "They said it was just for overnight, but she's gone."

She gave me the name of the hospital in Houston and said the service would be at the Sloane plot on Thursday. That was today. I was dressed; Will was taking me to the airport in Greenville. We'd sat a few minutes over a second cup of coffee, not talking a lot. He promised to hold down the fort. I promised to come back in one piece.

He had called Harriet's attending physician and got the story straight. They'd put her in to give her oxygen and some relief from the pain. The tumor, he said, had grown into a main vessel. She had drowned, four weeks to the day after her visit to Carolina, her warm heart beating and her great legs kicking no more.

Reading her death notice was like seeing a vivid life-size portrait shrunk to a dim miniature, and I crumpled it up after I read it. But Will retrieved it and smoothed it out, knowing I would want to keep it.

BANKER'S WIDOW DIES

Harriet Sloane Calhoun, 55, died Tuesday at the M. D. Anderson Hospital in Houston. A homemaker and member of St. Bartholomew Episcopal, she is predeceased by her husband, prominent area banker Knox M. Calhoun. Surviving are her parents, Nathaniel and Dolly Sloane of Cypress and La Salle, son Dwayne Knox Calhoun and daughter Pamela Sloane Calhoun, both of Houston. Services are to be held Thursday at the Sloane Family Cemetery in La Salle. Memorial contributions may be made to the charity of your choice.

I'd slept at Will's the night Doll called. The thought of being in that upstairs room where Harriet and I had had our slumber party that went so awry was too upsetting. I could see her again rocking my bed back and forth against the wall in anger, hurting in body and spirit. I could hear her wheezing breath mark the time like the ticking of a clock. But last night we'd come back here, to let me sleep in my own bed and know that she would never again scoot down beneath the covers of the other one. To let me get used to losing her.

"I brought you a little something to take along with you." Will was standing; it was time for us to leave.

"What?"

He handed me the little drawing I had done of Harriet's chest. "I made a copy before I parted with it," he said. "I thought you'd like to scatter it or some such thing."

I was touched and tucked it in my bag. I could see Harriet look at it, pleased.

"And I brought you a towel." He handed me a sack from which I pulled an old soft blue bath towel with *P* for Perry embroidered at the hem.

For that I gave him a serious smooch.

Walking to the car, I said, "You didn't have the summer party for your married friends this year." I was trying to patch the year back together, remember where I'd left off noticing.

"Some of my friends aren't married anymore," he said, starting up his Honda. He honked at the fenced pups, knowing they hated to see us take off without them.

"Some of us aren't." I'd pinned up my braid and worn the same suit I'd worn for Nolan's funeral, black, pleated, old.

"What about your Christmas party?" he asked. "You making big plans?"

The thought of the annual bankers' party seemed a scene from another lifetime. I smiled at him. "Were we giving those parties for each other?"

He reached over and took my hand in his. "How about a dinner at my place when Edith gets back? I'd like those mountain toys to come down my chimney this year."

I nodded. I knew what he was saying. That life goes on. Grandsons still want to open gifts on Christmas morning. Famous mothers approaching eighty still want a hearth where they can warm their bones against the chill. I dried my eyes for the tenth time this morning. "One of these years," I said, "we're going to have two new puppies under some tree."

"I'll hold you to that, Coop," Will said.

DRIVING OUT OF town, I saw that half the yards had already decorated their trees for Halloween, and it not yet October. Dozens of tiny white ghosts (strangled handkerchiefs) dangled from hardwood branches. I'd busied myself on the weekend cutting back the clematis and covering them with straw, packing the roses with peat moss and fertilizing the grass. I'd dug up what bulbs I wanted to replant next year—wearing my old gardening sneakers and heavy red socks, my dog-walking pants and a sweatshirt, with a scarf on my head and latex gloves on my hands. Something of a scarecrow.

I was "riding through my prosperity," the week after the funeral. On Long Creek Road I passed the signs that signalled the approach to the state park: HOT BOILED PEA-NUTS, PUMPKINS, SALMON EGGS, HONEY, HOT CIDER, U-PICK APPLES, CHAIRS CANED, FILL YOUR WOOD SHED. A new short-order cafe appeared after Rae's Cafe and the HIGHWAYS NOT DIEWAYS sign. Below its banner claiming BURGERS-HEROES-SUBS was a hand-painted likeness of a four-foot submarine gun.

On the radio, I listened to the call-in show. The deejay was telling his upstate listeners that Virginia to the north of us was the handgun supermarket of the East Coast. What, he asked, did they think about gunrunners able to buy handguns by the carload? I shut it off. Thinking that Knox's deer rifle and Harriet's .22 had provided her no protection after all.

The Sloane family plot had looked much the same as it had in April. Although the wildflowers were all gone, the pecans and willows were fully leaved. East Texas was short on seasons. I'd stood for a minute, before the crowd arrived, looking at the black granite stone that still awaited her name and dates. This time, there was a fresh mound of earth next to Knox's grave.

Harriet was not laid to rest alone. All of Birthday Club came, so a woman named Jo in a black turtleneck sweater and gray suit told me. "You can pick us out," she said, tears streaming down her angular face. "We all put on our jewels for her." And, sure enough, when I looked around the dry ground beside an open field shaded in the late morning by a thicket of trees, I could pick out the other women come to grieve for Harriet: they were all of an age, all had wet faces, and all wore sparkling gems on their fingers, on their lapels, at their throats and ears. I wondered if each, in tribute, had tucked a handgun in her leather handbag along with her handkerchief.

Nat was there, and I was amazed to see him after so long, even though I might have expected to find him there. He looked shrunken both in stature and in his face, and his teeth and eyes seemed to have receded into his head. But the two-tone shoes, bow tie and twangy voice were just the same.

"Not right for a man to outlive his child," he said. "It's not the natural order of things." He kissed my cheek as if it had been last week. "Have you met my friend here? David? He wrote up my radio." He said the last proudly, rounding out the syllables: ray-dee-oh.

I shook hands with Harriet's "young man," although he didn't, in fact, look much younger than most of us, forty being as adult as a man was liable to get. He was handsome, just as she had said, but, I thought, seemed uneasy with the fact. As though he awoke one day in a Kevin Costner suit and was still rattling around in it, wondering what he was supposed to do.

"You were a welcome addition to Harriet's life," I told him.

He took off his wire-rimmed glasses and cleaned them. "She was a fine lady," he said. "I wish we'd—we were—"

"Thanks for bringing Nat," I said, to save him some embarrassment. "I've missed him." Which was true.

He said, "I didn't actually. Bring him. I went to get him, Sarah—may I call you Sarah, she talked an awful lot about

you, as I guess you know—but he decided to drive himself."
He looked at the old man, somewhat confounded, but
fondly.

"You didn't?" I squeezed Nat's arm. "Aren't you sly?"
He seemed steady enough on his feet, not as wasted as I'd
been imagining him. Certainly not bedridden.

"It was the graph that did it. Did you see the graph? You
read the papers, don't you—?"

"I'm not sure—" I had no idea what he meant.

"The *graph*." Harriet's dad waved his hand, including
David and me in his audience. "There was this big article
claiming older drivers were a hazard and menace to the
road. With this graph that showed that the over-seventy
drivers had half again the accidents of the forty-year-olds.
But not a word about the fact that the under-twenties had
three times as many accidents. No mention that if they
followed their own figures they'd make the minimum age
to get your driver's license thirty years old. Take all the
twenty-year-olds off the road.

"It made me mad enough to get a mechanic out to the
house to jump-start the car and give it an overhaul. Then I
had to find myself a chiropractor to fix my back before I
could start up driving again."

"I'm truly glad you did," I said.

I saw Dwayne, whom I hadn't set eyes on since he finished
college. He caught sight of his grandfather and broke into
a lope, threading his way through people he didn't know,
past monuments to people too unrelated to note. "Granddad," he said. "I thought I'd seen a ghost."

"I've come back to life," Nat said. "There I was sitting
stewing in my juices while my girl was expiring. I'm not
proud of that." He sniffed and wiped his nose. "You
know these folks? Sarah? David here, who wrote up my
radio?"

"You got that stuff I sent you about Apple PIE?" Dwayne asked.

"I got it. It didn't make a lot of sense, but I appreciated the thought. They're over my head these days with what they can do. The last thing I wired together was a radio. I'm not likely to make it into the twenty-first century, but I have to tell you, if I did I still wouldn't catch up."

"Just listen, Granddad, and I'll give you the gist." And while Dwayne talked, I could almost see the polished broker's persona disappear and a pocket full of pens appear, and horn-rim glasses and a pencil behind his ear. How the course of history—one boy's anyway—would have been changed if he'd gone to live on the other side of the Big Thicket.

I thought I should say something more to David, who stood watching Harriet's kin with me, but I couldn't think what. I'm sorry you didn't get your trip to the Rockies? I'm so glad you stayed close until the last? But he, doubtless feeling awkward, too, moved on, nodding to Doll, then standing next to a small group of well-dressed older men. Perhaps he had his recorder in his pocket.

Doll was sitting under the same pecan tree where I'd seen her at the grave-cleaning in the spring. Her soft face crumpled under a small-brimmed felt hat. She was in black, a church dress with buttons up the front, and someone, as before, had buttoned a thick sweater about her shoulders as a wrap against the mild breeze blowing across the head-stones.

Uncle Bob, looking chipper in dress pants, a tie and wind-breaker, fussed around her, not seeming to take into account that his older brother had come all the way from the other side of the cypress swamps for the occasion, or even that he, Bob, was Nat's kin and not Doll's. The family plot seemed to be the badge of kinship; those who tended it and

frequented it were Family with a capital F, and the others—
Birthday Club, old friends, bankers who'd come out of re-
membrance to Knox, the dead woman's daddy and boyfriend and I—were outsiders.

"Hello, Doll," I said in a low voice, knowing that she
didn't need my words. "I'm sorry. I'm so very sorry." I
pressed my face against the old woman's, thinking how
alone she must feel, how out of line to be burying a child.
I could imagine the anguish it would cause my mother to
be standing by the kneeling lambs and fenced plots at home,
her hip stiff, her face set, burying one of her girls. It was
not the proper order of things.

That eventuality was not something you ever considered. Having children, you assumed for them a life opening up, flowering long after yours had closed. That was
the price you contracted for: your life for theirs. Who
wanted to be left? Who wanted to have the entire responsibility for children: giving birth to them and burying them,
too.

"She's over there," Doll said in the hollow tones of the
deaf. "She's going to be buried with him. She's a Sloane
on her daddy's side." She looked around, baffled by the
crush of strangers. "I married a Sloane," she said loudly,
as if claiming her right to be there. She seemed disoriented,
weaker than when I saw her last. The loss had shaken
something loose in her. "Are you going to stay with me?"
she asked, reaching up and pulling me down so my face
was next to hers. "I've got eight beds, all made up." She
looked in Nat's direction, and I wondered if they would
speak. "Nobody's sleeping in them."

"Next time I will," I said, "I promise." I bent closer until
my lips pressed her white cheek. "Next time."

It wasn't until Dr. Snow, the elderly slump-shouldered
vicar, was standing by the grave, the kin and friends arrang-

ing themselves in clusters, that I spotted Pammy. The one person I still hadn't seen.

The girl was huddled inside a heavy black jacket that came almost down to her knees and a straight skirt that hit the tops of the heavy shoes that had so bothered her mother. She'd cut her hair close to her head and she looked wretched. She held herself tight, her arms wrapped as if in a straitjacket. The Class Favorite, who was now a first-class attorney, was without makeup, her dimples obscured in her strained face.

I saw her wave at her brother—perhaps they'd come together and she had taken time to regroup. She didn't come up to the front of the half-circle of people; didn't stand with the family, Nat and Dwayne, Uncle Bob and Doll.

As I moved toward her, Birthday Club got out their handkerchiefs, while a group of portly, balding men coughed as if on signal. I heard a mockingbird, and the faint cry of a loon.

"Are you all right, Pammy?" I walked up to the solitary girl, not touching her.

"I'm lousy."

"It must be hard. My mother has lived long enough, she's almost eighty, that we've had time to say some things we couldn't say earlier."

"She hated me."

"No such thing. Nor you her."

Pammy's hands disappeared inside the sleeves of her jacket, and she rubbed her cheeks with her woolen arms. "I used to think she was more married to you than she was to Daddy."

I didn't know how to say what was on my mind. "You needn't blame either of them, Pammy. Marriage is—a destructive snare."

"You're telling me." She tried to tuck her chin out of

sight in her high collar, looking more like her mother than either of them would have been pleased to know.

I studied the troubled young face before me. "Maybe you're trying the hard way to avoid it."

Her eyes flared. "Don't tell me how to run my life," she said.

I strolled with her toward the grave, still keeping my distance. "I may try my hand at it, from time to time. You'll just have to put up with me."

Pammy sobbed. "They made such a fucking mess of it."

"We all do."

"Not me."

"Even you. Even you will make a mess of things."

She wailed, a pale tough stalk of a girl. "I didn't want her to die."

"None of us did," I said.

"The Lord giveth and the Lord taketh away. . . ." Dr. Snow, holding the Book of Common Prayer upside down, was reciting all too familiar words when we joined those at the graveside.

The last call I'd had from Harriet had been the day before she went into the hospital.

"Just because it doesn't last doesn't mean it didn't happen." Her squeak of a voice was faint. "Remember how we used to lie out in the sun and baste ourselves with baby oil, getting those deep glorious tans? Just because we know now you can't set foot outside without sun block 40, that doesn't change how it was then."

"Yes," I said, "we had those afternoons." I was on the bed upstairs and Will was rubbing my back while I talked and tried not to cry.

"I've decided I'm only going to keep those times I want and throw the rest away. I want the day we met at Pritchard's, the day I was your maid of honor, the week Knox and

I had together in Aspen, and the day David showed up on my doorstep like the answer to a prayer." She was coughing dreadfully and had to wait before she could go on. "I'm going to write each one on a slip of paper and tape them together like a filmstrip of the good times of my life. I'm going to hang it over my hospital bed so that when I wake up that will be the very first thing I see: the Best of Me."

When I returned from Texas, I began to make calls. I wanted to talk to everyone. I called my family—Mother, Bess, Fannin, George; and Harriet's—Doll, Nat, Dwayne, Pammy. I called porky Theo Kenton of the silly red suspenders to arrange a trust fund for my grandsons. I called Miss Pritchard's School for Girls (now Pritchard's Preparatory) to set up a Harriet Sloane Calhoun scholarship. I wanted to call every Stuart and Stewart from the old days. And every Bitsy and Binky, Muffy and Missy, Tiny and Teeny, to tell them that Harriet was dead. Harriet, the one who had more boyfriends than a tree has leaves. Harriet, who never let anybody but her husband touch her treasure. Harriet, who wrote her mom those weekly letters claiming: "I must lead a charmed life."

I wanted to call them all while it was still possible. People central to your life could vanish. We have so little time one with another.

In the state park this afternoon, the leaves were beginning to turn. The black oak and scarlet oak, ash and sumac, sweet gum and maple, sassafras, hickory, walnut, beech, turning red, yellow, rust, brown. In another two weeks Will and I would bring the dogs to tunnel under them, to chase smells and each other. We would rent a cabin and light a fire. An apple-wood fire to celebrate fall.

At the Wild and Scenic River overlook, I parked and got out of the car. In the distance, past the trees, I could see a four-year-old in her shorts and canvas shoes, gathering pine needles with her mother—already pregnant with her sister, Bess—and hear again her daddy, young and slim, call out to her, "Where's my Sarah?"

Looking out across the familiar hills of home, I was grateful for each and every one of us who had made it to the last chapter.

VINTAGE CONTEMPORARIES

WHERE I'M CALLING FROM
by Raymond Carver

The summation of a triumphant career from "one of the great short-story writers of our time—of any time" (*Philadelphia Inquirer*).   0-679-72231-9

THE HOUSE ON MANGO STREET
by Sandra Cisneros

Told in a series of vignettes stunning for their eloquence—the story of a young girl growing up in the Latino quarter of Chicago.

"Cisneros is one of the most brilliant of today's young writers. Her work is sensitive, alert, nuanceful . . . rich with music and picture."—Gwendolyn Brooks
0-679-73477-5

ELLEN FOSTER
by Kaye Gibbons

The story of a young girl who overcomes adversity with a combination of charm, humor, and ferocity.

"Ellen Foster is a southern Holden Caulfield, tougher perhaps, as funny . . . a breathtaking first novel."   —Walker Percy
0-679-72866-X

NOTHING BUT BLUE SKIES
by Thomas McGuane

This high-spirited novel, chronicling the fall and rise of Frank Copenhaver, is set in a Montana where cowboys slug it out with speculators, a cattleman's best friend may be his insurance broker, and love and fishing are the only consolations that last.

"So sizable in vision and execution, so funny, so tragically and truly about America . . . that one is moved to stand and applaud."   —*Boston Globe*
0-679-74778-8

THE JOY LUCK CLUB
by Amy Tan

"Vivid . . . wondrous . . . what it is to be American, and a woman, mother, daughter, lover, wife, sister and friend—these are the troubling, loving alliances and affiliations that Tan molds into this remarkable novel." —*San Francisco Chronicle*

"A jewel of a book."   —*The New York Times Book Review*
0-679-72768-X

VINTAGE CONTEMPORARIES

AVAILABLE AT YOUR LOCAL BOOKSTORE, OR CALL TOLL-FREE
TO ORDER: 1-800-793-2665 (CREDIT CARDS ONLY).

Printed in the United States
by Baker & Taylor Publisher Services